HOOKING UP

Elsie Young

2

www.BOROUGHSPUBLISHINGGROUP.com

HOOKING UP
Copyright © 2019 Elsie Young

ISBN 978-1-948029-64-3

For Carolyn. Always.

ACKNOWLEDGMENTS

Special thanks to Hugh Jorgan for his technical expertise.

HOOKING UP

Chapter 1

Baboon Butts Everywhere

Here's the thing. I've found the perfect man. Perfect in every way, except that my yearning remains unrequited. Despite my best efforts (a serious invasion of his privacy on social media and wistful glances from afar) and some seriously twisted daydreams, his affection remains as elusive as the fabled Chupacabra. He's never spoken to me. Never even looked twice in my direction.

That sounds pathetic, right? I'll tell you my story if you promise not to judge me. Although my judgment is questionable, it's not like I wear tinfoil hats or think my grocery clerk is secretly a spy. I've merely developed a ridiculous infatuation with a boy in a band who doesn't know I exist.

I know you've been there. Except you probably left this sort of thing behind in eighth grade. What can I say? Too many years spent focusing on my career rather than my social life has made me a late bloomer, and more than a little socially awkward.

The boy in question is the bass guitarist in a band called Stripper Monkey. They play somewhat off-key, but suitably loud, pop-punk music. They could play show tunes or polkas and I'd still be here. It's the skinny jeans—don't even get me started on the skinny jeans—and the tattoos. All girls from straitlaced Irish-Catholic families are suckers for tattoos and skinny jeans. It's a known fact.

This is why every Tuesday I sit in Not Frank's Bar at the same table, in the same chair, with the same plate of rubbery chicken wings staring back at me. Every Tuesday is *Groundhog Day*. The only new thing in my life is this lip gloss. I found it at my local drugstore perched on a shelf amid promises of perfect color, all-day shine, and kissable lips. I'd decided that those were all good things and that I needed them in my life.

Not Frank's, our neighborhood bar, provides live music, blazing hot wings, vats of blue cheese, and enough ambiance to make the pervasive wet dog smell bearable.

Week after week, I sit and I wait for *him* to show. It's not like I'm planning to cook anyone's pet rabbit or anything, but I've spent the last year at the same table hoping he'd notice me. The word "stalker" is starting to feel appropriate. Hell, it was probably appropriate six months ago.

Which brings me to tonight.

I was in my usual place. The wings had arrived. Valerie, late by her usual twenty minutes, wound her lanky frame through the crowded room. She shoved her curly brown hair out of her face with one hand and waved to me with the other, causing random patrons to duck. Her flip-flops flapped away over the noise of the bar as she approached.

"I'm not late, am I? Is Lance Manyon here?" She threw herself into the chair on her side of our beloved little wobbly-legged table. It was jammed among the other small tables on the side of the room with barely enough room for two people, but it had an excellent view of stage left.

"Lance Manyon" is our code name for the aforementioned denim-clad, ovary-melting bass player. Valerie doesn't know I know it, but his name is actually Trey.

Not that I would admit it to anyone, even Val, who has been privy to many of my more dubious life choices, but I've developed an extensive Google addiction. I'm like the Velma of the cyber-sleuthing world. None of Trey's social media was safe from my prying eyes.

I shook my head. "Soon, I hope." I rubbed my lips together to maximize the glimmer from my new lip gloss.

"I thought not. You're still in a seated and upright position and you're speaking in full sentences." She reached for my extra-spicy wings. "This better be blue cheese." She plunged a wing into the dip cup, sloshing a bit of it over the side.

I rolled my eyes. Of course it was blue cheese. When was it ever not blue cheese?

"New lip gloss, huh? I can smell you from here, even over the hot sauce."

"Yeah, it's good, right? It's called Angel Face. It's supposed to be shimmery."

"More like Baboon Butt Pink, if you ask me. Did you order the cheese fries?"

"Never doubt the cheese fries." I picked up my cup. "I'm going in search of a refill." I knew if I wanted a cold one before the music started I'd need to get up and go to the bar to get it myself. Except for delivering our orders of delightful deep-fried goodness from the kitchen, the waitresses had started ignoring us long ago. I was surely not going to get up during the show and miss any of the skinny jeans magic or any of the unhealthy food I only allowed myself to eat once a week. Okay, fine, twice a week.

I struggled through the throng of heavily perfumed women crowding the bar area, placed my empty cup on the bar, and tried to make eye contact with the bartender, who was chatting up a busty blonde.

"Excuse me?"

The bartender glanced at me and then turned back to the blonde. I tapped my cup on the surface of the bar a few times. The bartender turned to me and held up a "wait a minute" finger. I decided the beer could wait in favor of a fresh coat of Baboon Butt. I wanted to be shimmery from the audience. Not that Lance looked in my direction much.

I veered off into the restroom and began re-glossing my lips in the graffiti-covered mirror. I sighed. Too bad it was lip gloss and not a magic wand It's hard to be eye-catching when there's so little of you.

I tilted my head to the side and pouted. I rose up on my toes and stuck my chest out as far as I could. Compared to the blonde at the bar who was getting full service with a smile, I needed a little help. Before I could think too much about what I was doing, I stuffed a few feet of toilet paper into my bra. Couldn't hurt, right?

I walked out of the bathroom to find the lights dimmed and the hallway packed with people. My breast augmentation must have taken longer than I'd thought.

Clearly, I'd have to forego the beer because it was almost time for the band to start. I couldn't tell if they were already on the stage or not. At five foot nothing it's not like I can see over anyone's shoulders. Since there were no screeches from the amps and my ears weren't ringing, I figured I had a few minutes.

I gave my new breasts a squeeze to enhance their super-absorbent perkiness and began to skirt my way around the crowd. Scratchy. Who could I complain to about the quality of the toilet paper around here? Clearly, not Frank.

I was edging past the kitchen doors when someone grabbed me by the shoulders. Valerie must have come to find me. I thrust out my new and improved cleavage and spun around.

Right into Lance Manyon.

My mouth opened and closed a few times, but no words came out. He was even better-looking up close. My face flushed and I tried to subtly fan myself with my hand.

Lance didn't seem to be suffering from the same panic-driven aphasia. He grabbed my flapping hand and tugged. I stumbled closer to him, still tongue-tied and silent.

What was he doing? Did he have me confused with someone else with larger breasts? Or had he figured out that I was tracking him online and decided to confront me about it? That would be so much worse than being ignored.

"Hey, I'm really sorry about this." His voice was so quiet I could barely make out his words.

Sorry? About what? I was wondering what a man that hot could possibly be sorry for when his free arm wrapped around me and pulled me in close and his mouth opened over mine in a kiss.

Can women get erections? I was pretty sure there was no blood left in my head and I had no explanation for where it went. Maybe I was having a stroke. Thank God I wasn't required to do any long division at that moment. Or, like, ever.

I pressed myself against him indecently. In my favor, I'd like to point out that I had the presence of mind not to jump up and wrap my legs around him. If I could have figured out how to knock him over and lie on top of him, I would have. But at that moment the principles of basic physics eluded me and my brain was only capable of a buzzing noise that must be what gray matter sounds like when it's frying. The Discovery Channel should do a show on that sometime. (Call me, Myth Busters.)

Eventually, we broke apart. I waited for my pulse to slow and tried to stop my left leg from shaking like a nervous Chihuahua. I noticed there were several people standing around us and I tried to follow the conversation that was going on without me.

"Here she is," Trey said. His arm circled my waist and his fingers clamped uncomfortably onto my hip.

"This is the girl you've been keeping on the down low? The stalker?" Chad, the lead singer of Stripper Monkey, bit back a grin. I scowled at him.

"She's not a stalker, she's my girlfriend." Trey gave me another squeeze. *Girlfriend?* The lack of blood flow to my brain had apparently done some damage.

"Right, dude. Whatever." Chad ran his hands through his spiky black hair, causing it to stick up even higher. I had the feeling I was in the middle of a conversation I hadn't heard the beginning of. He shot us one last disgusted look before turning on the heels of his black boots and heading for the stage.

"I'll talk to you after the show," Trey muttered, and turned to follow. Halfway to the stage he paused and turned back around. He licked his lips and smiled.

"Bubblegum?"

I stood there, staring at his back (okay, his *ass* because skinny jeans, remember?) as he continued on toward the stage, the image of him licking the lip gloss off his perfect lips burned into my brain. *My* lip gloss. With his perfect pink tongue.

I worked my way through the crowded room back to Val at our table, confused, but unable to wipe a ridiculously goofy grin off my face. I'm not going to lie, there may have been a bit of prancing involved. I had no idea what was going on, but I was pretty darn happy about it. Thank you very much, baboon butts everywhere.

I slid into my chair. Valerie's mouth hung open and her glass of beer was suspended two inches away from her open mouth.

"Wow." She lowering her glass to the table, untouched. "I can't believe what I saw. You should've stuffed those babies long ago. Bigger boobs really do get more attention."

I glanced down. My cleavage was somewhat askew after my bout of upright wrestling with Lance Manyon. Ever so casually, I slid my hand down to retrieve a trail of two-ply quilted bosom when I heard Chad's opening remarks from the stage.

"And after months of believing he'd fallen in love with that blow-up doll at home in his bed, I'm happy to introduce Trey's new girlfriend to you all tonight. Stand up—Trey, what's her name?"

My glance darted to Trey, with my hand in mid-tissue-retrieval-mission. Trey was looking at Chad with the same expression I'd had when I'd found a fingernail in my muffin one day. Whatever had happened between them earlier seemed to be still going on. More importantly, he hadn't noticed me rearranging my left breast.

I dabbed at the wing sauce around my lips with the TP, as if I had picked up a napkin from the table. Yep. Nothing to see here—simply a woman wiping her mouth with tissues. Coming out of her bra.

Trey looked in my direction and smiled and winked. My pulse rocketed back to pre-stroke level. I wiped my forehead with my bra filler.

"Let's play some music." He strummed his guitar, drowning out further conversation.

I listened to their set and mentally doodled Trey + Eiley inside of a heart. Trey and Eiley, sitting in a tree. I would so totally do him in a tree. K-I-S-S... Or near some bees or on a box or even if he had the pox. I-N-G... I had turned into a lecherous Dr. Seuss.

I had worked out three more lewd verses by the time the show ended. Let's just say that there was no place I wouldn't consider. No sex act was officially off the table, and it rhymed.

The band left the stage and went into a back room. Several minutes went by with no sign of Trey. I poked at the puddle of blue cheese dressing on my plate with a soggy French fry. Valerie patted my arm sympathetically.

"How was work today?" I asked to distract myself.

"Great. Sold a Mini Cooper, and have a couple probably coming back tomorrow to fill out the paperwork on an M3."

Valerie's an excellent salesperson. She's relentless in her pursuit of customers and she's either oblivious to most social norms for politeness or she chooses to ignore them. Either way, it works. "Someday you'll be selling me one of those Bimmers."

"Honey, you're gonna have to do a lot of pirouettes to pay for one of those."

"Tell me about it." I threw the soggy French fry back onto the plate.

"How's Basil the Bitcherina and life at the tutu factory these days?"

"Terrible. He let me fall over three times today."

Valerie frowned at me. "You should tell him off."

"You know I can't." I shook my head for emphasis. "Even if I had the nerve, which I don't, I've got to work with this guy. I have to figure something out to make him like me."

"Why does he hate you so much? Did you kick him in the acorns like the last guy?"

I winced, remembering the feeling of my pointe shoe digging into my last partner's tender bits. "No. I swear. He thinks I can't handle the part."

"Can you?"

"Let's figure out a way to make him happy," I suggested, avoiding the question. "What makes you happy?"

"Sex."

I nodded. I had dim memories of liking sex. A lot. "I'm pretty sure he's not seeing anyone. Maybe we could fix him up with someone. He moved here a year ago. He probably doesn't know a whole lot of people."

"Okay. Who do you hate enough to stick with Bitcherina?"

"I'll get back to you on that one." I grabbed another wing for myself. "I'm optimistic. I think this could work." Also, I had no other ideas.

I saw Trey walking toward the table and frantically licked my lips to remove any lingering wing sauce. Unfortunately, I was out of napkins and my bra was empty. I looked at Val and tipped my head toward the bar a couple of times in the international symbol for "Go Away." I had no idea what was about to happen with Lance, but I didn't need Val watching it unfold.

"Not a chance in hell I'm leaving this table." She picked up the final wing from the basket and started to gnaw.

"Hey." Trey smiled as he approached us. My heart fluttered a little. The man I'd been staring at for the last year was actually speaking to me, and I hadn't even needed night vision goggles or an extendable ladder. I smiled and nodded, but kept my mouth shut. I couldn't think of anything to say that wasn't pornographic iambic pentameter.

"Well, thanks for all that." He grinned. I kept smiling and bobbed my head like a woodpecker in a grub-infested oak tree. I'm a bit of an over-nodder in times of stress.

"It's kind of a long story, but I appreciate that you went along with it. I owe you one." He started to turn away.

"Chimichangas."

The first word I'd ever spoken to Lance Manyon, and I'd screamed a Mexican entree at him like I had some bizarre form of food Tourette's. I demanded access to burritos, nature's gas-inducing, phallic-shaped meal. That's what happens when people have penis on the brain.

Lance's eyebrows shot up and his eyes widened. Even Valerie looked shocked, and that's a highly unusual look for her.

"I mean," I floundered, "you owe me a story. Let's get some lunch and you can explain all of this." My stomach clenched then because his face once again had the muffin-full-of-fingernail look on it.

"Um, yeah. I guess that would be okay, maybe." He ran his hand through his shaggy hair and his gaze darted around the room. Probably looking for witnesses in case I tried to throw him over my shoulder and run off with him.

Well. That was somewhat less than flattering. I could feel myself starting to blush. Every thought I have is always blatantly apparent. If there's an opposite of a poker face, I have it.

I was sinking like the *Titanic*: quickly and epically. The goddess of shimmery lip gloss threw me one opportunity and I blew it. Desperate to try to save the situation, I glanced at Val. Her face was red and a vein in her forehead throbbed. I could tell she was silently urging me to do something.

I said the first, and only, thing that came to mind. "Relax. I'm not trying to kidnap you. I have a boyfriend. I thought it would be fun to hear the long version of this story." I tried to casually flip my hair over my shoulder and ended up with a curl in my eye. I blinked the tears away, hoping that I didn't appear to be suggestively winking at him.

I didn't dare look over at Val again, but I knew she'd keep her mouth shut and go along with my lie.

"Oh." He smiled, looking relieved. Again, not flattering. At all. "Sure, let's meet for coffee. How about La Ruche, around one on Friday?"

Coffee? It sounded like he felt like he couldn't risk staying long enough for lunch. I mean, I'd only mentioned burritos, not a four-course meal. How does that throw fear into your heart? Other than the potential for chalupa-fueled gaseousness?

I didn't even like coffee, and I would have to figure out a way to sneak out of work, but I wasn't going to say no. To anything. It was probably stalker code or something. I agreed and he left to help the band gather up their gear. Valerie and I paid our tab and worked our way through the crowd to the parking lot.

"Dude, stalker JACKPOT," Valerie shrieked as soon as we were outside.

"I know, right? It's like when you're six and your mom says yes to the ice cream truck."

"That's one hell of a Good Humor man. You know, you really have to make an impression. Maybe you can parlay tonight's random encounter into something more."

I nodded enthusiastically. Parlaying Lance's clothes off sounded good.

"What are you going to wear? Do you have a push-up bra? Never mind, that's hopeless. You'll need a short skirt, the shorter the better. At least you have dancer's legs," Valerie said.

"At least?" Nobody was trying hard to make me feel that great tonight.

"Oh, oh, I know," Valerie continued on, oblivious to my wounded pride. "Drop something and bend over. Show off your little tushie."

"You know," I huffed, "he might like me for my personality."

Valerie looked at me blankly for a moment. "Of course, honey, of course. But we're going to have to work really hard to downplay your awkward side."

"I have no idea how to do that. That's sort of part of the whole awkward thing."

"Well, to be safe, don't tell him the pickle story. Or about the vacuum in the oven, or anything at all about the time you fell in the sea lion enclosure. I know you and your sisters think you're hysterical, but maybe save a little for a second date."

"Second date? You think I can get a second date with Lance Manyon?"

"Who knows? Maybe the patron saint of stalkers is looking out for you. If you make a good enough first impression…" she trailed off.

"What?"

"Well, why don't you swing by the dealership Friday for a little 'test drive'?" She made air quotes with her fingers. "I can set you up with a really sweet BMW. One like your sister's. That'll make an impression. But you have to make sure you get it back to the dealership within ninety minutes."

"Do you really think I should?"

"Sure, why not? Show up a few minutes late and park right in front, so he can get a nice long look. Then sort of slink out of the car, all legs and short skirt."

"No way," I gasped, "you're not going to suggest I 'forget'"—I made some air quotes of my own—"my underwear and flash him, are you?"

"I hadn't even thought of that. Now that you mention it…"

"Forget it. I'd have to go to confession and, with my luck, it would be with your cousin Thomas."

"But the car? You'll do the car?"

"It can't hurt, right?" I asked as we walked toward our parked cars, although I did feel a twinge of apprehension. My plans with Valerie had a tendency to turn into Lucy-and-Ethel fiascos.

I squashed down my worries. What the hell? This was Lance Manyon we were talking about. If anything ever called for throwing caution to the wind, this was it. Besides, I'd always wanted to drive one of those fancy BMWs, and my sister wouldn't let me near hers.

"Okay, then." Val clapped her hands. "Stop by around twelve-thirty on Friday and I'll hook you up." She opened her car door.

"I'll be there. I'll be the one in the push-up bra and short skirt."

We both got in our cars and started to leave the parking lot. I saw Valerie stick her head out her window and I lowered mine.

"Remember," she called. "No sea lions, drop something and bend over, and don't mention vomit."

Words to live by.

Chapter 2

The Dirty Grudge

Last night I went home on cloud nine. This morning I was definitely back on earth—literally and figuratively. I looked up at Basil from my position on the floor and blew out a sigh of disgust.

"Was that really necessary?" I waited for him to at least offer a hand up, but he merely shrugged and turned away from me. I looked over at Susan, our choreographer, and raised my eyebrows.

"Okay, people. We open this show in a month, ready or not. And I, for one, would like to not bomb. So, if we could all agree to put our personal differences aside and have a productive practice today, that would be great. Take five and come back ready to work." I couldn't help but notice that she sounded as stressed as I felt.

I crawled over to the corner of the room, too tired to get up, and reached for my water bottle. This was Susan's first major ballet as choreographer, and *Swan Lake* was a particularly difficult ballet to stage and perform. Never mind the grief she'd been getting from the big donors—arguments over choreography and casting decisions being two of the bigger challenges she faced.

I'd been a soloist and understudy for two years, but when our lead dancer came down with a sudden case of pregnancy, I was thrust into the role of temporary principal. After twenty years of lessons, thousands of ballet buns, hundreds of tutus, gallons of sweat, countless sore muscles, and no social life at all, this was my shot. If I did well enough in *Swan Lake*, I could remove the "temporary" from my job title. I couldn't let this friction with Basil cost me the goal I'd worked for since I was three years old. It was time to suck it up and make nice with the Bitcherina.

Toughen up, buttercup, I could hear my mom telling me. I wiped the sweat off my chest and arms, tightened my ponytail, and struggled to my feet. Basil met me in the center of the room, looking as fresh as he had when he had walked in the door six long hours ago.

"I'm so glad you joined our company, Basil. I'm really learning a lot from you." I smiled and nodded.

"You could be, but you're not."

My smile faded. I turned to walk away and caught sight of Susan, hands on hips, looking ready to choke someone out. Since I didn't want that someone to be me, I decided I could give it one more try.

"Well, I really appreciate having such a talented partner." I nodded my head a few more times. Maybe a compliment would soften him up a little bit.

"What is that supposed to mean?" He had me there. It didn't mean anything. I was trying to get him to like me.

"Oh, well, it means that I, uh, really value your experience and the, uh, level of talent that you bring to the company." *Assbutt.* I smiled again and nodded some more, despite the bright red blotches that were popping up on my chest.

"Wish I could say the same." He bent over to adjust his pink leg warmers. I walked away, in case I couldn't resist the urge to kick the smug French derriere he'd presented me with.

It was time for drastic measures, which pretty much described any plan that Valerie had come up with.

***

I snuggled into my couch, my dog, Barney, beside me, my feet in a pan of warm water and Epsom salt. My toes slowly uncramped in the soothing water, but there was no hope for my blackened toenails. I would have loved to sit there a little longer, but it was Wednesday night, and that meant only one thing: hump day at the Dirty Grudge Diner with the Murphy girls. I pulled my feet out of the water and dried them off. It was time to get going.

I wrestled my curls into a messy bun, slipped on some comfy old Toms, and headed out of my apartment. I live in Northeast DC. It's crowded, noisy all night, and parking is ridiculous, but I love it. I never thought I would after growing up in a tiny town in rural Virginia. The biggest sport there was meeting up on a Friday night to see which pickup truck could pull the other one. The first day of hunting season was an excused school holiday, and the largest club in my high school was the FFA. You probably don't even know what FFA stands for and I'm not telling you. You'll have to Google it. (Don't even bother with Urban Dictionary. It won't be in there.)

One reason I like living in my building is because pets are allowed. There's Barney, who's more of a live-in, lie-about boyfriend who snores, has an atrocious methane problem, and never cleans up after himself when he eats. And there's also my juvenile delinquent bird.

A few weeks ago I found a baby bird, more dead than alive. I didn't know if I could save it, but I brought it home and did a little research and discovered that what I had thought was a sweet baby dove is actually a less-than-friendly pigeon. I named him Frederic J. Pibb, because really, what else would you name a pigeon?

So now I have to spend a few minutes a day removing poop splotches from all over my apartment. I hope he's ready to make it on his own out in the wild soon, but to be honest, I'm not really sure how you can tell. I leave the window open a lot, hoping he'll get the hint.

Another reason I like my building is my next-door neighbor, Mrs. Radice. I can count on her to keep an eye on my apartment when I travel with the ballet, and she brings me treats during the holidays. It's really sweet and gives me a bit of my small-town upbringing back.

My building also comes with a secure parking garage. I made my way down the elevator, found my car, and drove on autopilot to meet my sisters. When we were kids, my sisters and I tried to kill each other regularly. Now that we're older we get together once a week to share our lives. And by "share our lives," I mean eat bacon. Bacon, cheeseburgers, mashed potatoes, and meat loaf at the greasiest greasy spoon in the tri-state area: The Dirty Grudge Diner. We only try to kill each other once or twice a year now, tops.

Upon my arrival, I scanned the parking lot but didn't see any familiar cars. I opened the Grudge's heavy door and let the smell waft over me. I took in a fortifying breath of grease and melted cheese.

The diner started out as a stainless steel rail-car-style building in the forties, but over the years various renovations had been done and now there's a dining room in addition to the original diner counter and stools.

I made my way to one of the larger round tables and waited for someone sharing my DNA to materialize. There are five kids in the Murphy family. I'm the youngest of four sisters and one brother. Also the shortest and least financially successful, but why dwell?

I dropped my phone onto the scarred Formica tabletop and checked for any text messages from my truant siblings. Then, three men sitting at the counter whipped their heads around in the direction of the door.

Glynnis walked into the room and casually glanced around. My oldest sister is tall, blonde, and beautiful. Sometimes I have to remind myself that she's family so that I don't accidentally hate her a little. She's one of the chief executives of a company in Georgetown called Fischer/Rowland. She runs marathons, drives like a maniac, and feels that the rest of us are two steps behind her. We are.

Although Glynnis seemed to not notice, I knew she had taken in the staring minivan jockeys, college students, and after-work suits. Just for fun, though. The Grudge isn't the right hunting ground for Glynnis. She's more at home at Café Milano or the Old Ebbitt Grill. I think she meets us here because no one she knows will catch her licking bacon grease from her fingers. She reached the table and slid gracefully into a chair.

"I'm kind of surprised you beat me here. I guess you saved some time by skipping hair, makeup, and wardrobe." She smoothed her impeccably straight hair.

I glanced at her typical designer outfit and high heels. "I'm wearing my special occasion leggings, you know," I told her. This pair had no holes and had the word "dance" emblazoned across the bum in glitter.

"I'm sure we're all grateful for that."

We both turned as my second oldest sister, Rowan, barged through the room, maneuvering a purse the size of a small suitcase behind her.

"Interesting fashion choice." Glynnis frowned. Rowan's lime-green pantsuit ensemble was a perfect cross between Hillary Clinton and Mr. Yuck.

"One of my favorites. I look like a businesswoman of the first water." Rowan sometimes speaks in colloquialisms circa 1758 Victorian England, thanks to a disturbingly prolific romance reading habit.

She heaved her bag across the back of a scarred wooden chair, and then caught the chair as the weight of the bag tipped it over. She planted her ample rear end in the seat to prevent any further chair calamities.

"Kyla's right behind me. She pulled in beside me blaring music out of her minivan windows."

Sure enough, Kyla rushed over to the table, her wispy curls escaping from a headband and several Lalaloopsy barrettes that had been randomly placed around her head.

"Sorry to be so late. I averted a last-minute kid-related emergency." This was no surprise. Kyla left her junior year of college because she got pregnant and never looked back. She also never saw her feet again, getting married and pushing out four more kids in rapid succession. She's like a Gatling gun of fertility. Who knows what she would have been had she finished college. As far as I knew she majored in beer pong. With a minor in boys.

We all sat and I looked around for Brett, the bacon bringer. Brett and I have been friends since college and I have no small love for the man who brings me a side of bacon larger than my head and doesn't judge me. Even when it's covered in cheese and sour cream.

"I have a goal tonight," I announced to my sisters.

"Other than hardening a few more arteries?" Glynnis asked.

I leaned in close to my sisters to avoid being overheard. "I need to find out if Brett would be willing to go on a blind date with a French sadist." They all frowned at me.

"The only problem," I continued, "is that I'm not one hundred percent sure that Brett's gay, which could potentially be what you would call a deal breaker."

Glynnis smirked. "You think?"

"So what's the plan here?" Kyla scraped at an orange stain on her shirt with a fingernail decorated with a tiny cat chasing a glittery ball of yarn. "They're Jamberry nails," she said when she saw me looking. "You know, one of those parties you go to at someone's house and everyone gets their nails done?" Kyla caught Glynnis's appalled look. "Never mind. Tell us about your plan." She looked at me expectantly.

"Simple. I need to work it into conversation that I happen to know a hot French guy who is not only available, but has leotards in every color of the rainbow, and seriously needs to settle down before he ruins my career and I kill him."

"Hey." Brett sidled up to our table. "I put the bacon order in when I saw Kyla walk in the door. What's everybody drinking tonight?"

All of my sisters looked at me expectantly, waiting for me to put my brilliant plan into motion. I decided to make a general reference to Basil to spark Brett's curiosity and then do a smooth segue into asking him if he'd like to go out with him. Assuming he was gay, and all.

"Do you have Pellegrino water?" I asked casually. "My partner Basil says it's refreshing."

"That's as subtle as a brick to the head," Glynnis muttered under her breath.

"Sorry, honey, fresh out. I can bring some Dasani in a bottle."

"I'll take it. Actually, make it a sweet tea." My sisters made their selections and Brett left to get our drinks.

"Fail." Rowan laughed. "And anyway, how do you not know whether one of your oldest friends is gay?"

I shrugged. "I never asked him."

"And people call me self-involved," Glynnis drawled.

"Why don't we start I Hate My Life?" Kyla asked, quickly changing the subject.

I Hate My Life is a game we play every week. We each tell a true story of our worst moment of the week and the winner doesn't have to pay for dinner. Glynnis almost never wins, and since Kyla doesn't know a story that doesn't include a diaper with poop of some volume or viscosity erupting from it, the real competition is usually between Rowan and me.

"I'll even start. Look at this." Kyla held up her left hand. Her ring finger was cut and swollen.

"What did you do?"

"I went to one of those stupid Pampered Chef parties last night. The hostess was going on about shaping butter into butterflies or something, so I pretended like I had to go to the bathroom. I was in there killing time when I noticed this beautiful sapphire and diamond ring someone had left on the vanity."

"You put the ring on?" I asked.

"Yep. And it got stuck. I tried everything. Wouldn't come off."

"Lotion?" I asked.

"Yep."

"Did you soak your hand in cold water?" Rowan asked.

"Tried it. Nothing worked. I had to go back out to the party and tell the woman I had her ring stuck on my finger in the middle of the vegetable spiralizing demonstration."

"And?" Glynnis prompted.

"And now fifteen frustrated housewives will never know that they can use zucchini in place of pasta in their spaghetti dishes. What do you think happened? We ended up having to go to a jeweler to have the ring cut off." Kyla's head drooped. "Her dead grandmother's ring."

"I threw a tampon at my boss," Glynnis chimed in. We all looked at her. "Earl came by my desk as I was looking for my keys in my bag. He's talking to me about this new project I'm working on and I finally feel my keys down at the bottom of my bag and I jerk them up and in the process a tampon goes sailing right out of my bag."

"That could be worse," I muttered, looking around for Brett, who should be coming back with our drinks soon.

"It hit him in the forehead."

"What did he do?"

"Caught it and threw it back to me, then turned and left my office without another word."

This was good information to have. Maybe I'd start keeping tampons handy to throw at Basil.

"Well, nothing from me tonight. I've actually got some *great* news. I'm celebrating my new commission." Rowan is an artist, which only partially explains her tendency to be a bit more free-spirited than sane.

"You mean the Urban Spaces commission?" Glynnis asked. A few weeks ago Rowan had been selected to create a series of murals around the DC Metro area.

"No, something that came up today. Something *awesome*. Last year I submitted some artwork in the *hopes* of being picked to design a Christmas stamp. Well, of course I was *way* out of my league."

"Don't say that," Kyla butted in. "I'm sure your artwork was as good as everyone else's. You're talented."

Glynnis rolled her eyes.

"*Well*," Rowan continued, adding more vocal extravagance to her winding story, "they have a new stamp campaign coming up and they picked *me*. I'm going to be on a *stamp*." She clapped her hands and bobbed up and down in her seat.

"I'm impressed." I smiled at her. "What sort of campaign is it?"

"Oh. Well, I don't really remember. I think it might be coin collecting, or it might be a herb garden."

"I thought you mentioned a Christmas stamp," Glynnis questioned.

"The stamp I submitted was a Christmas stamp. A bat. But that was for the Christmas contest. I didn't get picked for that one. This is for something else. Some hobby-type thing. I guess they kept my name in a file somewhere and called me when this came up."

"What does a bat have to do with Christmas?" I was stuck on that one.

"It's wearing a Santa hat." Rowan shook her head sadly at my slow-wittedness.

Glynnis drew her signature I-am-about-to tell-you-what-is-wrong-with-you deep breath, but Kyla interrupted before Glynnis could get herself fully wound up. "Well, you'll be great, and we can't wait to see what you come up with."

I didn't have to look up from my menu to know that Glynnis was rolling her eyes again.

Brett wound his way through the jammed tables carrying our drinks and appetizer. "So, ladies, what's next after the bacon?" I'd been so distracted by Rowan's stamp talk I'd failed to come up with an idea of how to turn the conversation naturally to Basil.

I decided to wing it and make one more valiant attempt to hook Bitcherina up. "Basil suggested that I try the portobello mushroom salad. With basil dressing," I finished lamely. Glynnis groaned.

Brett's brown eyes widened. "You're getting salad instead of the usual? You must really like this guy if you're going to miss out on the cheeseburgers tonight."

"Actually, Basil isn't my type. Or rather, *I* am not *his*." I was starting to sound like Rowan. "I think he might be looking for love though," I hinted.

"Oh, honey, aren't we all?" He finished taking our order and went off to another table.

"Well, that took care of it." Glynnis pulled a large piece of bacon from the appetizer plate.

"Are you really going to eat mushroom salad for dinner?" Rowan laughed. This night was not going my way. Why did The Grudge even have mushroom salads on their menu?

"Never mind that. Let's hear Eiley's moment of the week." Kyla absentmindedly rubbed her swollen ring finger.

"Remember that hot bass player I told you about?"

"You mean the one that you talk about every single week? Yes, we vaguely recall." Glynnis snorted.

"He saw me stuffing my bra. Well, actually, he saw me unstuffing it." I looked around the table. Everyone still happily eating bacon not paying much attention to my story. "And that was after he kissed me."

All three sisters stopped in mid-bacon frenzy to stare at me. I couldn't resist a bit of a gloating smile. That had gotten their attention.

"It's about time you finally made a move." Glynnis set her half-eaten piece of bacon onto her plate.

"Actually, he made the move." I added some smug eyebrows to the smile.

"Wow. Why didn't you tell us you had a date?" Kyla asked.

"Oh, well, it wasn't a date exactly, we were in Not Frank's."

"What you're telling us is that you hooked up with this guy. At a bar." Glynnis picked her bacon back up again. My smile was feeling slightly less smug at this point.

"That's okay," Kyla jumped in, "it could lead somewhere. I speak from experience."

"Can you guys smell my eyelashes? Wait." Rowan flapped her eyes open and shut several times. "Now, can you smell them?"

"Anyway…." Glynnis ignored Rowan. "Any future plans with this shining example of manhood?"

"We're going to meet for coffee on Friday." Hah. That was something, right?

"Coffee? You don't even like coffee," Rowan said, still flapping her lashes.

"Not lunch, only coffee?" Kyla frowned.

"You know," I told them, "this all sounded so much better in my head. Ask Valerie. She was there. It was actually pretty good."

"Oh, I know." Rowan clapped her hands. "Tell him that *hysterical* story about the sea lion enclosure. Men *love* funny women."

Glynnis looked horrified. "No. Wear a short skirt. No sea lions, no vacuum in the oven story, and for the love of all things holy, do *not* sing." She was probably right about all of those things.

"I have some news," Kyla interrupted. "Guess who else is going to be hating her life soon? Mom and Dad are going to go to LA to visit Aunt Psycho."

"Oh God, why?" Glynnis groaned.

"She's not that bad," I muttered. All three sisters turned to stare at me, bacon momentarily forgotten.

Aunt Psyche is my great-aunt on my father's side. She was born with the name Patricia and renamed herself Psyche after tuning in, turning on, and dropping out. However, she's been known to everyone who has ever talked to her for longer than five minutes as "Psycho" for as long as I can remember. She's a throwback to the sixties. Actually, I think she might still be in the sixties someplace, finding herself and balancing her aura. Aunt Psycho makes Shirley MacLaine look like a founding member of the Tea Party.

My sisters all find her greatly annoying, but I love her because she used to be a dancer. She was on the Jackie Gleason show with the June Taylor dancers back in the day. She does take some getting used to though, and by the time most people are used to her she's worn them out, blathering on about the illuminati, her past liaisons, and our great-uncle Seamus's lost treasure. But the truth is I admired her so much when I was a kid. She's the reason I became a dancer.

"Dad's worried. Psycho's been acting strangely," Kyla explained.

"How could he tell?" Glynnis snorted, which was impressive for a woman with a mouth full of bacon.

"Well, even more than usual apparently. Dad's going to take a look around and make sure she's okay on her own. Of course, Mom is beside herself. If Psycho isn't able to take care of herself, Dad wants her to move back here. Maybe even stay with them."

"Yikes. Do you think Mom can handle it?" Rowan looked doubtful.

"Not without a lot of alcohol," Glynnis deadpanned.

"Mom doesn't drink," I protested.

"She'll start," Glynnis stated. We all nodded solemnly at this thought.

"Now, before Brett gets back over here with your substandard dinner, why don't you explain what it is exactly you're trying to do to the poor man?" Kyla shoved a generous helping of bacon into her mouth, and then daintily wiped off her fingers on her napkin.

"Val and I have come up with a plan to make Basil like me so I don't lose my job."

"This should be good." Glynnis leaned back in her seat and crossed her arms.

I hurried to explain my plan before Brett returned with my miserable mushroom monstrosity. People had better appreciate the sacrifices I was making for love and art tonight.

"You want to hook up the man who faithfully supplies us with unending plates of bacon with a tool you gleefully refer to as 'Bitcherina'? Are you crazy? You'll get us kicked out of here."

It would be a real tragedy if my last meal here were a pathetic mushroom salad. "Basil only hates *me*, he's not that bad to other people. I admit I have selfish ulterior motives, but he really is hot, has a job and nice teeth, and Brett is all of those things, too, and you know, potentially gay. I thought I'd throw them together and see what happens, so to speak."

"This is one of the worst ideas you and Valerie have ever had," Glynnis said.

I crunched into my bacon and tried to ignore her. What an exaggeration. This might be a bad idea, but it was nowhere near the caliber of the worst idea Valerie and I have ever had. That had involved Palmolive, jumper cables, and several tense moments in the back of a squad car. Not to mention several days of picking lima beans out of my hair.

"You're a dimber damber." Rowan nodded at me.

We all stared at her blankly.

"An Abbess. A Cash Carrier." She threw her hands up dramatically. "A pimp."

I had a brief mental image of myself in a low-slung Cadillac wearing a purple satin top hat with matching platform shoes. And leg warmers.

"Lord love a chicken." Rowan took a breath and blew the bangs off her forehead. I considered stuffing my napkin into her mouth but there was no guarantee that would stop her.

"Hey, Brett," Rowan yelled across the diner. "You gay?"

"As a purse full of rainbows," Brett replied.

"Well, that's sorted then. Now pass the blue cheese."

That was one way to do it.

I decided to order a double side of fries to go with my salad.

I felt like I'd earned them.

Chapter 3

Coffee and a Class Four Felony

I stood in front of my closet, closed my eyes, and made a wish. When I opened them again, I was still staring at the same twenty leotards in varying stages of decay, three leg warmers, and assorted ratty shorts and jeans.

I'd gone over to Pentagon City Mall last night to try to find the perfect outfit for my coffee date with Trey. I'm usually a bargain shopper but I figured I could splurge since this was the single most important date in the history of the coffee bean. But I'd gotten serious sticker shock at the mall. Who pays eighty-five dollars for capri pants?

I was stuck with what I had in my closet. I pulled a box of random items from the top shelf. I found three pairs of yoga pants, several pairs of old underwear (don't ask me why, I don't know), my winter gloves, and one short black skirt. I straightened it out and examined it.

The length and color were good. This could potentially create the right look to convince Trey to profess his undying love. I flipped the skirt over and frowned when I noticed the pocket. It was huge and, even more undesirable, had a unicorn on it—in neon pink and purple rhinestones. I could vaguely recall having borrowed the skirt from one of Kyla's kids for a Halloween party. I must have forgotten to return it.

I'd called in sick from work this morning so that I'd have more time to get ready, but I'd spent a lot of it perusing Trey's social media accounts, hoping that he might have mentioned our coffee date today. He hadn't. Now I was out of time.

I pulled the skirt on reluctantly and added a cute pink shirt with a ruffle across the top that could almost be mistaken for cleavage. I could pull the shirt down to cover the pocket. I'm resourceful. I used to be a Girl Scout, you know. Too bad there wasn't a badge for online snooping, I would have had that thing sewn onto my little green sash in no time at all.

I used my last few minutes to put some finishing smudges on my eyeliner. I'd gone for an irresistibly sexy, smoky eye look. Hopefully I didn't have the more resistible "I didn't bother to take a shower" or, worse, the even less desirable "I got hit in the eye" look.

Frederic fluttered in and sat on my shoulder as I took a last survey of myself in the mirror. Not bad. I'd straightened my hair. I like how it looks straight but you kind of have to wonder about any beauty technique that makes your head smoke when you're doing it. I gobbed on a generous supply of Baboon Butt bubblegum gloss and did a few practice smiles in the mirror.

I hoped I'd appear like I had my act together today, and that after he explained why he kissed me at Not Frank's, Trey might want to get together again. It was a long shot, but compared to being invisible for a year, I felt like I was making some sort of progress.

Was it too much to wish he'd want to start an actual relationship? Probably the best I could expect would be a hookup. What should you do when the most gorgeous man you've ever seen offers you a night of mortal sin?

I'd never hooked up with anyone before. The two boyfriends I'd had were both long-term relationships. Maybe it was time. Lots of people did it. Glynnis never had any relationships that lasted longer than a month, give or take. Kyla had a one-nighter that happened to end up being with her future husband. It certainly didn't start out that way, though.

I'd been fantasizing about the man for a year, but was that really what I wanted? I pictured Lance sprawled across my bed and developed a sudden can-do attitude.

Gently, I removed Frederic from my shoulder, gave Barney a kiss, pulled my shirt down over my bedazzled pocket, and headed out to meet Valerie. It was time for coffee, subterfuge, and charm. And possibly some begging, if necessary.

When I got to the lot, Valerie was waiting beside a bright red BMW M4.

"You look great."

"Thanks. I'll be fine as long as I keep my shirt down."

"Uh, okay. I guess. Now, listen. You have ninety minutes. Drive carefully. I put temporary tags on and the dealership sticker on the window is barely hanging on so you can slip it off and shove it in the glove box. Put it back up when you bring it back."

My can-do attitude and I both nodded at her rapid-fire instructions.

"If you have any problems, hit the phone icon there. I pre-programmed it to connect right to me at the dealership. But don't have any problems."

The whole time I drove to Café La Ruche I heard Glitch Mob's "Drive it Like You Stole It" in my head. Although I had a furious urge to hit the gas and fly down the side streets, I made sure I didn't get a ticket.

I got to the café five minutes late, like we'd planned. I circled the lot for another several minutes trying to find a suitably obvious parking space. The only open space, however, was behind a dumpster. It figured. All our work on covert ops foiled by a steaming, festering hunk of metal filled with hipster coffee trash.

Determined to not be outdone by the dumpster, I took the key fob and casually slipped it into the waistband of my skirt, with the BMW logo facing conspicuously outward. It was shallow, but Valerie had gone to so much effort it was the least I could do. Tricky though, because I had to keep one side of the shirt down over the unicorn pocket and the other up to show off my ill-gotten key fob.

I carefully worked my way around the dumpster. Hopefully the smell wouldn't linger on me. That thing smelled worse than a latrine. In August. In the sun.

I went through the door and scanned the tables for Trey. I saw him at a small table in the corner, looking at his phone. If the whole rock star thing didn't work out, he could look into modeling. Underwear.

He looked over and smiled and gave me a small wave. As I got closer he stood up. "Hey, I'm Trey."

"Eiley."

He laughed. "How weird is it that we didn't even know each other's names and we were totally kissing, like, three days ago?"

"Yeah, weird." If by weird he meant totally the best day of my life. Plus, I wasn't going to mention the fact that I did know his name. And address. And I'd seen his house on Google Earth, courtesy of the satellite view. Seriously, I make the NSA look like amateurs.

"You want some coffee?"

I noticed he already had a huge cupful. "Maybe in a minute. I really can't stay too long." Or Valerie will get fired.

We both sat down.

"What do you do?" he asked me.

What do I do? What? Like, do I, say, sit around and Google you all day, drawing little hearts around your name? Yes, yes I do.

"Uh," I panicked. So far the caliber of my first impression was on thin ice.

Trey smiled. "I mean your job. What do you do when you aren't at Not Frank's?"

"Oooh." I blew out a sigh of relief. "I'm a dancer."

His eyes widened. "Really? A professional dancer?"

"Yep."

"Would I have seen you dancing anywhere? Like at a club, or a video or something?"

"Oh. Um, no. Not hip-hop. Ballet."

"Ballet. So no twerking and hip shaking?"

"Nope. More like hair nets and blisters." I couldn't help but notice that he looked a little disappointed by my not being a stripper.

"But I'm extremely flexible," I added, raising my eyebrow a little. "I mean, I can bend in all kinds of ways. Ever seen *Black Swan*?"

Trey choked a little on his coffee. I could feel myself start to blush. I'd gone from awkward to hot mess in ten seconds. I should have known better. I'd given up trying to be sexy in ninth grade when I tried to wink at Robert Turner, got nervous, and accidentally closed both eyes and he asked me if I was having a seizure. And although it would get me free dinner at the Grudge, it wasn't exactly what I was going for right now.

I needed to change the subject quickly. Sorry, Valerie, all that work for nothing. What a waste of eyeliner and a push-up bra. My can-do attitude was shaking its head in disappointment. I needed to do some damage control, but I couldn't think of a single thing.

The minutes stretched out in uncomfortable silence and my mind remained stubbornly blank of any possible topics of conversation. Trey glanced down at his phone again, probably wishing he were anywhere else but here.

And then, desperate to fill the conversational black hole, I lost it completely.

"So, this one time my sisters and I were visiting this aquatic animal park, and the funniest thing happened. My mother stopped to buy my brother a snow cone, and my sisters and I ran ahead to where they had this protected area for sea lions that had been injured and this one sea lion was attacking this other sea lion, so my sister…"

I paused to take a breath. Trey was looking at me like I might need a padded room. Ugh. More damage control. I took another deep breath and tried to refocus. What had we been talking about before my unfortunate reference to sexual contortionism? Employment.

"Never mind about that. Are you a full-time rock star, or do you have a day job?"

Trey blinked at the abrupt change of conversation. After a pause he answered, "I'm an EMT."

I caught my jaw before it actually fell open. Although it seemed impossible, he had somehow gotten more attractive. As I sat there contemplating this new kernel of information, a mom with an overloaded stroller brushed against our table and some coffee sloshed out of Trey's cup.

"Hey, got any tissues in there?" he asked, eyeing my ruffle.

"No." I tried to look offended, but then casually reached into my push-up bra and pulled a Kleenex out and handed it to him. "Well, maybe one."

He smiled and then we both started to laugh, which was kind of nice. He had a beautiful smile, with straight, white teeth. And when he laughed his eyes crinkled up at the corners. I pictured him in a leotard. It's an occupational hazard.

"So, I guess I owe you a story."

I nodded hoping the story would distract me from staring at him.

"I have this girlfriend my friends have never met."

So far this story sucked.

"She's out of the country right now. Her name is Lia."

I wanted to file his coffee spoon into a point and stab myself with it. In the eye.

"Where do I fit into all of this?" I asked, trying not to weep into his coffee.

"Chad wants me to go out with his sister, but that's a situation I'd rather avoid for a lot of reasons. I told him I had a girlfriend so he'd leave me alone about it."

"And Chad wanted to meet your girlfriend?"

"Right. I told him that she was out of the country but he didn't believe me. He thought I was lying about having a girlfriend and was blowing off his sister."

"Which you kind of are."

He hesitated. "Yes, but I'm trying to be nice about it. Anyway, he didn't believe me so I had to find someone to fill in until Lia comes home."

"So, I was your pretend girlfriend?"

He took the last sip of his coffee and slowly put the empty cup back down. "I guess that's one way to put it."

"I feel like I'm in a bad romance novel, or like I've been sucked into an episode of *General Hospital*." Not that I was complaining.

"It's more like a Hallmark movie, really," he said.

My eyebrows shot up. "You watch Hallmark movies? How very punk rock of you."

"No, that's what I've heard," he protested. He picked up his empty cup and tore at the Styrofoam around the edges. I gave him a skeptical look. "Once. With my grandmother, to keep her company." He made a little pile of the shredded cup.

"You decided to grab a random girl at Not Frank's and pretend she was your girlfriend?"

He looked up again and our eyes met. "Not so random."

My heart skipped a beat.

"I didn't think you would mind because you…ah. Well. You know."

"I know what?"

"I've noticed that you're usually at Not Frank's and you, uh, look my way a lot. I thought maybe you had a little crush or something."

"For your information," I scrambled to do yet more damage control and preserve my dignity, assuming I still had any left after the ill-advised *Black Swan* remark, "I wasn't looking at you. I was looking at your guitar. I happen to be interested in instruments. Especially guitars. I'm a…guitarophile."

Why do I never know when to shut up?

"Oh really?" He nodded at me. "What kind of guitar do I have?" The corners of his mouth turned up a little in a crooked smile.

Hah. I knew this one. You don't stare at a man's skinny jeans for months and not know the words on the guitar right in front of them. "It's an Epiphany," I crowed triumphantly.

"Actually, it's an Epiphone."

"Well, I was using the European pronunciation."

"European?"

I nodded. "And some parts of Scandinavia." We both started laughing again.

"I'm so glad this is all okay. You come to Not Frank's a lot, and I don't want it to be awkward."

"No worries. I admit I had a crush on you for like a minute, but I'm totally over it. And you know I have a boyfriend and all." I crossed my fingers under the table. "The big question here is how do we act in front of Chad and your friends? Will you need me to be your pretend girlfriend again?"

Trey frowned. "I didn't consider that. Hard to believe a plan I came up with in three seconds could have a downside."

I caught a whiff of his cologne and shifted, wedging myself against the tabletop, trying to subtly edge closer. I couldn't decide if his eyes were gray-blue or blue-gray. It probably depended on the lighting. In sunlight they were probably...

"Someone's car alarm is going off."

...more blue than gray. And his hair probably had golden highlights. And...

"That's a seriously annoying alarm. Can't you hear that?"

...in candlelight, he probably...

"Eiley, don't you hear that?"

Hear what? My ovaries crying?

And then it occurred to me. I had jammed the car keys into my waistband, to be casually conspicuous. All the shifting against the table must have set off the alarm—on the key fob that I didn't know how to work.

"Oh my gosh, I think that's my car." Mine for another fifteen minutes, anyway.

I pulled the keys out of my skirt and started frantically jabbing at buttons. "I never can remember which one it is," I improvised as the shrill alarm continued.

"That's okay, I can walk you out. I need to get back to work, anyway." He threw his trash away and we headed out of the cafè toward the dumpster. The car alarm had, thankfully, stopped on its own.

"There's my car," I chirped brightly, jabbing at the key fob and accidentally popping open the trunk.

"Nice." Trey walked closer to admire it.

I furtively shut the trunk lid and then opened the doors. "Hop in and take a look." I ignored the fact that I felt a little bit like a stranger trying to use candy to lure unsuspecting victims into my windowless van.

I made a mental note to get Valerie something really nice for Christmas. I hoped the extra few minutes might give him time to decide to ask me to go out with him again. That's right, "again." I was totally counting this as a date.

Trey walked around the car and climbed in the driver's side and I got in on the passenger's side. It was nice in there, Trey and his pretend girlfriend, in her pretend car. I took a deep breath of new car smell and tried to channel some of Glynnis's confidence. "So, this Lisa girl. Are the two of you exclusive?"

"Lia? No, not really."

My palms were instantly clammy. It would have been easy for him to tell me that they were exclusively dating each other even if they weren't. But he didn't. He'd left it open. Should I throw caution to the wind and go for it? *If you don't, I will*, my can-do attitude taunted.

I twisted in my seat to face him and tilted my head against the seat. "Well, that's good to know." I picked up a strand of my hair and twirled it around my fingers. Hint, hint. I smiled. I rubbed my lips together. I had officially exhausted my repertoire of flirting techniques. Baboon Butt was my only hope at this point.

Trey looked down at the steering wheel and fiddled with one of the buttons. "So, you're seeing someone, right?"

I couldn't decide if the question was meant to encourage me or discourage me. "It's more of an open thing, really," I hedged.

"Eiley," Trey hesitated, "I…"

Rats. Discouragement. I had to stop that sentence. That sentence wasn't going to end the way I wanted it to.

This is your last chance, my can-do attitude urged. *Seize the day.*

I grabbed his shirt and pulled him toward me, smashing our faces together. It was an awkward kiss—him in shock and me trying to determine if he was struggling to get away while I worked my tongue into his mouth.

I couldn't read how he was feeling, but I was too overwhelmed by a potentially lethal combination of lust and panic to care. There was only a whooshing sound in my brain. Sort of like one of those coffee bean grinders, or maybe a small handheld vacuum that isn't so loud it gives you a headache but is powerful enough to suck up dog hair and pigeon poop. (Call me, Dyson.)

I needed to get closer. I lurched myself awkwardly over the gearshift and onto his lap. The driver's seat was really close to the steering wheel to accommodate my five-foot-tall frame. Okay, fine, four feet eleven. And a half.

Using my left foot on the dashboard for leverage, I was able to reach down far enough to get to the seat controls. Finally, there was room for me to completely climb into his lap, my knees on either side of his thighs. I sighed happily at the contact my body was making with his. Carpe diem, indeed.

I was kissing him again when it occurred to me that all this shifting around had probably exposed my pocket. I sneaked a glance down, and sure enough, the magical flying rainbow unicorn was glinting in the sun. I tried to pull my shirt down without being too obvious.

Unfortunately, my right elbow hit the door handle and we both started to tumble out of the small car. I let out a girly squeal. More of a shriek, really. The two of us frantically leaned back into the car and my small hoop earring caught on Trey's shirt.

Any sudden movement would rip my earlobe. And then there would be…blood. I choked back a wave of nausea. Unable to see his face at the awkward angle I was trapped in, I frantically dug my nails into his arm. "Stop. Stop."

"What is it? What?" He moved slightly as he talked and my earlobe twinged in pain. I wailed in what some people might consider an unattractive manner. I was sure my ear was bleeding. Trey tried to raise his hands and I screamed again.

"You're hurting me. Please stop. Don't move. Stop what you're doing."

"I'll be absolutely still, if you'll tell me what's going on."

I let go of him and carefully removed my earring.

"Let me see." He turned my head to the left. "It's okay. You're fine."

"No blood?"

"Nope." He traced the edge of my ear with his tongue.

Who was I to argue? The man was an EMT. And the ear kissing was causing a rush of heat to my already overexcited anatomy.

More kissing followed, accompanied with heavy breathing, some over the shirt touching, and what would best be described as some minor moaning on my part.

I popped the button on his jeans and briefly considered calling Valerie to see if the car had been Scotch-guarded when something tapped on the window. I jumped back into the steering wheel and my bottom honked the horn. Trey groaned.

Two cops stood outside the car, one of them holding a nightstick.

"Oh my God. Oh my God," I squealed, my voice high and squeaky. I scrambled out of the car, being careful not to jab my knees into any tender anatomy while pulling my skirt down from around my waist. As soon as my feet hit the pavement one of the officers grabbed me and pulled me away from the car. Were they going to take me to jail for public indecency? Although it would be a great story to have a mug shot, this would not be a good thing. I looked back at Trey. He was on the ground up against the dumpster, his hands behind his head, the male cop's knee on his back.

"It's okay, honey. Where's your mother?" the female cop asked me.

"She's in Fauquier," I told her. "Oh no, actually, she's on her way to LA, to see my crazy aunt."

"And who's watching you while she's away?"

"Watching me?"

"Do you have a guardian?"

"I'm twenty-five."

The cop took in my flat chest and sequined unicorn skirt. "Do you have an ID, miss?"

"In the car, in my bag." I ran to get it, hoping they'd let Trey get off the molten asphalt.

I showed the cop my license and said a silent prayer that she wouldn't ask to see the vehicle registration or any proof of ownership. "Miss, do you know that we received an emergency nine-one-one call about an attack in this car?"

"I didn't call nine-one-one. Someone was mistaken. There was no attack. It was…just some…you know, we were um…"

The cop with his knee on Trey's back was grinning at me now.

"I think we get the picture here, miss. We're going to let this go this time, but in the future please remember there are laws against this sort of thing."

Someone mumbled something about getting a room. The officers walked back over to their cruiser and I helped Trey brush off his clothes.

"Well, that was interesting," I said.

"Yeah, interesting."

I glanced at my watch. There was no time to try to figure out how he was feeling. I was late to return the car. "Well, I guess I'll see you at Not Frank's." I scrambled into the car.

"Yeah, sure."

I would have liked to hang around for a few more minutes to smooth things over with him, but I needed to hurry back. I used my tardiness as an excuse to test out the car's powerful engine. I blazed through a red light on my way back to the dealership, cringing as I replayed everything in my mind.

It was definitely a bad ending to our date. But on the plus side, kissing Lance Manyon was even better than I'd imagined it would be, and believe me, I've had a lot of practice imagining it. I never thought that I'd kiss him like that in this lifetime without the use of a blindfold and chloroform.

Chapter 4

Patton Does Not Prevail

I stumbled into the studio at three thirty, only an hour later than I said I would be when I'd called in sick this morning. I rushed into the changing room, threw my ruffled blouse and unicorn skirt into my locker, and pulled on tights and a leotard as quickly as I could. I had a brief pang of disappointment when I had to twist my hair into a bun. It had taken me over an hour to accomplish silky smoothness.

My chest, neck, and cheeks were bright red and blotchy. Did I mention that stress also causes the blotch phenomenon? Stress, embarrassment, anger, happiness, anything really.

I ran out of the locker room and down the hall, passing a practice room filled with cygnets rehearsing the dance of the swans from the second act. I paused a second to watch the four dancers link arms and complete a series of sixteen pas-de-chat in perfect unison. It was one of my favorite parts of the ballet.

I hurried on to the main practice room and flew through the door, my pointe shoes skidding on the worn floor. I took a deep breath and let it out slowly as I assessed the room. Late afternoon sunlight filtered through the tall windows and added to the June heat. Dancers clustered around the room, some stretching at the barre, others watching Basil as he did a series of brisé, his massive thigh muscles contracting to make the small leaps controlled and beautiful. Honestly, Brett could do worse.

Susan turned and saw me lurking in the doorway. Hopefully she wouldn't be too upset that I'd taken most of the day off.

"Eiley, so nice of you to join us." Uh-oh. That didn't sound promising. "You can take over for Corinne now."

My gaze swung to the corner where my understudy was toweling off. "Corinne?" This was not one of the scheduled practices for understudies.

"We expected you after lunch. It's almost four now. You can't expect the entire company to shut down when you're tardy."

"I'm sorry. Of course not. I came as soon as I…" I paused, looked down at my pointe shoes, and swallowed the lump in my throat. "…as soon as I felt well enough to get here." I crossed my fingers behind my back. I looked up again at Susan, who said nothing. My gaze flicked to Basil and then to Corinne, standing smugly in the corner, smiling slightly.

"I'm here and I'm ready. What are we working on?" I wiped my sweaty forehead. It really was stuffy in the studio.

"Act Three. Let's start with Siegfried's dance with Odile."

I managed to suppress my groan, but it wasn't easy. The dance began with a maneuver that's like doing a split in midair, one foot on the ground and one on Basil's shoulder. The foot on the ground is en pointe, or on my toes. Then Basil walks slowly backward, pulling me along with him. The problem? I'm five feet tall. Okay, fine. Four eleven. And a half.

We took our positions and Susan started the music. I took three small steps toward Basil and began to lift my leg. Then put it right back down again. This was exactly how I'd kicked my last partner right in the chicken nuggets. The last thing I needed was a repeat of that. Basil already hated me and, let's face it, Valerie would never let me live it down.

"Eiley?" Susan's voice had a bit of an edge to it. I'd been back for two minutes and was already causing problems.

"Maybe I could raise my leg and Basil could sort of slide his shoulder under it?" I suggested hopefully.

"Try it again." Susan turned the music off and the room was still and quiet and hot. All eyes were on me and the stupid smirking Bitcherina.

"Right. Okay. I'm on it."

All I would need to do was kick as high and as quickly as I could so that my foot would be in position as Basil stepped toward me. Quick and high. I could do this. I jogged in place for a few seconds like a boxer, psyching myself up. I could do this.

We took our positions again. I took my three small steps toward Basil as he moved toward me. I kicked as quick and hard and high as my short legs allowed. My knee crashed into my chin and my head snapped back. My arms flailed as my pointe shoe slipped underneath me and I hurtled backward toward the ground. There was an audible gasp from somewhere behind me as I bounced off the wooden studio floor. Followed by some muffled snickers.

I sat up gingerly, rubbing my chin, a little dazed.

"Did you just…" Susan paused, took a small breath and continued, "kick yourself in the face?" She covered her mouth with her hand.

"It's okay. I'm totally fine. Only a little mishap." I glanced in the mirror. My lip was swelling and I had a huge red mark on my chin.

"Go get some ice. Corinne, why don't you finish out the day with Basil. Eiley, you watch."

Corinne slinked over. She gave me a small nudge and took position where I had been standing. "You're so graceful," she muttered under her breath before turning to face Basil.

I trudged into the locker room, the pout on my face helped along by my ever-increasing lip size. I got some ice and, in no hurry to go back to the studio and watch Corinne dance with Basil, went to my locker and found my phone.

I had four messages from Valerie that all started with *URGENT*. I decided those could wait. Valerie's idea of urgent and my idea of urgent are two totally different things.

The only other message I had was from Kyla. *Last day of school. Let's celebrate tonight at the Grudge? Usual time?*

I typed out a quick reply. *I'll be there.* Grudge bacon twice in one week would not be good for my thighs, but it would give me a chance to make up for the substandard dinner I'd had on Wednesday night, not to mention today's humiliation. Perhaps a corndog was in order. They always made me feel better when I was upset. There's probably a scientific link between carnival food and endorphins. Psychologists should study it someday. (Call me, Dr. Phil.)

***

"And so," I paused dramatically, wiping bacon grease from my fingers, "we ended up in the car, kissing for like twenty minutes." I looked around the table to see the reactions to this bit of news.

"Is that what happened to your lip?" Glynnis finished the text she had been writing, threw her phone down, and reached for the bacon.

My hand flew to my lower lip. "This? No. A little accident at work today."

"Did Basil do that?" Kyla asked.

"Sadly, I did this to myself. My leg kind of got away from me." I regretted my words as soon as they were out of my mouth. I probably should have fibbed that I ran into a door.

Glynnis hooted with laughter and Kyla and Rowan were both grinning. "That'll be some performance this fall," Glynnis said after she'd caught her breath.

I shot her a look. "But you're all coming, right?" I left off the thought that had been circling my head since today's disastrous practice—assuming they actually let me keep the lead role.

Kyla looked at me sympathetically. "Of course we'll all be there. I'm going to do you a favor and leave my kids at home with my husband, but I'll be there and so will the rest of the Murphy family." She looked at each of my sisters pointedly. "Right?"

Rowan and Glynnis both nodded. "I'll even throw you a celebratory dinner afterward," Glynnis told her.

I smiled. "Really? Thank you. That would be really nice." What a generous offer. I couldn't think of a better way to celebrate opening night as the lead. Unless it all went horribly wrong. Then I'd be stuck at a party with my whole family. No pressure. I resisted the urge to fan myself.

"Never mind that. What's it like to fondle the hottest guy you've ever seen in your life?" Glynnis grinned.

I considered that for a moment. What had it been like?

"Amazing." That pretty much summed it up. Although it would have been better if he'd been the one to initiate it.

"Don't you think it was a little…you know…?" Rowan asked. "I mean you've kind of turned into a light skirt."

"Oh no, not really." Kyla frowned at me. "Well, maybe a little bit. This is out of character for you, Eiley. You must really like this guy."

I shrugged.

"Okay, so you're in the car, and you're kissing. What happened after that?" Glynnis asked.

"I'm saving that part for I Hate My Life." I crammed a few more pieces of bacon into my mouth, rendering myself incapable of further incriminating self-disclosure.

"It must be pretty bad if it's worse than kicking yourself in the face," Glynnis teased.

"Let's get this special Friday night edition started then," Kyla suggested. "I'll go first. As you know, today was the last day of school. A half-day. And although there were only three hours of actual school time, Finn managed to get into trouble."

Despite being the cutest red-haired, freckle-faced first grader in the country, my nephew Finn had a rap sheet at Sandy Pines Elementary School that was a mile long. The office secretary has my sister on speed dial.

Kyla continued, "Mrs. Krebbs tried to get him to come to her desk without drawing too much attention to him. She was making the come here sign," Kyla bent her index finger back and forth.

"Then Finn crooks his finger back at her and yells, 'Arrr, I'm a pirate too.' like his finger is a little pirate hook."

We all laughed. Secretly, Finn is my favorite nephew. He loves to tell jokes and he keeps boxes of odd collections and treasures stuffed under his bed. He's autistic and super smart and has the kindest heart of anyone I've ever met. The only problem is that he sometimes doesn't fit into the structure of the typical school day, and sometimes his sensory issues cause meltdowns that not all of his teachers are equipped to handle.

"Then he insisted on talking in pirate the rest of the day."

"That doesn't sound all that bad." I was indignant on my nephew's behalf.

"Well, there was an unfortunate plank walking incident on the playground. Mrs. Krebbs was not amused. She made a point of mentioning the self-contained classroom for next fall several times during her phone call, so now I've got that to worry about."

"She needs to chill out. That's harmless, and it's the last day of school. Who cares?" Glynnis shrugged.

"I love that story. It's better than mine." Rowan set down her half-eaten piece of bacon. "I was on my way to meet the lady in charge of the Urban Spaces Commission and I was starving, so I ate some peanut brittle out of my purse on the way there."

"You carry peanut brittle around in your purse?"

"Not usually, but I was out of beef jerky so I had to improvise. I forgot to grab a bottle of water and let me tell you, it isn't *easy* to get peanut brittle out of your teeth. I was in a bit of a sticky wicket, you know. I was *hoping* to find a water fountain, but of course, I was in the District, so *none* of them worked, and I was running a wee bit late. So I had to talk to the lady all brittled up."

"And?" Glynnis prompted.

"I accidentally *spit* on her when I was talking. *Three* times, right in the face. I suggested we perhaps do a portrait of Patton."

"Well, that could've been worse," Kyla said encouragingly.

"One of them went into her mouth."

We all paused in our pursuit of pork to consider that.

"That's pretty bad." Glynnis shook her head.

"Don't vote yet. I think I have the winner. Let me finish my Tale of Lance Manyon."

"Ah, yes. Lance Manyon. The pinnacle of male perfection. Could we all pause for a moment of silence for Lance?" Glynnis requested.

"Yes, let's hear it for Eiley's double-breasted water-butt smasher." Rowan picked up her forgotten bacon and dipped it into the ranch dressing. We all stared at her. "You know? Her true Corinthian?" Our blank stares continued. "A young blade? A dashing rakehell? You people should really do a little more reading. They're in, like, *every* Regency romance novel."

"Okay, so we're sitting in the car and there was a lot of body contact going on." My face warmed thinking about it. Okay, maybe my face wasn't the only thing heating up. I fanned myself with my napkin.

"Right in the middle of everything, someone starts pounding on the door. It's the police. They think Trey is a pervert, and I'm a twelve-year-old girl."

"Can you blame them?" Glynnis asked.

"What happened?" Kyla asked.

"They throw him to the ground and cuff him, while I have to show my ID and prove that we're both adults." I rushed ahead at this point to cut off whatever remark Glynnis was going to make concerning the validity of my adult status. "And then I had to leave to get to work." I conveniently left out the part about borrowing the car from Valerie. "So I have no idea if he hates me now, or what."

"Keep throwing yourself at him and see what happens," Glynnis suggested.

"I'm not throwing myself at him." I looked at Kyla for support. She was suddenly too busy getting the last bit of sour cream on the last piece of bacon to look at me.

"Fine. I am. I've wanted to be with this guy for a year. Is it so wrong to take the opportunity when it finally presents itself?" I glanced from sister to sister.

"Go for it." Glynnis nodded. "Don't forget safe sex and try to hang onto a little of your self respect." Condoms and dignity, I could do that. The condom part, anyway.

Kyla frowned at me. "I'm sorry, Eiley, I don't think this is a good idea. You're going to end up with a broken heart. Why don't you try to slow things down and get to know him? Maybe this could turn into a relationship."

"Maybe." I shrugged. I didn't think Lance was really offering anything more. He had a girlfriend out there somewhere. And it had been me who had initiated everything except for the first kiss. But I didn't want to admit any of these not-so-flattering facts to my sisters.

"That's actually a great idea," Rowan concurred. "Hooking up is great, but if you had a relationship, you'd have more time to fool around with him."

"Sure. Fine. I'll make an effort to focus more on getting to know him and less on, uh…"

"Getting to know his—" Glynnis began.

"Well," Kyla interrupted. "I guess Eiley is our winner this time. Although spitting in someone's mouth is pretty bad."

"Thank you," Rowan beamed. "But the police thinking your fake boyfriend is a pedophile has to be the winner."

Free dinner for me. A dubious honor to get a free meal for having a life that sucks the most, but when you're chronically short of cash, it's not the worst thing. It was time to find Brett and order that bacon cheeseburger.

"Now that we know for sure that Brett is gay, should I ask him to go out with Basil?"

"Have you asked Basil if he'd go out with Brett yet?" Kyla asked.

"No, not yet. Today was kind of awful."

"What, with kicking yourself in the face and all?" Rowan snorted.

"Yeah. Probably not the best time." My words came out sounding a little short and sarcastic. "Should I start with Brett? To get an idea if he might be interested?"

"Ask him what his ideal date would be," Rowan suggested. "It'll get him talking about dating. Maybe you can segue."

"Hey, Bacon Bringer. We're ready to order," I called out.

Brett walked over with his order pad at the ready and gave my ponytail a tug.

"How are my favorite ladies tonight?" He pulled out his pencil then paused, crinkling his nose. "Who smells like they used a whole bottle of perfume?"

I took a deep sniff. Sure enough, there was a strong floral smell coming from Kyla's direction.

"Oh, that's probably my Scentsy," she answered sheepishly.

"What is a Scentsy, and why are you wearing so much?" Glynnis asked.

"It one of those melted wax things you get from one of those parties at someone's house. You heat it up and it makes your house smell good. I accidentally spilled it on myself and didn't have time to change."

"You've been walking around like that all day?" I asked her.

She nodded. "Bees chased me home when I was walking my dog."

After Brett wrote down all of our dinner choices, I decided to give Rowan's idea a try. "Brett, what would your ideal date be? If you could go anywhere, with anyone, you know. That sort of thing."

Brett pulled an extra chair up to the table. "We're talking romance tonight, are we? Okay, let me see. Confidence is attractive."

This sounded good already. Basil was more than confident. He was like the Kanye of the ballet world. Although what did that say about me? Was I the Woody Allen of the dance world? Probably better to think about that later.

"My best first date ever," Brett continued "was in the summer."

This was good, it was summertime now.

"Like, the perfect summer night. You know what I mean, big moon, stars in the sky, finally cool after a long hot day. We went for a walk through an orchard, and the air smelled like fresh, ripe peaches."

Were there peach orchards in Adams Morgan, the DC area where Brett lived? Probably not.

"There was a pond in the middle of the orchard and we sat there, listening to the frogs and crickets. You know how they sound in the summer. We spent hours talking and looking for shooting stars."

By the end of Brett's story, all four of us were staring at him dreamily with our mouths open.

"Well, that beats the never-ending pasta bowl at the Olive Garden all to hell," Rowan said.

"What about a dancer? They're pretty confident and they, uh, have nice legs." I smiled brightly at Brett.

He patted me on the head. "Sure you do, honey. You have beautiful legs. Now, if only you had a great big beautiful penis to go with them." He winked outrageously. "Now let me get on those cheeseburgers before I get fired. Unless you'd like another mushroom salad?" I scowled as he walked off laughing. I'd have to come up with a better plan and try again.

"You guys," Kyla exclaimed. "I got so distracted by Eiley's whole fake boyfriend situation I totally forgot. I talked to Mom today. You'll never believe what she's doing tomorrow."

"Having Psycho committed?"

"Starting her career as a drinker?"

"Nope. You're all wrong. She's going to be in the studio audience for *The Price is Right*." Kyla crowed.

"Maybe she'll get to play Plinko," Rowan squealed. "It's too bad Bob Barker isn't the host anymore. He's a sexy guy."

"I'm sure she'll have some good stories to tell when she gets home." Glynnis blinked several times. "Wait, what? On what planet is Bob Barker a *sexy guy*?"

After two weeks stuck with my dad and Aunt Psyche, I had no doubt there would be many stories to tell. But I didn't know if they would be good ones. Maybe my mom might have to join us for a night of "I Hate My Life—the Alcohol Edition."

Kyla turned to Rowan. "Tell us more about the meeting with the Urban Spaces lady."

"It was kind of hard to focus after I spit in her mouth, but we did decide on a theme. Sort of a theme, anyway."

"Which was?" Glynnis asked impatiently.

"Urban street art. Sort of Banksy style. Using existing features to create pictures. It's been popular in other cities."

"Existing features?"

"Well, for example, picture a cement wall with a tree over it. The artist paints a face on the wall, and the tree is the hair for the face. Things like that."

"And you can make this happen?" Glynnis asked.

"Of course she can." Kyla stacked our appetizer plates to make room for Brett, who was heading our way with a cubic ton of ground beef smothered in American cheese. We each claimed our prize and began to eat.

"And some of the paintings," Rowan continued between bites, "will have a political message. I'm particularly good with those. Or they might reference popular culture. The arts as well." We all nodded as we concentrated on chewing.

"In fact," she nodded at me, "you know that retaining wall outside of your studio? I plan to do a line of ballerinas in tutus doing something dancer-ish."

I thought back to the practice I'd seen briefly today from the hallway. "You could do the cygnets from Swan Lake. It's beautiful. They all hold hands in this crisscross pattern, and they wear short feathery tutus and feathers in their hair, and they all dance in unison…" I trailed off as I realized that no one was really listening to me anymore. Rowan and Glynnis were scuffling over the last onion ring and Kyla was dabbing at ketchup on her shirt.

"Yeah," Rowan replied, "that sounds like a perfect idea. I'll touch base with you later, when I'm doing my sketches."

"I like it," Glynnis proclaimed. "I mean, for God's sake, you weren't really going to paint Patton, were you?"

"So you like it, or you think Patton would be awful? Because we owe our freedoms to those generals and military type people, you know." Rowan's voice had an edge to it.

"I like it. Bring some sketches with you next week. Maybe we can help you with some of the ideas. Oh, I know. You should paint workmen on a wall that has public water fountains. Because typically, everything is broken in DC."

"And you could do a queue of silhouettes at a bus stop, like a line of people waiting for the bus," I chimed in.

"Or a heaping plate of bacon," Brett yelled from the counter.

Now that would be a true work of art.

Chapter 5

Earwigs, Banana Pun Not Intentional

Every morning I have a ritual. Most dancers do. Foot care is serious business when you rely on your feet for a living. Some dancers I know use vinegar soaks and put on fake toenails and even go as far as to put bandage tape covered with makeup on their foot imperfections.

But my morning routine is purely for functional, rather than cosmetic, reasons. I trim whatever toenails I have left, slather Lucas' Papaw lotion all over my feet, and inspect them for fungus. I also use a pumice once a week when I shower to smooth down the worst of the rough edges and rub coconut oil on them every night before bed.

Unfortunately, all that pampering doesn't lead to beautiful feet. My feet could star in their own version of *Nightmare on Elm Street*. It's one of the many downsides of being a professional dancer.

You might think it's all glamour and glitter, but in reality, professional dance is a competitive world that requires perfectionism and a serious work ethic for little compensation.

In addition to the toll it takes on your personal life, you have to learn hours of choreography and then there's flexibility, stamina, body control, and weight to worry about. Not to mention figuring out when you're going to pee.

After finishing with my feet, I got myself ready to head to the studio. I was determined to not be late this week. Yesterday had gone fairly well. No major mishaps. It felt like the time was right to find a way to talk to Basil about Brett.

I fed my animals, made a half-hearted attempt at wiping up bird poo, walked Barney, and wheeled my bike out of the parking lot in record time. The bike is crucial around here. Not only can you park the thing almost anywhere and save on the exorbitant parking fees in DC, but you can also zip past all the cars stuck in traffic. Pointing and laughing at them as you go by is optional. The downside, however, is that about six months out of the year the weather is abysmal.

Bike riding in the ice and arctic temperatures is no one's idea of a good time, least of all mine. Not to mention, it's never a good idea to arrive at the studio with frozen muscles. So, when it's cold I usually drive. It can sometimes add an hour to my commute, but it's worth it not to be a popsicle upon arrival.

Today, however, was perfect bike riding weather. I tipped my head back as I pedaled. With the sun and summer breeze I could almost pretend I was at the beach. I had one more long day to get through before skinny jeans time tonight. How would Trey act when he saw me? What should I wear? Did he have an innie or an outie? I hadn't managed to get a look at his abs yet, but it was on my list of things to do. My can-do attitude and I were going to give it our best shot to get closer to him.

I locked up my bike and made my way into the studio. I worked my way past a small crowd of dancers in the hallway in various stages of lacing up pointe shoes and finishing French braids. I turned into the main practice room. Basil and Susan were already there. I went to the barre and began stretching.

"I will show the appropriate emotion during the performance. Do not doubt that I know my job," Basil yelled with his French accent. I bent over in a low stretch, trying to eavesdrop. It appeared that they were arguing.

"It's not about bringing it at the performance," Susan returned fire. "You need to be emotionally present during rehearsals or you throw off the entire cast."

Emotionally present? The man barely made eye contact. The real problem was that it was hard to sell the idea that his character was willing to die for my character when he couldn't stand being in the same room as me.

"I do the best I can with what I have to work with," he responded sourly. I straightened from my stretch to find them both looking at me. My face flushed. Today was definitely the day to put my plan into motion. I would find a way to hook Basil up with Brett and all his bacon fulfillment glory, and then he'd be happy, and like me, and everything would be better.

We spent most of the morning perfecting lifts, and things were going well. It was probably the only upside to being a shrimp, but at least Basil couldn't complain that I was too big or too heavy to lift. Susan finally called a break and I gratefully took off for the locker room.

I relieved my bladder, checked my phone, and got a new bottle of water from my locker. On my way back to the practice room I saw Basil exiting the men's locker room. I glanced around. It seemed to be empty. There was no time like the present. I might not get a chance to speak with him privately again today.

"Basil, I was hoping to talk to you alone for a minute." I pasted a big smile on my face. Basil's eyes widened in surprise. He nodded his head but I couldn't tell if it was a yes nod or a no nod. He made some sort of gesture I couldn't interpret and took two hasty steps back into the locker room.

Had he been waving me off or telling me to follow him? I didn't want to go into the men's locker room uninvited. But on the other hand, if he was in there waiting for me to follow him, he'd be even angrier if I walked away. Which scenario was worse?

I forged ahead. I stalwartly pushed the door to the locker room open. Basil was standing right inside.

"Oh *mon Dieu*," he exclaimed and took several more steps backward.

Okay, he had been trying to avoid me. But I was here now, and I might as well get this over with. Too bad I hadn't prepared what I should say. As I tried to collect my thoughts, Basil looked toward the door, probably calculating his chances for escape. I needed to act quickly.

I took a deep breath and put my hands on my hips. "Basil, how would you like to go on a date?" I gave him a big friendly smile.

"Oh *merde. Dieu ait pitié*." He looked horrified.

I patted his arm reassuringly. "I promise you'll really enjoy it." I continued to pat his arm and smile. "You know, you've got really huge biceps."

Basil's face was white. "I am sorry, I am not interested," he choked out from between gritted teeth. He pulled away and darted past me, escaping through the door. Well, at least I'd tried. How was I supposed to know he'd be ridiculously afraid of a blind date?

Things only got worse when I got back to the practice room.

"Let's go back to the lift Eiley had trouble with on Friday," Susan said, with a small grin on her face. Sure. It was all fun and games until someone kicked her own eye out.

"Maybe we save that for tomorrow?" Basil looked even more uncomfortable than I did. I had somehow managed to make things between us even worse.

"No, it's okay. I can do it. I'm ready." I smiled, nodded, and tried to exude confidence.

We took our positions. Susan started the music and I took my three small steps toward Basil in preparation, but he remained rooted to his spot.

"Again," Susan directed.

She restarted the music and I resumed my position. My hands were clammy and my heart was pounding. I did not want to make a fool of myself yet again. On cue, I took my three small steps toward Basil. I could see that he had started to move as well. I quickly shot my leg up, high, but not into any major organs—mine or his. As my leg started to come back down to rest on Basil's shoulder it met with only air. I began to fall awkwardly, unable to regain my balance.

Basil's face registered surprise as he realized he had not gotten close enough to me to complete the sequence. I made a frantic grab for him, but it was too late. We both crashed to the floor in an ungainly tangle, my leg still extended over Basil's shoulder, his face most unfortunately pressed into my crotch.

Basil looked up at me from between my legs. "I told you. I do not wish to go out with you," he whispered angrily.

We untangled ourselves quickly and got to our feet. What in the world was he talking about? I had asked him to go out with Brett, not with me. Hadn't I? I tried to replay the conversation in my mind, but I couldn't remember whether I'd mentioned Brett's name.

"You know," Susan said, ending my silent horror, "why don't we try it another way. Eiley, you kick your leg up and Basil, you sort of slide underneath it."

Perfect. One problem down, about a million to go.

***

I made the trip home quickly and had my swollen feet in a tub of Epsom salt as I mentally planned my outfit for the evening.

Tonight's outfit was important. I wanted to look hot but act cool, something I'd never mastered, or even come close to, really. I knew the trick was to look great but not like you'd tried too hard to look good.

I was drawing a blank. I grabbed my phone and sent a quick text to Valerie. *Help. What do I wear to Not Frank's tonight?*

She answered back right away. *Be dazzling, but not bedazzled. What then?* I replied.

I don't know. Play to your assets.

That sounded like good advice. I took a quick mental inventory. I must have some assets. I have small feet. Would that get his attention, assuming he could overlook my mangled toes? If he did, he was probably not the guy for me after all.

I dumped my foot water and went to look at myself in the mirror that hung on my closet door. I turned to examine myself from all angles. Perky breasts had not materialized since the last time I'd checked, and my trunk remained junkless.

I threw my hands up in defeat almost smacking Frederic out of the air as he zipped past my head. It wasn't like I had the budget for a wardrobe anyway. I decided to wear one of my black leotards with some jeggings and heels. At least I wouldn't look as if I'd tried too hard. Plus, the Baboon Butt lip gloss would provide any added flash my outfit lacked.

I was at Not Frank's at our usual table with wings and blue cheese at the ready when Valerie arrived. "Okay, look," she said as she sat down. "Don't be mad."

Conversations that start this way are never good.

"Okay," I replied, with fear in my heart. "Tell me."

Valerie twisted her handbag nervously. She hadn't even made a move toward the wings, which was another bad sign. Nothing keeps Valerie away from chicken wings.

"The thing is," she started again, "and you should know, I had nothing to do with this. Nothing."

"Yes?" A bead of swat trickled down my forehead.

"It's viral." She covered her face with her hands. This was a lot of drama, even for Valerie.

"What is?" I asked. "Shingles? Is the virus already inside me? Something on my laptop?" I gulped. "Plantar warts?" I may need a paper bag to breathe into.

She lowered her hands a fraction, so that I could see her eyebrows and the top of her eyes. "Your little, ah, romantic interlude last Friday."

"But," I asked, "But how? I mean who? Why would anyone? How?" I fanned myself with my hand.

"Apparently, when we heard you through the Bluetooth on the car, someone at the dealership made a recording with his cell phone, in case we needed it for the police or insurance. And when he realized what was really going on, he put it on YouTube."

"It's on YouTube?"

"And. Um. This morning, I heard it on the radio. Elliott played it, during Elliott in the Morning."

"Elliott? Everyone listens to Elliott. My *dad* listens to Elliott."

"Really? I can't see your dad listening to Elliott. Isn't he more of a WASH FM kind of guy?"

"Valerie. Focus. Did they mention anyone by name? And what exactly can you hear on it? Did it sound like we were, you know?"

"Playing hide the salami? Here, see for yourself." She whipped her phone out of her pocket. She spent a moment looking at it and then handed me the phone.

Since this was an audio recording, some individual had helpfully supplied several still shots from pornographic movies while the YouTube clip played.

There was a lot of breathing, some groaning, and some random scuffling, followed by my voice yelling "stop" and "you're hurting me." Then I could hear someone, probably one of the car lot employees, calling 9-1-1, and Valerie's voice trying to convince that person to hang up the phone.

The kissing and breathing sounds went on for a while, and then you could clearly hear the officer knocking on the window with his nightstick. As the conversation continued, it became obvious what was going on, and the car lot employees were hooting with laughter. When I recognized Valerie's snorty laugh, I gave her the evil eye. She shrugged.

"On the bright side, you can't tell it's you. It doesn't sound like you, and it sure doesn't look like you," she said, eyeing the well-endowed blonde on the screen.

"I guess you're right. It could have been a lot worse." I scanned the room. The bar was starting to fill up. I wondered where Trey was. I could use the YouTube video as an excuse to talk to him. "I'll be back with beer," I told Valerie. I took her mobile with me and walked toward the bar, hoping to see Trey.

I finally found him in the kitchen talking to one of the dishwashers. "Hey, fake boyfriend. Do you have a minute to talk?"

"Sure" he answered, leaning against a stainless-steel counter filled with food prep items. I couldn't help but notice that some flies were milling around the appetizers. Carlton the dishwasher leered at us from behind his industrial-size pot scrubber.

"Uh, maybe privately?" I asked, looking around.

Trey grabbed my hand and pulled me out the back door into an alley that reeked of old grease and overfilled trash dumpster. I didn't want to think about what vermin might be lurking. I was especially not going to think about rats the size of small children waiting to bite my ankles.

"What's up?" He was wearing gray cargo shorts and a tight white T-shirt that emphasized his tan and his abs, and his bluish-gray eyes. I had been right. They were bluish gray in the sunlight.

I sighed and handed him the phone without explanation. He watched the clip through twice.

"How did this get on YouTube?"

"Well," I crossed my fingers behind my back, "apparently when we were in my car on Friday I must have accidentally hit the OnStar button. And they made a recording of what they heard."

"BMWs don't have OnStar."

"Well, whatever it's called." I smiled nervously. Hopefully he didn't know that it was almost impossible to accidentally press the emergency button in a BMW.

"So someone took the recording and then put it on YouTube?"

"I guess so. And then somehow it ended up on a nationally syndicated radio show with thousands of listeners."

"But they didn't use your name or anything, right?"

"No. You and I are the only two people who know who is on the video. And my friend Valerie. And the cop who knocked on the window. And my sisters." I swatted at a huge fly from the dumpster that was swarming around my head, probably attracted to my Baboon Butt lip gloss.

"Oh, is that all?"

"And Brett, my bacon supplier."

"I don't even want to know what that means." He ran his hands through his hair.

"What's wrong? Are you worried about this somehow getting back to your secret girlfriend?"

Trey glanced away from me. "No, not really. But I was a little surprised to hear that my private life had been broadcast on a morning radio show."

"It's actually kind of funny, when you think about it." I took another swat at the fly. It's kind of hard to look seductive when a buzzing spawn of Satan is circling your head like you're a rotting carcass.

"Yeah, I guess. Send me the link." He looked like he was about to turn to go back into Not Frank's.

I scrambled for some way to make the most out of my current situation. I was alone in an alley with Lance Manyon, trash heap and pestilence be damned. I needed to keep him talking. I coyly tilted my head to the side and flipped my hair. "What songs are you going to…" The accursed fly flew right into my ear. I shrieked.

"Help. Help." I flapped my hands in the air helplessly. I was afraid to touch my ear, not sure if I'd be scaring it away, or pushing it deeper in.

Trey slapped his hand over my mouth. "Do *not* yell that. The last thing we need is another cop coming to your rescue." I could feel him searching my hair with his other hand, trying to determine the fly's whereabouts. Slowly, I opened my mouth and bit the inside of his hand. You know, in a sexy way, not in a Hannibal Lecter way. He took his hand off my mouth but didn't say anything.

Without breaking eye contact, I stepped closer until there was only a sliver of space between us. I was so close to him I could swear my skin was vibrating. If he rejected me, I would throw myself into the dumpster with the flies.

I put my hands on his shoulders, pulled him down, and kissed him one time, softly. He still hadn't initiated anything, but maybe he'd choose to continue. That was probably the best I could hope for.

I looked up into his beautiful blue-gray eyes. Neither of us moved. His gaze held mine, and the moment hung in the air. A second passed And then another. I was pretty sure the entire world had slowed to a stop and was waiting to see what would happen in the next moment.

In one sudden movement his hands were on my hips, lifting me as he walked forward. I slammed into the brick wall and my breath came out in a whoosh. He leaned into me, crushing me against himself, and kissed me. *Woo hoo.* My can-do attitude cheered.

I was pressed so tightly I couldn't move. Not that I was going anywhere. How long does it take for people to die of thirst? They could peel my cold dead corpse off the bricks in a week or so. I wasn't even thinking about the fly anymore. It could have crawled into my brain and burrowed into my cranium for all I cared.

I wrapped my arms around his neck and my legs around his waist. There was a blur of kissing and hands accompanied by some grunting. You know, sort of like a pig rooting for truffles, but sexier.

My hands were under his shirt, feeling his abs. He's an innie, if you were wondering. I felt his hands go to my waist and start pulling at my top. "How does this thing come off?" he asked between kisses.

Ugh. Stupid leotard. "It doesn't. It's all one piece."

I felt his hands go to my shoulders and push the straps down over my arms. Had I stuffed tissues in there? I couldn't remember. I also couldn't hear anything over the pounding of my heart. Which probably explained how neither of us noticed that the door to Not Frank's had opened and Chad was standing there, hands on hips.

"Dude," he yelled. "I've been looking for you for ten minutes. Put down the girl already." He turned around and went back inside, mumbling something about getting a room. I was starting to get tired of hearing that.

Trey stepped away from me, and I slid down the wall to my feet. I pulled up my leotard straps. Fortunately no breasts (or tissues) had been peeking out for Chad to see.

Trey wiped his hands over his face. "I don't know what to say," he told me with his hands out, palms up. "I mean, this wasn't part of my plan. This whole fake girlfriend thing is getting out of control." Fortunately, he was unaware that he'd been the star of some fantasies that were far more out of control than this. He dropped his hands to his sides. "This is the second time this week we've been standing next to a dumpster, kissing. Do you have some weird thing for dumpsters?"

"Uh, I like dumpsters? You know, give a hoot, don't pollute?" I made a vow to stop talking. Maybe forever.

"We can talk about it later," he said.

I nodded and he turned to go back into the building. I followed after him, Carlton ogling me as I passed. I walked through the kitchen and back to my table with Valerie, a happy little smile on my face.

"Where's my beer?" Valerie asked, turning to look at me. Her jaw dropped open. "Did Lance do that to you?

"Do what?"

"Uh, let's see, your hair's messed up, your face is all red, your shirt's on crooked, and you're grinning like an imbecile. And what are those imprints on your back?

"I did what you suggested. I went with my assets."

"And what's that?"

"Being small and easy to lift is useful in more areas than ballet," I answered smugly.

"Ew. Stop right there. I need beer." She got up from the table and walked off toward the bar.

"Get more wings," I called to her retreating back. The wing plate and both vats of blue cheese were empty. Valerie had even eaten the little garnish on the plate. I guess you really can eat anything with blue cheese on it. Then I remembered the flies in the kitchen. "Never mind," I yelled over to her, casually scratching inside my ear where the fly had been. It had probably laid eggs in there.

I focused my attention on the band. It was too hot for skinny jeans, but there was still plenty of magic on stage. When Trey glanced in our direction he smiled at me.

"You'd better settle down," Valerie tipped her cup back to get the last dribble of beer.

"What do you mean?"

"Every time that boy looks at you, you break out in hives."

"I'm a little worried. The last thing he said was that the fake girlfriend thing is out of hand and we'd need to talk about it," I told Valerie as I fanned myself.

"Do you think he's going to fire you?"

"If he does there'd better be some sort of hookup severance pay."

When the set was over, Trey jumped down from the stage and headed our way. I swilled down the last of my beer and girded my loins. Do women have loins? Fine, then. I girded my metaphorical loins.

"Hey," Trey called as he got closer. Okay, so far, so good. I smiled and tried to keep myself from over-nodding. "I wanted to talk to you about something." Uh-oh. I cut my eyes over to Valerie, who merely raised an eyebrow and shrugged. "Chad's having a get-together this weekend, and his sister is going to be there. So, I need you for fake girlfriend duty."

I said nothing for a moment as I grimaced in pain from Valerie's size ten foot ramming into my shin. I was trying hard to stop my eyes from watering. This was so not the moment to appear to be crying tears of gratitude.

"Sounds like fun." I did nothing to give away the fact that on the inside I was dancing like Snoopy when he sees his supper dish coming. Which was probably confusing, considering not forty-five minutes before I was in a back alley climbing his body like a monkey on a banana rampage. (Banana pun not intentional.) (Well, mostly not.)

"Great. I'll text you later and give you all the details. It's sort of an outdoor pool party type thing, so bring a bathing suit."

"Sounds good." I smiled, giving myself a mental pat on the back for my calm exterior. I wrote my address down on a scrap of paper from Val's purse and handed it to him.

We finalized our plans and Trey left to pack up his gear.

Valerie grabbed my arm, her mango orange nails digging into my skin. "Oh my God. HE LIKES YOU." she hissed out in a strangled rasp. Whispering has always been tricky for Valerie.

"What do you mean? It's only to keep Chad's sister away." I shook my head.

"Stupid, think about it. He could have told Chad you had to work. He didn't have to ask you. He asked you because he *wanted* to ask you." She emphasized each word with a little stab of her pointer finger.

"That could have something to do with the fact that I keep throwing myself at him. If it wasn't totally clear that I am willing to hook up with him, it is now." Kyla would have been so disappointed if she knew.

Valerie nodded slowly. "Okay, that may be true. But now you know for sure he's interested in at least one great night."

"He has a girlfriend, remember?"

"Huh." She snorted. "Outta sight, outta mind."

I liked the sound of that.

Valerie picked up her empty cup and licked a drop of liquid off the rim. "You could use the opportunity to make him fall in love with you."

"Fall in love with me? Like a Disney movie? Am I supposed to put him in a rowboat with singing frogs? Eat the same strand of spaghetti until our noses bump? Go riding on a magic carpet with my pet tiger…" I was getting a little worked up.

"Okay. That might be a tall order. Go to the party. Have a good time, get to know him, and he'll realize that he needs to change your status from fake to real."

It couldn't hurt to try. Plus, it was another day spent with Lance, and I could honestly tell Kyla that I'd made an effort at getting to know him.

"And it doesn't hurt that you look pretty good in a bikini."

"You think so?" I asked.

"Sure. With two percent body fat? Of course you do."

I left Not Frank's feeling a little ray of hope.

Maybe I could pull this off.

Chapter 6

Huge in France

Kyla nodded her head in Brett's direction. "How's the big plan coming?" She shoved a mound of bacon into her mouth then licked the grease from her fingers.

"I hit a small road bump. Basil may be under the mistaken impression that I asked him to go out with *me*, and now he's afraid of me."

Glynnis rolled her eyes. "How did that happen?"

"I may have accidentally forgotten to mention Brett's name when I suggested the date."

"Well that's a fifteen puzzle," Rowan said. I looked at her in confusion. "A mess. Or as Basil would say, *Quel désastre.*" We all looked at her in surprise. "What? I know things. Continue your story."

"In my defense, I was flustered. I hate going into the men's locker room. It makes me feel so icky."

"You cornered him in the men's room and asked him out? No wonder he's afraid of you. What happened after that?" Glynnis asked.

"It turns out fear may be worse than hate. I ended up falling on my behind yesterday because he was too scared to get close to me."

"You're blaming him for you falling on your own bottom?"

"It was his fault."

Glynnis looked at me skeptically.

"Remember my swollen lip last week? We were working on the same move that caused that. This time, I kicked my leg up but his shoulder never turned up in time for my foot to land. He stepped in three seconds too late and we both fell over."

"You took the captain down with the ship?" Rowan asked.

I scoffed. "Worse than that. His face landed right in my No Trespassing area."

"Well, that's one way to get to know him." Glynnis deadpanned.

Kyla giggled. "What did he say?"

"He was furious. He said that he'd told me that he didn't want to go out with me and I needed to leave him alone."

"Wait. Let me get this straight. He thought you fell on purpose to… to… entice him?" Glynnis threw back her head and laughed. "And he ran away in horror?"

I threw my napkin at her. "Fear, horror, and hate, the trifecta of dysfunctional work relationships. You can see why I still need to fix him up with Brett, can't you?"

"And how do you plan to do that, now that the man won't even speak to you?" A glob of blue cheese dressing fell onto Kyla's sweatshirt and she quickly wiped it away with a napkin.

"I'll get Brett on board first and then take another stab at Basil later. When he comes over to the table again, I'm simply going to ask him if he'd be interested in meeting someone. That's the best way, right?"

"Well, it would certainly be the fastest way," Glynnis grumbled.

"Good luck," Kyla said. "I hope you're doing the right thing."

I hoped so, too. I scanned the crowded room until I found Brett, huge round tray in hand, delivering plates to another table. I smiled and gestured to him to come over.

"I have it right here," he called, arriving at our table a few minutes later with an extra cup of blue cheese.

"Oh no, not that."

"Speak for yourself." Rowan reached for the extra dipping sauce. I hesitated for a moment, studying her wardrobe choice for the evening. She was wearing a low-cut dress that was a cross between a Victorian gown and a dominatrix outfit. Where did the woman shop?

I shook off my distraction. "Brett, I was wondering. I have this friend, and I think the two of you would be great together. Would you consider meeting him sometime?"

Brett put his hand on his hip and looked at me suspiciously. "Depends. Does he have a great personality?"

"No," I told him excitedly. "He's hot."

"Is he one of your dancer friends?"

"Yes. In fact, he's the male lead."

"Got any pictures?"

"Of Basil? Well, no. But you can Google him. The ballet was really lucky to get him. He's huge in France. And he's tall…"

"*Huge* in France, huh? I like the way that sounds." Brett waggled his eyebrows. "Hang on. Tall as in tall, or as in taller than you, Miss Five Foot Nothing?"

Four foot eleven. And a half. But a true friend gives you the benefit of an extra half inch.

I was stumped over the question of Basil's height. "Well, I think he's about five ten, at least. Brown hair, blue eyes." Brett's eyes narrowed. "Dancer's body. Rock-solid muscles," I hastily threw in.

"I think that's enough to work with." He smiled. "I'll meet your Bitcherina. Tell me, does he have a French accent? I love an accent."

A brief memory of Basil swearing at me in French flashed across my mind. "Yes. It's totally charming."

"Okay. I'm in. Set it up and let me know. Now, that appetizer plate is looking almost empty. Let's get on with dinner. Orders, ladies?"

We gave Brett our list of demands and he went off to the kitchen in search of our cheese-coated, calorie-laden desires.

Glynnis smoothed her impeccably smooth, flat-ironed-to-within-an-inch-of-its-life hair. "Let's get on with 'I Hate My Life.' Eiley, are you going with molesting your dance partner?"

"Actually," I drawled, "I have something else for tonight, but I'd like to go last. Trust me when I say I have tonight's prize all sewn up."

"Must be a good one if it beats accidental sexual harassment," Rowan said.

"Oh, it's a prize winner. Hall of fame. Not to mention it comes with a visual aid. Well, audio, anyway."

"Okay then," Rowan offered, "I'll start. I was at the grocery store the other day right around lunchtime. Right as I pull up, a fire truck parks in the lot and a crowd of *adorable* firefighters pile off the truck and head into the store. So I'm kind of following behind them, watching them shop."

"That's kind of creepy," Kyla interjected.

"I was *hoping* that one of them would notice me." Apparently a fondness for rescue personnel ran in our family. "I was trying to look alluring so I bypassed the Lean Cuisines. And I didn't put on my glasses. When they stopped to look at something I stopped nearby to look at something."

"Seriously. That's creepy," Kyla said again.

"One of them notices me staring and *smiles* at me. I got so excited I dropped a huge jar of gravy on the floor. It didn't simply break. It was like a Thanksgiving *explosion*. By the time I had the mess sorted out, the firemen were gone."

"Does no one else find this creepy?" Kyla asked. "Really? Fine. I'll go next. Our church does a drop-in day care. Yesterday I was dropping off Jamie when the priest stops by. So he does a little blessing and then walks around the room to interact with the kids a little. When he gets to Jamie, he has a puppet and he's making the puppet talk in a funny voice. So Jamie looks him right in the eye and says, 'You're dickless.'"

"What?" I asked. "Why would he say that?"

Rowan propped her elbows on the table and rested her chin on her hands. Any conversation about penises had her full attention. "Were you totally shocked?"

"Shocked, humiliated, prepared to be excommunicated, all of the above. So Father gives me the hairy eyeball and asks where my three-year-old might have heard such a word. While I'm telling him how wholesome our family is and that I have no idea, Jamie says, 'My mommy says my dad is dickless.' At this point I'm completely mortified. I was as red in the face as Eiley gets when talking about Lance Manyon."

"Gee, thanks."

"I'm trying talk to Jamie the way you do when you're pretending to be calm and collected but you're dying inside and you really need your kid to shut up. Jamie thinks the whole thing is hysterical. He starts yelling 'My dad is so dickless,' as loud as he can. I had to pack our things up quickly and get out of there before I ended up in the Adoration Chapel doing penance."

"Why do you call Mike dickless? Was there an unfortunate weed eater incident we haven't heard about?" Glynnis asked.

"I don't. It wasn't until the drive home that I realized that Jamie was talking about what happened after dinner the night before. I was washing dishes and Mike was tickling me and I told him that he was ridiculous. Ridiculous. Rotten kid."

Brett returned with our heart-attack-inducing entrees. "Stay a while, Glynnis was about to tell us the worst thing she did all week." I pulled my cheeseburger off his tray.

"I can only spare a minute. It's busy tonight." He passed around the rest of our food. I slid over and he perched on my chair with me.

"Mine isn't all that exciting really. I walked in on my boss while he was in the bathroom."

"Earl? I'd call that pretty exciting," Rowan mumbled through a mouthful of Salisbury steak. "Did you see anything good?"

Glynnis's face flushed. "Oh, I caught a glimpse before I slammed the door shut and ran away like a wildebeest being chased by a pack of rabid hyenas." She turned to face me. "So tell us your award-winning story. It has to involve our good friend Lance, correct?"

I spilled out my story, capping it off with a presentation of our clip on YouTube. "So you see," I told them, "I think this is Guinness Book level 'I Hate My Life.' Am I right?"

Kyla patted my hand sympathetically, leaving behind smears of fried chicken grease. "Well, how did Lance react to all of this?"

"He was a little surprised, but overall it ended on a good note."

"All's well that ends well," Rowan said vaguely.

"What kind of good note are we talking about here?" Brett asked. I had a brief flashback of hot kisses, fast hands, and a brick wall digging into my back. My face flushed.

"Oh you didn't. Don't tell me that you hooked up with him again. What kind of girl is he going to think you are if you shove your hand down his pants every time you see him?" Kyla asked.

"The best kind," Glynnis stated.

"I didn't shove my hand down his pants. Not ever. Not that I'm against it or anything. The opportunity hasn't presented itself and those skinny jeans are pretty tight…but he asked me out. We're going out on a date." I conveniently left out the detail about Chad's sister.

"That's great," Rowan enthused.

Brett gave me an awkward side hug. "Good luck, honey."

"Try to keep both feet flat on the floor," Kyla suggested. I scowled at her.

"Why don't we have a Mom and Dad update. Kyla, have you talked to them? How did they like watching the *Price is Right*?" Rowan asked.

"Well, it's pretty exciting. They didn't only watch *Price Is Right* get taped. Mom got called to 'Come on Down.'"

"I knew it." Rowan pumped her fist with glee. "I knew she'd get called. She played Plinko, didn't she? Didn't she?"

"Oh for the love of all things holy, put your arm down, Snookie," Glynnis snapped.

"She didn't play Plinko. She played this game where you have to slide numbers over and figure out the price of three prizes. And if you get it right you get to keep the prizes."

We all started talking on top of one another. Even Glynnis was excited. Kyla let the moment drag out, enjoying having all of us in suspense. Finally, she said, "She won. She won all three prizes."

Once again we were all clamoring for more information. "You won't believe it. She won a juicer, one of those huge fancy barbeque grills, and…"

Brett grabbed a piece of fried chicken off Kyla's plate and took a big bite out of it. "I'm going to eat your dinner until you spill the details," he told her.

"She won an RV."

"That's a lot of taxes to have to pay." Glynnis scooped a spoonful of cheesy hash browns into her mouth.

"How are they going to get it home?" Brett asked. He gathered up the ten Sweet and Low packets Rowan had emptied and set them on his tray.

"They're going to drive it home. And you haven't heard the biggest news yet."

"What's bigger than a Winnebago?" Rowan looked perplexed at the mere thought. Or maybe she was distracted by her push-up bra. I know I was.

"There will be three people on the ride back to Virginia."

A hush fell on the table as we all stopped to ponder the reason for the third traveler. Aunt Psycho was coming home.

"Poor Mom," I muttered.

"Poor Mom, poor *us*," Rowan asserted. "We're going to be the ones who have to keep Mom from losing her mind. Psycho will be nagging Mom to henna her hair and take pictures of goats and go on a hunt for Seamus's lost treasure and Mom will be spending weekends, weeks, and months at our houses to get away from Pyscho."

"It'll never happen," Glynnis stated. "The drive across country will fix it. That Winnebago will arrive with two people and a mysterious smell in the lavatory."

"Isn't there always a mysterious smell in an RV lavatory?" Rowan asked, frowning.

"I think we need to offer up a toast for our mother," Glynnis said. We all lifted our glasses.

"To Mom." Kyla toasted. "What doesn't kill you makes you stronger."

"A lasting peace, or an honorable war," Rowan chimed in.

We all drank to that.

Chapter 7

Un Soupçon Gay

The next morning I did a perusal of Trey's social media accounts while I soaked my feet. We'd exchanged numbers last Tuesday at Not Frank's but I hadn't heard from him at all. This would have to do.

There weren't a lot of new things on Instagram since my last visit so I focused on who had liked and commented on his photos. Chad commented frequently, as well as some other guys I didn't recognize but assumed were fellow EMTs.

I was able to recognize Chad's sister, Nicole, out of the many female commenters. I'd like to say that this was thanks to my keen intellect and excellent detective skills, but really it was because she and Chad had the same last name and dark hair.

I took a few minutes to scan her profile. And her Facebook and Snapchat, if you must know. Hey, attention to detail is a virtue. I learned that she'd moved back into the area recently after being gone for several years. She was also apparently an aficionado of tube tops and she either had a serious immune system disorder or she liked spray tans. She also had no problems with body image judging by her semi-nude profile picture that was barely this side of Facebook legal. She probably hadn't stuffed tissues into her tube tops since third grade.

I turned off my laptop and hurried to get ready for the studio. I didn't want to talk to Basil today, but if I didn't, my next opportunity wouldn't be until Monday. As much as I dreaded it, it was probably better to clear things up sooner rather than later.

I pedaled to the studio and tried to formulate a game plan. Unfortunately, my brain decided it would much rather think about seeing Trey in a bathing suit tomorrow. No matter how hard I tried to focus on the task at hand, my mind wandered back to naked abs and suntan lotion. It was probably some new form of perversion-induced ADD. Doctors should diagnose this disease so that sex-starved women all over the globe can be helped. (Call me, World Health Organization.)

I locked up my bike and went to the locker room to change. It would probably be better to talk to Basil privately but I didn't know how—he gave new meaning to the word standoffish, lately. I would have to do the best I could. Brett was on board and it was time to make a love connection. If Brett couldn't improve Basil's mood, a pointe shoe to the kidney was my next strategy.

I wandered out of the locker room and looked around. Practice for the day hadn't officially started and the hallway was filled with clusters of dancers. I walked past two of the cygnets leaning against the wall outside of their practice room, looking at something on one of their phones. I found an open space sufficiently far enough from the men's locker room to not appear that I was lying in wait. I bent to fiddle with the satin tie of my shoe as I began my stakeout.

After a few minutes, Basil emerged from the locker room and strode down the hall. I straightened from my crouch. I crossed my fingers.

"Basil," I called out, my voice only a little shaky. His head swung in my direction. I could swear his skin tone paled when he caught sight of me. Not a great start.

"Not now." He picked up speed and was down the hall before I could say another word. Definitely not a great start.

I raced after him and caught up to him at the door to the main practice room. I grabbed his elbow before he could disappear inside. He spun around on his long bony feet, his worn dance shoes making a circular scuff mark on the burgundy carpeting.

"Yes?" he asked warily, not making eye contact.

"I wanted to talk to you a minute to explain something."

"What is that?" His eyes remained glued to his shoes.

I lowered my voice so that we wouldn't be overheard. Although Basil was under the impression I'd propositioned him, I hoped that none of the other dancers knew about it. Luckily for me Basil probably thought it would be more embarrassing for him than for me and had not talked about it to anyone.

"The other day, when I asked you what I asked you, I wasn't really asking you for me, you see." Basil said nothing. "It was really a misunderstanding. You see, sometimes, when I get nervous, I can be a little awkward."

"I hadn't noticed," Basil deadpanned. Score one for the Frenchman.

I cleared my throat. "Yes, well. Anyway. I wanted to take the chance to clear things up. I feel like these misunderstandings are getting in the way and causing us to perform poorly together." I nodded and smiled. Basil still wasn't making eye contact but plenty of other people were.

"That would be one explanation for it."

Ouch. I decided to let that one go and forge ahead. "You see, I have this friend…"

"Really? I find that surprising." I heard a muffled snicker from one of the cygnets.

I decided to let that one go, too. "I think you and my friend would really have a good time together." I was feeling a little more confident, despite the crowd of dancers that was now listening intently to our conversation.

I had been clear and concise. He couldn't misunderstand that. And he couldn't be upset either, right? It was a kind gesture. I was doing something nice for him. I smiled and nodded some more. The plan was back on track.

Basil wrinkled up his nose and crossed his arms. "You aren't referring to Valerie, by any chance?" He said "Valerie" like some people say "contagious skin lesions."

"Oh no, not Valerie," I stumbled. "S-someone else."

"Huzzah. Who, then?"

Well, this was confusing. I blundered on like Ray Charles driving a getaway car.

"It's actually a friend from college who works at the Dirty Grudge Diner. You'll really like him. He has a great sense of humor, but that isn't code for ugly. He's really attractive, and not only a waiter, either. He's starting his own software company. And he, he uh. Well, he always has bacon. I mean, it isn't his bacon, it's his job and all, but he brings it to us, as much as we want." Hopefully Basil wasn't kosher or found bacon repellant for some other unfathomable reason.

Basil's face turned a violent shade of red. Even the bits of scalp that I could see beneath his brown hair were glowing. He grabbed my arm and pulled me into Susan's small office and slammed the door. Susan looked up from her desk but before she could say anything Basil erupted.

"What do you think you are doing?" Each word was a staccato, angry blast.

"I was trying to help." I fumbled for words.

"Help who?"

Well, myself actually. But there would have been some benefit to him and Brett as well. I glanced over at Susan and then back to Basil. "I thought that you might be having trouble meeting people since you're new in town. I have a friend I thought you'd like, so I wanted to see if you were interested."

"So you assume that I'm lonely and gay?"

Had I horribly miscalculated? I never have a clue about men and their feelings, so the potential to make a mistake of this magnitude was definitely there. I'd had to ask Brett if he were gay and I've known him for years.

"Well, you're in the ballet, you wear leg warmers in all the colors of the rainbow, and you use words like 'huzzah.' Yes, I assumed. I mean, you kind of seem like you might be gay." I heard Susan gasp. "A little bit," I added nervously.

Basil gritted his teeth. "Are you saying that all men who dance and wear leg warmers are gay? How perfectly provincial of you. I was right about you all along."

What did he mean, right about me all along? "Of course not. I'm saying *you* are gay. Cause you are." I hope.

His eyes narrowed. "It's really none of your business, is it?"

"Not exactly, no." I hung my head. Glynnis had been right. This had been a terrible idea.

"Not at all. Never." He jerked the door open and left the room.

"What exactly were you trying to do?" Susan finally spoke.

"Make things better," I mumbled in a small voice.

"Oh. It was kind of hard to tell from where I was sitting."

No kidding.

Chapter 8

The Tutu Fluffer

I lathered up my legs and pulled out my razor. I planned to be as smooth as a naked mole rat for this party. With this new five-blade razor I could have probably harvested the pelt of a wooly mammoth. Whatever Trey's reasons were for inviting me today, I planned to look good in a bathing suit.

Looking good would be the easy part. Having a clue about what was going on would be harder. Maybe I'd get lucky and develop telepathy. It would be the only way I was going to be able to figure out what Trey was thinking. And if the whole ballet thing fell through, I could land a job on the Psychic Friends Network.

I didn't have vast experiences with past boyfriends to serve as guidance. I've had exactly two long-term relationships. Both of them were fairly serious but neither ever took priority over dancing. I should have read more than the headlines of *Cosmo* in the grocery store checkout lane. Maybe if I'd opened a copy, I'd have a few ideas right now.

I rinsed off, wrapped myself in a towel, and flopped onto the couch with my phone. Barney jumped up beside me and laid his straggly head on my leg. I pondered my options. If I called Kyla, she'd tell me to behave myself. Glynnis would tell me to grow up and figure it out for myself. Rowan would probably want to talk about the ghost living in her attic.

It would have to be Valerie. You know the train is off the rails when you're calling Valerie for moral support. I texted *Need advice emergency call me* before I could talk myself out of it. She was working at the dealership today and I was half hoping she'd be too busy to talk.

The universe continued its campaign against me and the phone rang almost instantly.

"What's up?" Valerie asked before I could say hello.

"Valerie, listen. Seriously. I need help. Why do you think Trey asked me to this party?"

"I thought you said he asked you to keep Chad's sister away?"

"That's what he said. So that's probably it, right? I should relax. This is the fake girlfriend decoy thing."

"Or he wants to sleep with you."

"So you're saying he either has zero interest in me or he wants to fool around? That's so helpful."

"You'll figure it out. Go have fun. Get to know him. Report back as soon as you get home." And with that she was gone, probably off to harass some poor unsuspecting old lady into buying a turbo-charged coupe with paddle shifters and leather seats.

Valerie was overestimating my ability to figure things out on my own, but she did have a point about getting to know Trey better.

I needed a game plan—a mental list of questions to ask Trey, sort of like a first date quiz. I brainstormed a few basic questions. I actually already knew the answers to most of them, courtesy of social media, but I didn't want Trey to know that. Luckily there wasn't a guest counter on Instagram or I'd be forced to enter rehab and change my name.

I had a few solid topics sorted out. Where did you go to college? Do you have any pets? My perversion-induced, ADD-afflicted brain drifted to an image of myself rubbing sunblock on his back. Or his front. I couldn't concentrate. I wasn't Gandhi, or some other person known for self-control. It probably said a lot about my personality that I couldn't think of any better examples.

A quick check of the clock told me I'd have to put off pondering these deep philosophical questions until later. I was running out of time to get ready. Putting on a bikini and a little mascara shouldn't take me a lot of time. However, panic and perfectionism are never good friends when getting dressed in practically nothing for the most important party in the history of hookups. But no pressure.

Forty-five minutes later, I still didn't know what I was going to do about the likelihood that Trey's only interest in me was either for my Nicole-repelling properties or for my loose moral code and vague references to being flexible enough to have mastered most of the Kama Sutra, but I did know what I was going to wear.

I'd settled on a black and hot pink Nike two-piece. It was tiny enough to show off the things I considered assets—good abs and serious thigh muscles—sheer enough to aid the negatives, like my barely there breasts, and athletic enough to look as if I weren't trying as hard as I actually was to look good.

I pulled my hair up into a ponytail and left it curly. No sense flat-ironing hair that's going to get wet anyway. I slid a flowered mini-dress on over top, dabbed on some Baboon Butt, and found some flip-flops. I was ready to go when Trey buzzed to be let in.

He knocked a few seconds later and I pulled open the door, trying to get the big goofy grin on my face under control. Lance Manyon was picking me up for a date, and no matter what his motivations were, it was pretty amazing.

"Hey," he greeted me.

"Hey, yourself." I leaned against my doorframe and looked him over. He was wearing a white T-shirt and blue Hurley board shorts. I wiped my sweaty palms on my legs. I glanced around for Frederic, hoping he didn't make a sudden appearance. Sometimes it was hard to explain why I had a pigeon as a pet.

"You ready?"

For anything. Technically, I'd been ready since February. Of last year.

"Sure." I pulled the door closed behind me and followed him down the hall.

"What have you been up to this weekend?" Casually, he reached over and took my hand in his.

His hand was warm and soft and so large it totally encompassed mine. My inner twelve-year-old gasped for air. I had forgotten how nice it felt to hold hands with someone. Not to mention, it made it much easier to pretend this was a real date.

I knew I shouldn't read too much into it. It was probably a guitar player thing and he liked to keep his hands busy. Idle hands are the devil's playground and all that. Although, when you think about it, busy hands are more likely to get you into trouble than idle ones, aren't they? I could think of several things he could be doing with those warm hands that would require some serious time in the confessional. A small shiver ran through my body.

I realized the silence had stretched on a bit. I glanced up at Trey. He looked at me expectantly. What had we been talking about? I tried to rewind the conversation in my mind but everything after he had touched my hand was lost.

I'd talk about the weather. That was safe, right?

"Nice day for a pool party," I ventured.

He laughed "Yeah, should be fun. It's at Chad's parents' house. Should be a pretty good crowd of people there."

We made our way out of my building. He led me across the parking lot to an older, grungy-looking Jeep Cherokee. The black paint was covered in mud splatters and the bike rack on back was duct-taped together. "We can take your car, if you want," Trey offered.

"My car?" I glanced around the lot nervously.

"Sure. It's a great day for a convertible."

"Well, yeah, but I don't have any gas." Or any BMW. I smiled nervously at Trey. "What's that?" I pointed to a small sticker in the back window with the letters "WEMT" on it.

I climbed into the passenger seat carefully and threw my small bag onto the floor mat. The upholstery was ripped in a few places but it was clean and smelled okay.

"Wilderness EMT. It's an extra certification beyond basic EMT training."

"What things are different than regular EMT training?"

"Basically, you take a year of courses that prepare you to deal with things like animal bites, lightning strikes, and hypothermia, things like that. Once you're certified, it's a lot of off-road stuff and usually ends up in the parks and trail areas in the Shenandoah Valley, so I only have time for it in the summer."

"Wow," I gushed. I had a brief, but hot, mental picture of Trey sucking snakebite venom from an unmentionable area of my body.

Trey's cheeks reddened and he looked away as he started the car.

I tried to downplay my enthusiasm and rampant snakebite fantasies. "I'm impressed by anyone who can do that. I could never be an EMT or any type of medical professional."

"Sure you could." He turned back to me and smiled. "There are plenty of EMTs who are your size who are great at it."

"My size isn't the problem. The problem is that I sometimes panic in emergency situations. Not to mention the serious phobia I have about bodily fluids." I shuddered a little thinking about it.

I looked around for a diversion. No way was I going to let him know what a psychotic fear of blood, injury, and toe fungus I had, not when he was practically Superman.

"What's with all the ropes?"

Trey carefully eased the Cherokee into the traffic. "Climbing gear. Do you ever rock climb?"

"I haven't in a while but I used to. When Kyla was at college at James Madison, they had a day where they let people climb the clock tower. That was my first time. It was so much fun." I could already picture the two of us scaling mountains together. Or tying each other up. Either way.

"Kyla is your sister?"

"One of three, plus a brother. Have you ever had to use your climbing skills on a rescue call?" I changed the subject again. I was getting good at this conversational spy and evasion thing. It's best to introduce my family slowly and carefully. Or not at all.

"A few times. Once a car went over an embankment and landed in a steep ravine. There was no other way to get to the people."

"That sounds pretty exciting." It had probably been more exciting for the person being rescued by the calendar model of EMTs.

"It can be. I'd really like to do some of the water rescues. I'm working toward getting certified to be a police diver."

"That's impressive. My biggest goal right now is to watch all of the *Dr. Who* episodes in order." I studied his profile as he drove. "How long does it take to certify?"

"I can only work on the training during the summer because I'm a full-time grad student. It's taken me two summers but I should be finished by this September."

"Where are you in grad school?"

"George Washington." He shot another quick look in my direction.

"I went to GW too." This was great. We were already finding things in common. Maybe I didn't need *Cosmo* after all. "I finished with a BA in dance four years ago. What program are you in?"

"Med school," he said as he changed lanes. "It's taking me forever, working and taking classes. But I'll get there eventually."

Of course he was going to be a doctor. The man was perfect. He probably also spent weekends teaching disadvantaged children to ride horses and spit polishing the pews at the local church.

"What type of doctor do you want to be?" I asked. "Emergency medicine?"

"Yeah, great guess. Most people don't figure that out." We sped along on 495, the traffic heavy but not as bad as the weekday congestion.

Trey took his eyes off the road for a moment to glance at me. "Tell me what you do when you aren't watching *Dr. Who*? I had no idea you could get a BA in dance."

"Yeah, you can, but there's not much to tell. Dance all day, every day, and then graduate and dance some more all day, every day."

"Where exactly do you dance?"

"I'm at the Washington Ballet Company. We do several shows a year, some are local and others are in different parts of the country. Once a year a show will tour, so it'll go to multiple cities."

"Sounds like a big deal," he said, and I flushed with pleasure. "Are you working on a show now?"

"We open *Swan Lake* in a month or so, then it will run for two months at the Kennedy Center."

"I don't know much about *Swan Lake*. Actually, to be honest, I've never seen a ballet before except watching *The Nutcracker* on PBS with my grandmother at Christmas. Tell me about it."

"It uh…" I faltered. No one ever asked me about dance. I almost didn't know what to say. "Well, it's a story about a prince who's supposed to find a wife."

"Sounds like a Disney movie so far."

"Yeah, but instead of Cinderella he falls in love with a swan."

"That could be awkward at family reunions," he joked.

"The swan is actually a girl named Odette who's been enchanted by the prince's advisor, Von Rothbart. She swims in a lake made from the tears of her parents." I paused. This was usually the time that Valerie's eyes were glazing over and drool was dribbling down her chin.

Trey glanced away from the road again. "Then what happens?"

"The only way to break the spell is if a man with a pure heart professes his love. The prince wants to, but Von Rothbart stops him. Are you sure you want to hear all of this?" I hesitated. "It's kind of a long story."

"Sure, don't leave me hanging now."

I turned in my seat to face him, no longer caring if he caught me staring. "Okay, the prince is in love with Odette the swan. Von Rothbart wants the prince to marry his daughter Odile. He enchants her so that she looks like Odette. So the prince dances with her at this big party and the whole time the real Odette is watching. When the prince pledges himself to Odile, Odette runs away and the prince sees her."

"Then he knows he's been tricked, and Von Rothbart reveals what he's done. The prince chases after Odette and finds her at the lake. Von Rothbart follows and tells the prince that he has to marry Odile because of his pledge. So the prince and Odette jump into the lake and drown. And then the other swans, who are Odette's friends, force Von Rothbart and Odile into the water and they drown."

"So, it's a comedy?"

"Funny." I rolled my eyes.

"Seriously, not a happy story. Kind of like *Romeo and Juliet*."

"Well, at least they ascend into heaven together at the end. Plus their sacrifice breaks the spell for the other swans and kills the bad guys, so all in all, not too bad. Although it isn't really one of my favorite ballets to perform."

"Why not? Aren't they all pretty much the same?" he asked.

"Oh no. Not at all. The choreography for *Swan Lake* is really challenging, one of the hardest to do. And it's long. Really long. There's a lot of dancing, and it's taxing on the left leg."

"So what part will you be doing?"

I fiddled with the towel in my lap. "I'm the swan. Odette. And Odile."

Trey looked over at me in surprise. "You're telling me that you're dancing the role of head swan at the Kennedy Center?"

"It's my first lead. It's a huge opportunity for me. The principal dancer took a sudden leave of absence and I took her place. If things go well I might be considered for the principal dancer position."

"Well, congratulations then. You'll have to dance for me sometime."

"Sure." I tried to not read too much into that he hadn't offered to come to watch the performance. That was probably expecting a little too much, especially when you considered the fact that I wasn't even sure if this were an actual date or not.

While I was regaling Trey with the slightly psychotic and completely depressing story of Odette and her fellow waterfowl, we had turned into a quiet Arlington neighborhood. Trey navigated the tree-lined residential streets with ease and turned into a cul-de-sac of older family homes. Definitely not the wild city singles community you'd imagine a hot bass player would live in.

"We're almost there." He pulled off to the side of the road. "This white house with the blue shutters," he pointed out his window, "that's my house. Well, it's where I live with my grandmother." (Like I didn't already know that. Thank you, Google street view.)

"Are your parents here too?"

"They're in England. My dad's from the Oxford area. He met my mom when she was taking a graduate class there and we lived there until I was thirteen."

"You don't have an accent."

"I used to but it wore off. We came to the states because my mom wanted us to go to college here, so we moved in with my grandmother."

"Have you lived with her since then?"

"Sort of. I stayed on campus for the undergrad years of college, but when my parents returned to England, I moved back in. She's turning eighty soon and she's had some memory problems. As long as I'm here, she can stay in her house safely."

My heart melted. He really was almost too good to be true. It was a good thing he didn't still have that accent. It would have singed the clothing right off my body.

"How do you like living with your grandmother?"

"It's good, really. She's so sweet. I have to stop her from doing my laundry and trying to cook for me all the time. She still calls me by my full name like she did when I was a kid."

"Full name?"

"Uh, yeah. I'm the third. That's what Trey stands for."

"The third what?"

"William. My dad and grandfather were the first two." He toyed with the keys dangling from the ignition.

"William what?" I asked, suspicious.

Trey made a face. "William Cuthbert Layton."

"Now I know what to call you when you're in trouble."

He leaned closer and traced the edge of my jaw with his finger, stopping below my lips. "Am I going to get into trouble?"

"I hope so," I said breathlessly. I also hoped that he might decide to kiss me, but instead he turned to look out the window. I wished I could read his body language better. Or at all.

"See the little part over the garage?"

I nodded.

"That's where I live."

"You sure it's safe, leading your stalker to your house?" I lowered my eyebrows and tried to look scary.

"Hey, I never called you that." He started the car and we pulled back onto the road. "That was Chad. Besides, I invited you here so I think we can forget all about that stalker stuff. Maybe I'll be your stalker now. Do ballerinas have groupies? Maybe I'll wait outside of your ballerina place and ask if I can walk you home and carry your little pink shoes. I'll be your tutu fluffer. I'll polish your barre."

"You'll polish my barre?" Was that like spit polishing the pews at church?

"Or you can polish mine. I'm flexible. Well, not as flexible as you apparently. Hey, can you put both feet behind your head?"

I groaned. "Do you know how many people ask me that question? How many drinks I've won at bars with that?"

We'd pulled to a stop in a crowded driveway a few houses down from Trey's. Cars were parked in the lawn and in the street in front. Trey slipped a finger under the strap that was holding up my sundress and rubbed my collarbone underneath. "So that's a yes then?"

"Uh-huh," I breathed. He bent his finger around my strap and slowly pulled me to him. His head tilted and our lips met. The kiss was soft and sweet. Before things could escalate to hair pulling and a feet-behind-the-head demonstration, someone knocked on the window. Fortunately this time there were no law enforcement personnel involved.

"Hey, Noah," Trey opened his door and slid from the car. I climbed out too. "Eiley, this is Noah. He's the drummer in our band. You probably recognize him from Not Frank's."

Nope. Never looked past the skinny jeans to the back of the stage. "Sure, of course. I knew you looked familiar," I lied.

The three of us walked around the house to join the crowd of people roaming the large backyard. A small group was crowded onto the back deck of the house filling red Solo cups. Several people relaxed in colorful lounge chairs organized around the pool watching a rowdy volleyball game in progress. Chad was manning an oversize grill under a huge lemon-yellow beach umbrella.

With a jolt I recognized some of the regulars from Not Frank's. Valerie and I called them the Not Frank's Skanks. Unlike us, who sat respectably at a table, the NFS hovered around the band and the stage in barely there tank tops and skintight jeans like a herd of 80s hair band devotees. There was a fine line between obvious groupie and demure stalker, and I never crossed it.

"Eiley, this is Brandon, Ryan, his girlfriend Tara, and Jake." I nodded and smiled. I'd never be able to remember all their names. "And you already know Chad, the master chef." I nodded again. Yes, I did. Unfortunately.

"There's some cups on the table if you want to get started." Tara gestured to her own red cup. "The keg's on the porch."

I took a cup and handed one to Trey. A sweating pitcher of ice water sat on the table and I filled my cup from it. "I'm going to stick with this, I think," I told him. He smiled and held his cup out for me to fill. Alcohol could only work against me and my never-ending struggle against social awkwardness. Not to mention, I'm a total lightweight. One cup in and I would probably be trying to sneak a peek down Trey's bathing suit.

"Hey, man." Chad slapped a huge chunk of meat onto Trey's plate and eyed me suspiciously.

"I'd like the chicken," I said pointedly to Chad.

"It's spicy, you won't like it."

"I'm sure it's fine," I insisted, not backing down. If I had to take a stand, it might as well be for chicken. (Call me, Colonel Sanders.)

Chad looked over my head to Trey. "Hey, make sure you say hi to Nicole, she wants to talk to you. She's over there by the keg." Chad nodded his head in the direction of the crowd of band flies around the edge of the deck. He scooped a breast off the grill with his giant spatula and put it on my plate. Seriously, was this guy overcompensating?

"Good to know," replied Trey, obviously embarrassed. "And thanks for the warning," he muttered as he pulled me toward a picnic table.

I checked out the crowd of girls clustered around the keg on the deck. No way was I going to bring up the subject of Nicole. The less said about her the better. If he didn't want to talk about it, neither did I.

I picked a shaded chair and sat down. I take any chance I can to protect my milky white skin. I used a plastic fork to pull a piece of chicken off the breast and secretly eyed the Not Frank's Skanks. It was easy to pick Nicole out from the rest because she was staring at Trey like she wished she could strip the clothing right off him.

Did I look at him like that? I'd have to work on my poker face a little if I did.

I took a tentative bite of the chicken and my mouth immediately erupted into flames. This chicken would have two chilies drawn next to it in a Sichuan restaurant menu. Chad smirked at me from his grill. I smiled and gave him a little wave. Hopefully, from this distance he couldn't see that my eyes were watering. I wanted to stick my lips into my water cup but settled for a casual sip.

"What's up with Nicole?" I blurted. I took a huge gulp of water. I really needed to work on my willpower.

"Nicole is Chad's sister." I nodded as if this were new information. "The one he wanted to fix me up with. She's a little…intense."

Noah sat down with us and the conversation turned to the band. I refilled my water cup then shoveled some macaroni salad into my volcanic mouth while casting a few more furtive glances at the girls on the deck.

Nicole was still staring at us from beneath the brim of a floppy straw hat. Her bracelets jingled as she raised her hand to her mouth and whispered something to the girls next to her. They all looked at me and giggled. I looked back at them pointedly and scooted closer to Trey. I closed my eyes and leaned over so that my head was resting on his shoulder. Score one for me. If my bladder weren't so full from all the water, I could fall asleep like this.

Trey's voice roused me out of my stupor. "Let's go for a swim before I fall into a food coma." We stood and threw away our paper plates.

"Okay, give me a few minutes to run inside and change." I really needed to use the bathroom. I'd plowed through the whole pitcher of water, plus I'd finished Trey's cup when he wasn't looking.

Trey turned to face me and put his hands on my shoulders. He dipped his head, blocking out the rest of the world. "Don't be shy. I can help you with that." His low voice rumbled in my ear as his hands slowly traveled from my shoulders, down my body, to the hem of my sundress. He took hold of the edge and pulled it over my head in one deft maneuver.

"Snrvkl." It was the only sound I could manage. My cheeks were as hot as my charred mouth. I risked another look at the deck, but the crowd had disappeared.

One side of Trey's mouth went up in a half grin. He pulled his own shirt over his head. His bared skin radiated heat onto mine. My hands were inches from his hot flesh when he suddenly stepped away from me. A crowd of girls surrounded us and I took an elbow to my straining bladder.

"Break it up, you two. I need to talk to you, sweetie," Nicole near swooned in a breathy baby voice. She stepped neatly between Trey and me, giving me an unwanted view of her suntan-oiled-up behind hanging out of her thong-style bathing suit bottom. Ugh. I'll take Things You Can't Unsee for $200, Alex.

Her circus-peanut-orange body oozed against Trey and her hands splayed across his chest, as she leaned in to kiss him on both cheeks. I didn't know what to make of this. I looked around at the crowd that had gathered around us. All of the guys there were staring at her in dopey admiration, too distracted by her tiny yellow bikini to notice that her behavior was outrageous. I found Tara in the crowd and she rolled her eyes at me and shook her head in disgust.

"So glad you could come today," Nicole said in a low voice, as if she were talking intimately to him even though we could all easily hear her. She was clearly marking her territory. Hopefully she wouldn't pee on him.

Trey took a step back from her. "It's nice to see you too, Nicole. Have you met my girlfriend, Eiley, yet?" He gestured toward me, and after a brief hesitation she turned around.

Then she did that clever thing that bitchy tall girls do—pretended to not see me by looking over my head. She then looked down at me, her mouth rounding into a dramatic O when she made eye contact. I successfully avoided sticking out my tongue at her.

"Nice to meet you. I've heard so much about you," I lied. Like how Trey is desperate for you to leave him alone.

"Oh really? That's nice. I've heard nothing at all about you." She scrunched up her nose. "Absolutely *nothing*." She emphasized the word while looking directly in my chest area.

I was ready to comment about how lucky it was for her that she looked like a blow-up doll when Trey took my arm. "Come on, let's play some volleyball."

"Make sure she's on the shallow side," Nicole cracked as she walked off.

Trey wrapped his arm loosely around my shoulders. "Ignore her, okay?" I nodded. "I can't waste any time on her when all I can think about is how hot you look in that suit." It sounded like he had perversion-induced ADD, too. Kyla would be so happy to hear we had something in common.

We joined the group at the edge of the pool. Teams were established and the game was about to begin. "I'll be right back," I told Trey. "I'm going to run inside to the bathroom." I had to cave. I really had to go and the sound of sloshing water wasn't helping matters any.

Trey jumped in the pool and I headed to the back door of the house, groaning as I got closer. Nicole and all her friends were once again clustered on the deck, which was unfortunately also the way into the house. I quietly crept past the crowd. I eased open the sliding glass door and a blast of icy air flowed out of the small crack.

"Hold on a minute." Nicole clamped a hand on my shoulder, her red nails digging into my skin. I turned to face her reluctantly.

"You need to know that Trey and I are going to be getting together. You're a tiny little speed bump in the way. We have a long history, and we *will* end up together." She poked me with each word for emphasis. Her friends circled around her, arms crossed. Maybe we'd have a dance-off like *West Side Story*.

"You may as well run along home, little girl, because the truth is he wants to be with me. Always has." She smiled smugly at me.

"That's funny, Nicole." I took a step back to avoid her poking finger. "Cause it seems to me that if Trey wanted to be with you, he would."

"Oh please. You're the flavor of the week."

I crossed my arms and narrowed my eyes.

"Don't believe me?" She looked around at her friends. "Everyone who's gone home with Trey, raise your hand." Several of the girls put their hands up.

"Whatever." I gave in to my inner coward and pushed my way through the crowd and walked back to the pool. If I went inside now

I'd have to walk back through that mongrel horde again on my way out. I'd have to wait until they cleared off.

I got in the pool and joined the volleyball game. Luckily my team was on the shallow side. As we played I kept an eye on the back door of the house. As soon as the coast was clear I started making my way out of the pool.

"Wait," Noah called, "You can't leave now. We're two points away from winning." I turned to see Noah, Trey, Chad, and the rest of my team looking at me expectantly.

"Yeah, but I…" What? I couldn't finish that sentence was what. I'd have to either admit that Nicole had bullied me away from answering the call of nature or act like I had to go for the second time in five minutes. Cowardice or incontinence? Neither option was appealing when you were trying to make a good impression on the man of your dreams.

"Right, it can wait." I sank back into the pool in defeat. And I did wait. The teams battled it out for five long minutes before the last two points were scored and we won the game.

There was no way I could make it out of the pool, dry off, and get into the house in time. I was going to have to pee in the pool. Disgusting. I shuddered thinking about the pee touching my body, but it was desperate times.

Everyone grouped together in the shallow end, talking and choosing up sides for the next game. I swam to the deep end and hung on to the side, pretending to admire a nearby Chinese planter filled with pansies.

Nothing happened. I had performance anxiety.

I closed my eyes and focused on relaxing. Finally. Relief. I let it all out at last, hoping fervently those rumors of pool water turning orange when it came into contact with urine were merely urban legend.

The water erupted into a huge splash behind me. Trey surfaced next to me, bending down to take a big mouthful of water and spit it at me playfully. A big mouthful of peed-in pool water.

My mouth dropped open in horror. He must not have noticed the look on my face because the next thing I knew he was kissing me with a lot of tongue involved. I gagged. Chad popped out of the water behind me as I struggled to pull away.

"Hey. Do you want to play again?" Chad asked, trying his best to break us apart. "They're setting up teams for the next game. If you want... Hey, I felt a warm spot. You totally peed in here, didn't you?"

I looked from Trey to Chad and then back to Trey again. My mouth opened and closed a few times. I had no words. Was there an apology that could suffice for this kind of horror?

Trey put both his hands on Chad's shoulders and dunked him. Into my urine. He came up sputtering and spitting pee-filled water all over both of us. With a sudden burst of joy, I realized that it had been a joke. I breathed a long sigh of relief and managed a wobbly smile. That had been a close call, but luckily I wouldn't need to find a way to apologize for the fact that I had used the pool as a roadside rest area and inadvertently supplied them both with a urine hair rinse and gargle.

"Funny, Chad." I tried to look slightly irritated.

"You should have seen the look on your face, Eiley." Chad laughed. "You were totally freaked out." Still laughing, he climbed out of the pool to pull together his next team.

"You did look completely panicked. You really do have a phobia of bodily fluids."

"Well, yeah, like I said," I stammered.

"You're blushing."

Thanks, opposite of poker face. "It's embarrassing."

"I'd almost think that you had actually peed in the pool and thought you'd gotten caught." He leaned over and started kissing my shoulder.

Oh no. I felt my cursed red-haired-girl skin blotching up like a color-coded lie detector.

"Well, I mean, it's like this…" I stumbled along with no real idea of how to finish my sentence. Of all the things I'd pictured going wrong today, this wasn't one of them.

The kissing stopped abruptly. I floated feebly, praying for divine intervention. With all those rosaries I'd said as a kid I figured God owed me one right about now.

I watched helplessly as the look on Trey's face went from confused to nauseated as he put the pieces together. "It's not that big of a deal," I tried.

"Ugh," he gurgled as he jumped out of the pool to scrub his face with a beach towel.

"Bear Grylls from *Man Versus Wild* loves it," I yelled out to him helpfully. I wanted to remind him that he wasn't the only one with a mouthful of urine-tainted pool water, but that seemed counterproductive. Besides which, I didn't want to think about pee having been in my mouth. Never mind that it was my own.

Nicole slinked over to Trey, her bracelets, which looked a lot like a pair of handcuffs, glinting in the sun. "What's the matter, babe?"

"Nothing. I'm fine." He stuck out his tongue and wiped it with the towel. Nicole took the towel from his hands and rubbed his chest with it. She was such a tart. If I didn't find a way to get rid of her, I was pretty sure that towel would be headed for dangerous territory and I would have failed in my mission as fake girlfriend and bodyguard.

I had a sudden inspiration. "Trey, honey, what time are you coming over for dinner tomorrow night?" I smiled up at him innocently.

Their heads swung in my direction. I could tell by the look on Trey's face that he knew what I was up to. If he said he wouldn't come, Nicole would be on him like a dung beetle on an elephant turd. He almost had no choice but to agree to come over, at least in front of Nicole. "Seven o'clock?"

I looked at him suggestively. "Make it five. I won't want to wait that long." There. I could mark my territory too. And hey, I'd *actually* peed on him, so he was mine, right?

***

Trey didn't say much in the car, and we pulled into my parking lot in silence. I wasn't sure if he would walk with me to my door or slow down and kick me out of the car.

He parked and I let us into the building with my key card. I couldn't help noticing there was no hand holding in the elevator this time around. We stopped at my door as I rummaged around to find my key. For once, I wasn't eager for any kissing to happen.

"Look," I started, "I'm so sorry. It was an emergency. I never meant for any of that to happen. You don't really have to come to dinner tomorrow. I said that so Nicole would leave you alone." Tears prickled the corners of my eyes. "Tell everyone you broke up with me, and I'll stop coming to Not Frank's on Tuesdays." I sniffled. I would miss those chicken wings.

He put his arm around me and pulled me into him. "Never, ever speak of this again. Okay?" I nodded against his chest. "I'll be here tomorrow night."

I looked up at him in surprise. "At *five.*" He grinned crookedly. He gave me one last hug before walking down the hallway.

I let myself into my apartment and leaned against my door fanning myself with my towel. It was like *Swan Lake*. Whether or not Trey's heart was pure was questionable, but he fit the handsome prince role. I was Odette, trying to keep my man away from Nicole, who was Odile, and instead of a lake filled with tears we had a pool filled with…well, I'd work on the metaphor.

Chapter 9

In Bed with a Deaf, Drunk Pirate

I gave the couch a last flick with the lint roller, trying to remove all traces of Barney fuzz. I'd vacuumed, scrubbed, and bleached most of the day. I'd showered, shaved my legs again, and coated myself in my favorite lotion. My hair was flat, and my eyelashes were black. Baboon Butt was in full effect.

I had a kitchen full of supplies and three pages of recipes I'd Googled and printed out. I was ready.

Trey buzzed a few minutes after five o'clock. He was still dressed from work, wearing a white and navy T-shirt with the Fairfax County Fire and Rescue insignia on it. Barney and I both greeted him enthusiastically. However, I had the decorum not to sniff his crotch. Besides, Barney beat me to it.

"Hey." I wiped my sweaty palms on my shorts. This was one of my fantasies coming true. Lance Manyon was in my apartment and he was dressed like a Rescue Hero. It was a little hard to take it in all at once.

"Hey." He gave me a quick kiss and my heart flipped over. We were kissing hello like we were a couple and it was a thing we did.

"I brought some dessert." He handed me a grocery bag with a cheesecake inside.

"Thanks. Come on over to the kitchen." I pulled him over to where I had two stools set up at the counter that divided the kitchen area from the rest of the apartment. "Would you like a beer?" I stood in front of the fridge for a minute, letting the air cool down my overheated face. Too bad it couldn't work on my dirty mind. I handed Trey a beer and then turned to the food on my counter.

"I'm going to start with this gourmet blue cheese and grapefruit bruschetta." I'd found the recipe when I'd Googled "How to impress the hot guy you invited to dinner." The Internet can be oddly specific at times.

I pulled a knife out of the drawer. It was a waste of perfectly good blue cheese, but it sounded fancy. I subtly double-checked the recipe I had taped to the side of my cabinet out of his line of sight. Barney came over and laid his head on Trey's knee.

"Who's this guy?"

"Barney. Well, technically, his full name is Barney Awesome Rocket to the Moon Fife."

"That's quite a name."

"My nephew Finn named him. He mainly goes by Barney, or Bad Dog."

"How old is he?" He scratched Barney below his ears and I could swear the dog was smiling—not that I blamed him. My tail would have been wagging, too.

"I don't know. I rescued him two years ago. At least, I think I rescued him. He was alone in an alley in the mornings when I biked by to go to work. One day I brought him home with me."

"Lucky Barney," Trey said. His glance lingered on me for a hot minute.

"Do you have any pets?" I asked, flustered. If he was trying to charm me, it was totally unnecessary. I was charmed. Well, actually, I was charmed six months ago. Technically, at this point, I was besotted.

"My work hours are all over the place. It wouldn't really work out right now."

"Being able to have pets is the best thing about living in this place, even if I do pay a fortune in rent. And it's close to the studio, so that's good, too."

"With the traffic in the District it's probably worth it."

"My parents picked this building, actually. They liked that it's locked all the time and you need a remote to get into the parking garage. They worry about me being alone in a big city full of sexual deviants and the morally ambiguous."

"They worry about you living alone?"

"I choose to believe it's because of my young age and small stature, rather than my Neville Longbottom-like tendency to screw things up."

Trey nodded. "I'm sure they think it's safer to live in a huge building like this with more people."

"You have to think though, that if you live in a building with a thousand people in it, aren't you really living with *more* perverts? You know, mathematically speaking? I mean, if one in every one hundred people has criminal intentions then by percentages, ten people in my building are potential felons."

"Good point." Trey laughed, and I couldn't help noticing how his eyes crinkled up at the corners in exactly the right way. If I didn't start focusing on the recipe, we'd never make it to dinner.

"Looks like you came right from work?" I nodded at his T-shirt. "Good day?" Hopefully that wasn't a stupid question. I had no idea if paramedics had good or bad days.

"Pretty good. I got to fill in today on the medevac helicopter for a heart attack in the suburbs and a traffic accident on the Beltway."

"I didn't know they sent a medevac for heart attacks." I chopped the fruit with flair, showing off my dazzling knife skills. Thank you late night reruns of *Iron Chef*. (Bobby Flay, call me.) I was dicing the life out of the grapefruits.

"Yeah, they have to sometimes because of the traffic during rush hour. An ambulance would take too long." I casually glanced over at Trey to make sure he was seeing exactly how talented a domestic goddess I really was. I had one skill in the kitchen, unless you counted my uncanny ability to turn literally anything into a pizza, and I wanted to make sure he was watching.

He was still focused on Barney, scratching behind his ears. The fact that he was so easily able to find the spot that made Barney's eyes glaze over with happiness boded well for me, but he was missing out on me working my fingers to the bone to make this incomprehensible recipe that included blue cheese but no chicken wings.

"Have you done medevac before?" I asked, trying to get his attention back to me.

He looked back in my direction. "Did you know that you're bleeding?"

"What?"

"You're bleeding."

More accurately, I was *cutting* my fingers to the bone.

I squeezed my eyes shut immediately. Maybe if I didn't actually see the blood I would be all right. I stood still and tried to take some deep breaths. A wave of heat like a hot flash engulfed me and I wobbled unsteadily, unwilling to move my hands to steady myself.

"Eiley?" Trey's voice sounded far away but there was no mistaking the concern.

I risked a quick glance at my finger through one half-opened eyelid. It was like the Texas Chainsaw Massacre on my cutting board. Everything was covered in blood. I did the only possible thing I could do under the circumstances. I screamed.

Trey jumped up and ran to me. Barney, unsure whether Trey was hurting or helping, barked loudly, jumping at him and biting the hem of his shirt. My hero. I'd have to buy him some more of the peanut butter treats he loves. (Barney, not Trey.)

I kept right on screaming because, hey, it might help and let's not forget I needed to be heard over the dog. While I was screaming, I figured it would also be a good idea to do the stationary panic dance. You know the one, arms flailing, legs running but not going anywhere? Frederic picked that moment to swoop low over us and leave a deposit on the countertop.

Trey pulled off his shirt, wrapped it over my hand and dragged me into the bathroom, closing the door to shut out my poor yelping dog. He picked me up and sat me on the edge of the sink, leaning against me to stop my flailing arms and legs from decapitating him. He grabbed the back of my head with his free hand and pulled my face right up to his.

"Look at me."

I stopped screaming and opened my eyes.

"Are you okay?"

"That was so much blood," I explained weakly. "You know I don't like blood. Or your bedside manner. Do they teach you to yell at hysterical people in EMT school? Because that is not cool."

"Honey, I'm not yelling."

"You're not?" Trey wiped his hand down his face and took several deep breaths.

I leaned in a little closer and could smell a hint of musky cologne coming off his shirtless body. Even though I had totally humiliated myself and was at serious risk of developing gangrene from my knife wound, things were really not too bad at that moment.

"I'm going to take a look at your hand. Are you going to stay calm?"

"Probably." They should have taught him to take his shirt off in EMT school. It was totally distracting me.

"Probably?"

"I mean, yes. I will. I promise." I hoped I wasn't lying. It would be bad to start breaking promises this early in our relationship. And yes, I was totally considering it a relationship at this point.

He unwrapped the shirt from around my hand and bent it back behind me where I couldn't see it, leaning against me to look over my shoulder. He turned on the warm water and began to rinse away the blood.

I lifted my non-injured hand toward his hot, ridged flesh but hesitated before touching him.

"This may sting a bit." He angled my hand so that the warm water flowed over it. I lowered my free hand. I needed to think about this. He'd been in my apartment for five minutes and I was ready to maul him.

"That's okay," I told him. "Pain I can do. But not blood." Actually, he could have cut a few other fingers off right then with my five-blade razor and I would have gladly sat there balanced on the hard edge of the sink, inches away from his bare chest, his hips between my knees.

My eyes drifted back to his chest. There was a dent between his collarbones, right under his Adam's apple, where I could see his heart beating. What was that spot called? I couldn't stop staring at it. I really should know the name of that awesome spot.

"Do you have any bandages?"

"Cabinet behind me," I mumbled vaguely. I was definitely feeling this.

He pulled me forward onto his thighs, balancing me there with one muscular arm while he removed the first aid box and set it on the counter. I could see the edge of his underwear peeking out from his waistband. What were they? Boxers? Boxer briefs?

Clearly, I was not a well person. I needed to seek professional help. Later.

"It isn't too bad. If I put a butterfly closure on it you should be fine."

"Okay." I would have agreed to cauterization by curling iron at that moment.

He slowly wrapped a bandage around my fingers and placed tape over it.

"I covered the butterfly with tape. You won't be able to see it," Trey assured me.

My fake boyfriend was so thoughtful. Hot and thoughtful, and so good at taking care of me, I decided, still staring at that sweet little spot.

Sometimes you didn't need to think too much to make a decision. Sometimes you needed to go with what you were feeling. *Think long, think wrong*, as my friend's dad always used to say when we were kids. Although he was talking about pinochle and not issues of morality, I felt like it still applied here.

I leaned forward and ever so carefully licked that spot where his heart was beating.

Hell yes, my can-do attitude said.

Trey slowly pulled back and looked at me seriously. "We're going to do it in the bathroom, aren't we?"

"Yeppers," I gleefully shouted through the weave of my shirt as I tried to jerk it over my head, one-handed. Now that I'd made the decision, I couldn't get naked fast enough.

Trey helped me pull off my shirt. I stood up and we tore at buttons and zippers. Within a few seconds there was a pile of clothing all over the floor.

He cupped my bottom and lifted me back up onto the sink. He trailed kisses from my jaw to my collar, each one hotter and more aggressive than the last. His teeth skimmed my skin and my back arched. My legs found their way around his waist. His skin, his body—everything about him—was male perfection.

He held me suspended, millimeters away from the thing I had wanted for so long. Or was it centimeters? I was never good with the metric system.

I reached into the shelf the bandages had come out of and pulled out a condom, praying it wasn't years past the expiration date. Trey gently lowered me to my feet. I pushed him onto the toilet lid that was, fortunately, closed.

I did not want to take the time to move to my bedroom. I wouldn't have made it as far as the hallway, or even the bathroom floor, which was a good thing, really. There could have been stray eyebrow hairs down there, or God forbid, some of my toenail clippings. I was pretty sure that would have been a boner killer.

So much for foreplay. All things considered, this was so much better than my plan to get to know him. We started to move together, although it wasn't exactly a coordinated effort. Sure, my living is based upon my grace and physical ability, but I wasn't usually required to work in such a confined space. I would have probably been less awkward if I'd had some leg warmers on.

I wedged my knee onto the toilet paper holder and raised myself up. My head crashed into the shelf behind the toilet. The door swung open and tampons rained down around us. I really needed a bigger bathroom.

"Are you okay?" Trey asked as I continued to move. I was saved from answering as my elbow made contact with the flushing lever and the toilet gurgled to life with a loud floooshing noise.

"Oh my God," I groaned at my body's quick response. Think of baseball, I told myself.

Floooosh went the toilet as I moved again. I tried to slow down, to calm down, but I couldn't stop, the gurgling toilet punctuating my every move until it ran out of water.

I squeezed my eyes shut and yelled out some expletives. It was over almost before it started. I quickly detangled my right foot from the towel holder on the shower door, freed my hair from the cabinet door hinges, and jumped to my feet.

We'd knocked the trashcan over and my toothbrush was on the floor. That would need to be thrown away later. The "some bunny loves you" needlepoint my mother had sewn and framed for me was hanging crookedly.

I stood in front of him, painfully conscious of my lack of clothing. I resisted covering myself with my hands, but it was difficult. This was so awkward. What was I supposed to say now? "Hey, nice penis" felt inappropriate, and it seemed like the wrong time to bring up the weather.

"That was..." Trey paused.

I gulped. What? Great? Awkward? Like being molested? I studied his face but as usual couldn't read his expression. Finally he shook his head. Being at a loss for words can be a good thing, right?

He glanced around the room. "You want to?" he asked, gesturing toward my small shower with his head.

I breathed a sigh of relief when I realized he meant together. I smiled and nodded.

It was possibly the best shower in the history of showers. I'll never look at a loofah the same way. Bed, Bath, and Beyond should really consider a new marketing strategy for those things.

When the glass door popped out of the frame and shattered onto the tiles we moved carefully into my room, wet and soapy. Maybe if I supplied my maintenance man with a case of beer he would fix the broken door without the landlord finding out. And fining me.

I scooted onto my bed and Trey followed, pushing me onto my back, poised above me. His wet hair was dark, his eyes even bluer in contrast. I sighed. How could one man be so beautiful? It was a little hard to believe he was actually there with me.

"You don't know how many nights I fantasized about you being in this bed," I blurted.

"Really?"

I nodded. A warm blush rose up on my cheeks and crept down my chest.

He smiled. "Show me how those fantasies ended up."

"You want me to go get a pint of Ben and Jerry's?" I asked in surprise.

"No." He shifted so that he was beside me and took my hand in his. "I want you to show me." He put my hand between my legs.

"Oh, paddling the boat?"

"Yeah. Flicking the bean. Petting the kitty. Double clicking your mouse."

"Playing with the gerbil?"

"Drowning the man in the canoe. Polishing the pearl."

I was out of euphemisms. "I can't. I'll go blind and everyone will know why because I won't be able to shave my hairy palms."

He stroked the damp hair away from my face and a smile spread slowly across his face. My thoughts trailed off and evaporated. He was like the Riddler, hypnotizing me with that crooked grin.

"Show me." He leaned over and kissed me. "What was it like when you were here," he kissed me again, "on this bed thinking about me?"

I pondered that. What had it been like? Nowhere near as amazing as the real thing.

"You know you want to."

I hesitated. Did I?

"I'll help you." His eyes roamed the length of my body.

Help me? As in, shout out encouragements? That would be some awkward cheerleading. I couldn't even think of anything that rhymed with clitoris.

I made some tentative motions. Just a little. And then a little more. I opened my eyes enough to catch the unguarded, hungry look on his face and grew a little bolder. Trey shifted beside me, watching in silence.

After a few minutes he took hold of my wrists and held them above my head as he moved over me. As fine and upstanding citizens as they may be, neither Ben nor Jerry could compete with that, not even on their best day.

My upstairs neighbor pounded on the floor when I shouted expletives a few minutes later. I couldn't make out exactly what he was saying, but apparently, all the commotion had interrupted *Wheel of Fortune*.

Trey settled beside me and pulled me close to him. "Do you always yell profanities like that? It's like being in bed with a deaf, drunk pirate. And who's Lance Manyon and why have you yelled his name twice?"

I fluffed my pillow, stalling for time. I decided to tackle the less embarrassing of the two questions. "The swear words were Valerie's idea. I used to have this terrible habit of yelling out 'I love you' in bed. Believe it or not, that sort of thing makes people uncomfortable, no matter how many times you tell them you didn't mean it. So I switched to swearing."

He shook his head and smiled. "That's a new one. Are you as hungry as I am? You did promise me dinner, you know."

"I'm starving. But I have a confession. I can't cook gourmet food. I can barely cook regular food. I was trying to impress you. But now that you've taken your chastity belt off, the truth can come out. And while I'm at it, I don't have a boyfriend, and that's not my BMW, either." I sighed with relief. It was good to get it all out in the open.

"Who's Bimmer is it?"

"Valerie's. Technically, Valerie's car lot's."

He nodded. "I'm kind of glad to hear you don't have a boyfriend, considering how we spent the last few hours."

I felt a surge of guilt. I'd forgotten he actually did have a girlfriend out there somewhere, even if they weren't exclusive and she wasn't on the same continent at the moment. "But you do."

He nodded uncomfortably. "Kind of. It's nothing serious, although I do try to not go around hooking up all the time. Tonight was…unexpected."

"Unexpected five times," I gloated. He smiled and shook his head. "I understand what you mean, though. I never do this."

"So when you say 'never' you mean…?" he asked.

"No one in the last year. Two serious relationships in the past, and that's about it."

He frowned, but didn't say anything. Had I made myself sound horribly inexperienced? Had he been disappointed? I'd thought it had been amazing, but I didn't have a lot to compare it to.

He'd said he tried not to hook up "all the time." I had a flashback to the deck full of Not Frank's Skanks raising their hands. How many women had he been with? Hopefully it was less than the population of Delaware, but it didn't sound likely.

I imagined myself asking him, "According to the latest research by the experts at *Cosmo*, on a scale of one to ten, how much of a man-whore are you, *really*? Take this quiz."

I had to ask. "So, when you say 'all the time'?"

He untangled himself from me and the sheets and got to his feet. I felt cold in the sudden absence of his body next to mine. "That's not really your Bimmer, huh?" he asked. "What kind of car do you have?"

I sighed, figuring the evasion meant more in the range of the population of New York.

"A Jetta. Do you want to go to Five Guys?" Five Guys is my favorite place to get a burger. Their food is so good I'd kiss each of those guys right on the mouth. I almost never go there but I figured I'd burned enough calories tonight to make it okay.

"I love Five Guys, but I'd rather stay here."

"Stay here in bed?" That did sound a lot better than getting dressed and leaving the apartment.

"Hang on. I'll go clean up the, uh, bodily fluids in the kitchen so you don't have to deal with it later. I'll come back with dessert." I watched him walk across my room toward the door. The view was even better without the skinny jeans.

I rushed to fix myself up while he was gone. Score. Sex and cake, and it wasn't even my birthday. I grabbed a T-shirt from my laundry basket and ran to the mirror to do some damage control. My hair had dried in a mass of crazy curls and my makeup was mostly washed off. Hopefully Trey hadn't noticed. The lights were on, but I'd had my eyes closed most of the time. Had he?

I sprayed my hair all over with some TIGI No More Bed Head, hoping for the best. I picked up a brush and tried to work it through my curls, but I couldn't budge the rat's nest in the back. I've always gotten a stubborn tangle in the same spot. It's so bad my mom named it Old Nasty when I was a kid.

I gave up and clipped it into a loose, messy bun. I dabbed on some more Baboon Butt and then grabbed my eyeliner and went to work. I had one eye done when the door to my apartment crashed open and hit the wall. I jumped and the eyeliner pencil poked my eye. Barney howled. I slapped my hand over my aching eyeball and raced out of my bedroom.

Ivan Morely, my building superintendent, was standing in my doorway holding a baseball bat.

"What's going on in here?" he asked, looking around the apartment. I hadn't realized it was such a mess. Bird tracks and blood covered my kitchen counter and there was a trail of it leading toward the bathroom. The broken shower door was lying in the hallway and shards of glass were mixed with spilled apple-scented shampoo. My clothes were strewn about with Trey's, covered in my blood.

Mrs. Radice appeared in the space behind Ivan. "I heard you yelling for help, so I called Mr. Morely to come up here and I opened the door with your spare key. Why is this naked pervert in your kitchen cleaning blood off your knife?" She glanced at me and took in my watering eyes. "Oh Eiley sweetie, are you okay?" She wiggled around Ivan and came to stand beside me protectively.

"Mrs. Radice, wait. I think there's been a misunderstanding. I wasn't being attacked. I was, um, it was consensual."

"Consensual? Oh honey, I'm sorry." She looked at Ivan. "He put it in the back door, poor thing."

"No, Mrs. Radice, consensual, not back door. Two totally different things. Consensual means everyone is happy." I'll take conversations you don't want to have with your elderly neighbor for $200, Alex.

Trey moved to stand behind the island in the kitchen. Mrs. Radice and Ivan exchanged a look, and Ivan choked up on his bat a little.

"Stop that. It was only a private moment between me and my fake boyfriend." I threw up my hands in exasperation.

"Fake boyfriend?" Mrs. Radice shook her head slowly and made a tsking sound. "Not even a real boyfriend, Eiley?" She looked disappointed. I probably wouldn't be getting any zucchini bread from her this Christmas.

I tried to explain. "Mrs. Radice, it wasn't…anything perverted," I choked out. "It was regular, average sex. I mean, better than average," I frantically amended, trying to read Trey's expression.

Ivan lowered his bat. "Boy, put your Johnson away." Trey darted out of the kitchen with a potholder strategically in front of himself. He picked his way around the broken glass and went into the bathroom and pushed the door closed.

"No more noise." Ivan slung his bat over his shoulder and turned to go. I looked at Mrs. Radice.

"I'm sorry about this." I took her hand in mine. "You know I'm usually quiet."

She patted my hand. "It's okay, dear." She glanced toward the closed bathroom door. "I think I can understand your motivation."

"I'll still be getting zucchini bread for Christmas?"

She nodded and smiled. "And a bigger pot holder."

"It's safe to come out," I yelled after Mrs. Radice had gone.

Trey opened the door and peeked out cautiously. He had his shorts and shoes on, bloody shirt in hand.

"You still hungry?" I asked.

"That's okay, I'll get something on the way home. It's getting late."

I blew out a long breath. It was 8:30. This wasn't exactly how I'd pictured our first night together ending. After all that amazing sex, he was going to run off because of one little near-death experience with a baseball bat? He seemed a little too eager to leave.

I swallowed back my disappointment and plastered a fake smile on my face. "Thanks for coming over, Trey. Sorry dinner didn't work out."

I was happy to note that my voice sounded firm and cool. I could do this. I'd wanted to hook up with him and I had. Mission accomplished. Now I'd have to live with it.

"Keep an eye on that finger, the cut's pretty deep. Check for any signs of infection like pain, redness, swelling, or pus."

I gagged a little but stood my ground. He grabbed the front of my shirt and pulled me to him.

I gave a little bit of ground.

"Take care of yourself." He kissed me lightly.

"Of course."

I didn't know how to interpret the good-bye.

He left and I curled up in bed with Barney and Jimmy Kimmel. Tomorrow was another day.

Chapter 10

The Cheese Grater

I stood up on my bike pedals as I worked to make it up the hill. It was a beautiful sunny day, but instead of enjoying the slightly smog-tinged summer air, I was obsessing over Trey's parting words.

Take care. Take. Care.

On one hand, he could have meant "you are so special to me, so precious, please take good care of yourself until I see you again." I pictured myself walking into Not Frank's with Trey walking beside me, staring lovesick into my eyes, his arm around my shoulders. I considered taking my hand off the bike to fan myself, but decided against it. Probably better not to think too much about that right now.

On the other hand, he also could have meant "see ya, wouldn't want to be ya, I'm calling another woman on my way home tonight."

Considering the fact that it had been two days since we'd done the greased weasel tango and I hadn't heard a peep out of him, he probably meant "have a nice life I never plan to see you again." I really needed that telepathy to kick in so I could stop worrying.

I stopped at the crest of the hill and checked the traffic on the side streets. When I was reasonably sure the coast was clear I coasted forward, my hand on the brake in case. The bike picked up speed, rocketing over the bumps in the sidewalk. The wind lifted my hair and cooled the sweat running down my back. It had only been two days, that wasn't that long, really. Guys usually had some stupid rule about not calling too soon, right? That was probably all it was.

I turned into the studio lot and walked my bike into a slot in the bike rack. I'd see Trey tonight at Not Frank's. He was waiting to talk to me in person, that was all it was. I snapped the lock around the wheel and made my way into the studio. I pulled open the heavy door and headed toward the locker room. As I passed Susan's office Serena walked out. Serena designs and creates all the costumes for our productions.

"Practice ends tonight at six, right?" Serena asked, smiling at me warmly. It was nice to see a friendly face in the studio.

"Yes, we're working on some staging, so it'll go long today." I'd have barely enough time to get home and get ready for Not Frank's.

"I'll meet you in the locker room around six fifteen. Does that give you enough time to shower before your fitting?"

My heart sank. I had forgotten all about my fitting. "Actually, I was wondering if we might be able to move that to tomorrow night?"

"Sorry, I have Jake and Regina's preschool graduation tomorrow night."

My face fell and Serena looked at me with concern. "I tell you what, sweetie, I have Basil down for Thursday. Why don't you see if he'll switch with you? I'll do his tonight and you can go on Thursday."

I gaped at her. "Basil?" Asking him for a favor might be a little tricky when he wasn't speaking to me. But if I wanted to see Trey, I'd have to figure something out. Something like groveling, begging, and a liberal dose of insincere flattery. I wrinkled my nose at the prospect. "Okay. Thanks. I'll check with him and see if he'd be willing."

Basil was already warming up at the barre, his long leg extended as he stretched from the waist. I approached him reluctantly. The sacrifices I made for love. Could sainthood be far behind? He continued to stretch, giving no indication that he'd noticed me standing beside him.

"Good morning," I said hesitantly, clasping my hands in front of me to keep myself from fidgeting. "I was hoping to talk to you for a minute."

His head tilted ever so slightly in my direction and one eyebrow raised in question. I took that as encouragement.

"I wanted to apologize for last week. I thought we should clear the air." I smiled in what I hoped was a friendly and totally nonthreatening way.

He turned to face me. "So apologize, then." His arms were crossed in front of himself and he was not smiling.

I blew out a sigh. "Okay, well. I'm sorry for upsetting you last week."

"That's your apology?" His face remained stony.

Well, there went plan A. He wasn't ready to forgive me and it didn't look like any amount of sucking up was going to help. There was no way I could ask him to switch nights with me so I could get to Not Frank's tonight. I had no plan B.

I'd have to wait to talk to Trey. He'd call me when I didn't surface at Not Frank's tonight. There was nothing to worry about.

Cosmo would say I should be a modern woman and make the first contact, however, *Cosmo* didn't know I had recently been called a stalker. I didn't need to add "desperate" or "stage five clinger" onto my already questionable reputation.

***

By Wednesday morning it was starting to look like Trey's "take care" really had meant "have a nice life, I never plan to see you again."

I'd kept my phone with me all through my fitting last night, but he didn't call. If it wasn't so pathetic, I'd admit that I'd fallen asleep with my phone on my pillow, and I'd checked it every chance I'd had at practice today. But it was pathetic, so I wouldn't admit it.

I'd have to deal with the fact that it appeared as though he'd slept with me and then moved on. I should walk away with a smile on my face and something to brag about at the Grudge. That was the plan.

Unfortunately, I was having some trouble sticking with that plan.

I decided, under the circumstances, it was perfectly acceptable to do a little cyber sleuthing, purely in an information-gathering sort of way and not invasive at all. Not to mention, I would probably get arrested if I tried the binoculars-and-bedroom-window routine. A little social media exploration was the safest way to see what Trey was up to.

I went to his Twitter page but found nothing interesting.

I checked out Instagram but there was nothing new there either.

I'd saved the best for last, good old reliable Facebook. Sure enough, there was a status update a few minutes old.

Looking forward to tomorrow—special night at The Palm. Nicole had liked it. Even more incriminating, she'd posted a comment: *Can't wait.* She'd even followed it up with a <3.

I felt a pang in the general vicinity of my heart. Was this why I hadn't heard from him—because he was meeting Nicole for a special evening? One night with me and he'd changed his mind about her?

I heaved myself off the couch and, not bothering to change out of my grubby T-shirt or brush my sloppy hair, took off to meet my sisters. Thank goodness it was Wednesday night. It was going to take a lot of bacon to make me feel better—and possibly a corndog.

My sisters had all arrived and had already ordered the appetizer by the time I got there. I slunk over to the table and flopped into a chair.

"What's wrong with you?" Glynnis asked.

"Nothing," I groused. "And I don't want to talk about it." I caught a strong whiff of something familiar I couldn't quite identify. "What's that citrus smell?"

"Why? Is it bad?" Rowan asked.

I leaned in closer to her and took a deep breath. "Why do you smell like a field of lemons?"

Rowan held her wrist out to the table. "Is that a new perfume?" Kyla asked. "It's…potent."

"I was at a friend's house yesterday and I was in her bathroom and she had this wonderful spray called Poopourri. Of course, I *had* to try it. I love how fragrant it is."

"You mean potpourri," Glynnis said.

"No, I don't. I mean Poopourri." She pulled a small spray bottle out of her giant purse.

"You know that's not perfume, right?" Glynnis smirked. "It's meant to go into the toilet to mask the odor."

Rowan shrugged. "If it can make *that* smell good, then it will make me smell even better." She smiled happily and put the bottle back into her bag.

"Okay then…" Kyla dipped some bacon into the blue cheese. "One of us has to help Mom with Psycho"

We all groaned.

"They've finally gotten home and they're trying to get her settled. Mom says she packed about a hundred boxes and they need to go through them all. Do you guys want to Rock, Paper, Scissors it?"

"Don't bother," I grumbled. "I'll do it. My life sucks anyway." Images of me sorting through my aunt's collection of Troll dolls flashed before my eyes. It couldn't be any worse than sitting around moping over Trey. Maybe I could use the opportunity to look for the clues that Great-Uncle Seamus had left about his hidden treasure. Psyche probably had all that stuff squirreled away somewhere. I'd never actually seen anything, but I'd heard about the treasure often enough. I perked up a bit at the thought. Finding a treasure would be a nice distraction, and Psyche would finally stop talking about it, and then I'd be Mom's favorite. Win, win, win.

"Spill it," Rowan ordered. Her hair was in two pigtails like Cindy Brady that bobbed around her head as she switched her attention from the bacon, to me, and back to the bacon again.

I sighed loudly. I might as well get it all out in the open. Talking about it couldn't possibly make me feel any worse than I already did. "You were right. You were all right. I shouldn't have slept with him."

"Wait a minute. You did the blanket hornpipe with Lance Manyon?" Rowan's pigtails vibrated with excitement.

"I don't know what that means, but if it means sex then yes, I did, and there was plenty of pipe."

"What's wrong, honey?" Kyla asked. "Was it not any good? Oh no. He was Quick Draw McGraw. The hot ones always are." She patted my hand sympathetically.

"What's wrong is that it happened three days ago and I haven't heard from him."

"Wait, *plenty* of pipe as in well endowed, or as in number of times of pipe exposure?" Glynnis asked.

"Both," I clarified.

Brett was at the table next to us, stacking dirty plates onto his tray. "Hang on, ladies," he called over his shoulder. He abandoned the full tray with a clatter. "I've got six tables right now but I think you ladies require my undivided attention." He pulled a chair over to our table to sit with us. "Now back up to the hornpipe."

"Eiley is having some sort of man trouble," Kyla told him.

"Of course she is, she's Eiley." Glynnis rolled her eyes.

Brett looked at me affectionately. "Let's hear it, kiddo."

I poured out the whole story. I gave them the *Cliff's Notes*-on-meth version, rapid-fire detailing a tale of handcuff bracelets, bursting bladders, bloody grapefruits, baseball bats, and the aforementioned pipe laying. I ended with Trey's ominous parting message and the suspicious Facebook activity.

"Aw, honey," Brett said, putting his arm around me. "You may have given the milk away a little too soon."

Kyla nodded. "There's other fish in the sea."

"If it wasn't meant to be, it wasn't meant to be," Rowan added.

"Get even with the jack wagon," Glynnis stated.

Finally, a voice of reason.

"Get even? Why? *How?*"

"Hang on a minute." Glynnis dug her phone out of her Kate Spade, scrolled through her contacts, and tapped an icon.

"Who are you calling?"

"Hush. Watch and learn. What's Trey's last name?"

"Layton," I supplied.

"Hello," Glynnis said into her phone. "I have reservations with you tomorrow evening and I want to check on the time. The name is Trey Layton. Okay, thank you." She looked around the table at us triumphantly. "Six o'clock."

"So I'm supposed to show up at The Palm tomorrow night at six o'clock and crash his date with Nicole?"

"Of course not. You show up at The Palm looking better than you've ever looked before on the arm of a hot guy and walk past Trey's table without giving him a second glance," Glynnis explained. "Because he was so insignificant, you've moved on."

"Oh yes," Brett said, "I can see it now. New dress, hair done, push-up bra…" I thought I saw Glynnis roll her eyes at the term "push-up bra" but I let it go since she was being so helpful.

"Okay, but where do I find a boyfriend on short notice? And what if I can't get reservations? That place is probably booked."

Rowan sucked in some air. "Brett will be your boyfriend."

Glynnis was already on her phone again. "I'll get you a table through my company. We take clients there all the time, they'll open something up for us."

I looked at Brett. "Well, would you?" I liked the idea of having a fake boyfriend of my own. Not to mention, having a plan to focus on was so much better than feeling sorry for myself.

"Of course I will. I'll go let my manager know I'm going to have a family emergency tomorrow night. Now hurry up and order before I have a hungry mob on my hands." He glanced over his shoulder at his other tables.

I opted for water and a green salad. I had to limit my gluttony to two nights a week, tops if I wanted to fit into my tights. If I was going to eat at The Palm tomorrow night, I'd have to take it easy tonight. Besides, I didn't feel like I needed corndog therapy any longer. I had a plan.

"Speaking of Brett and boyfriends, have you talked to Basil about going out with him?" Rowan asked when Brett had left.

"I don't think that's going to work out. He's not interested."

"How could he be not be interested?" Kyla picked up the dip cup and licked the last bit of blue cheese from around the edge. "Did you show him a picture?"

"I didn't get the chance. He didn't want to hear anything about Brett. He didn't even want to admit he was gay."

"Wait, what?" Glynnis sounded shocked. I looked from her to Kyla to Rowan. All of them were staring at me.

"I know, right? I mean, it's so obvious he's gay," I said nervously.

"Because he's openly gay?" Glynnis asked.

"Well, it depends on what you mean by open. He doesn't talk about it or anything, but it's obvious." My sisters were still staring at me, wide-eyed. "I was trying to do something nice. I explained that I wanted to introduce him to someone special, but he said I was stereotyping him and it was none of my business. He was so mad he was yelling at me, right in front of our choreographer. Can you even imagine?"

"Can I imagine it being none of your business? Yes, I sure can," Glynnis answered her own question. "What did you say, exactly?"

"Well, I mean, I can't remember exactly," I hedged. "Something about leg warmers and him being born that way."

Rowan did an overdramatic face-palm. "You're lucky he's still speaking to you."

"Well, technically, he's not." Or looking at me.

Brett delivered our dinners and we all ate in silence for a few minutes. "As soon as we're done here," Glynnis told me, "I'm taking you to Tysons Corner."

My eyes widened. "The mall? Why do we need to go to the mall?" Tysons was not simply a mall, but the largest, most upscale mall in the metro area.

Surviving Tysons with Glynnis would be iffy, and that was assuming I arrived there alive. Dale Earhardt had nothing on my sister. I'd have to say a quick Hail Mary in the bathroom before we left. And by "we" I meant me, my sister, and the Angel of Death. My sister's favorite car game is "Driving with Your Eyes Closed." She says it makes you feel closer to the road. Personally, I think it makes you feel closer to God.

"You need a new dress and shoes, and a pedicure. Maybe a little waxing."

"Waxing?" I asked dubiously, my fear level increasing.

"Yeah, a little here and here." She pointed to her eyebrows. "And a little here." She pointed to her crotch.

"Why? I think we've established that Brett isn't interested in that piece of anatomy. No one is going to see down there but me."

She tossed her hair off of her shoulders. "I'm about to share with you one of the pearls of my wisdom, not that you people ever listen to me." She looked around the table to be sure we were all paying attention before continuing. "When you know on the inside that you look your absolute best, it shows on the outside. Men are drawn to self-assurance like moths to a flame." This explained why my flame had remained generally mothless for quite some time. "Every detail is important to help you look and *feel* your best."

We all nodded in understanding. "That way you can really crush his spirit and make him rethink his life choices."

I looked at her in awe. "You're a little scary sometimes."

She shook her head. "Imagine you have to go somewhere and you're feeling a little insecure, like a cocktail party or an interview for a job that you don't know if you're qualified for," she began. I couldn't imagine my sister ever feeling unqualified or insecure, but I nodded. "You should put on your best outfit, have your hair done, and pull your designer bag out of the closet," she continued.

"People don't pick job candidates based on what they're wearing," Kyla protested. She glanced down at her faded Blink-182 concert T-shirt from 2008. "Do they?"

"That's not what I'm saying. What I'm saying is that when you look your best, your confidence level is much higher. And employers *do* notice that."

I mulled this over. "That's actually pretty good advice," I conceded. "But are we sure making him feel bad is the way to go here?" Maybe this situation required more of a go-away-with-your-tail-between-your-legs approach. What if I went to all the trouble and he didn't even care?

"He slept with you, never called, then hooked up with your nemesis. A subtle bit of revenge is required."

I remembered the little heart emoticon on Nicole's message. Maybe I was in the mood for a medium-rare filet after all.

***

I followed Glynnis into the pedicure place unhappily. I didn't want anyone touching my feet. However, judging by the way she'd ignored my earlier objections regarding what can only be described as a truly harrowing Brazilian wax, I knew my protests would fall on deaf ears. She'd also start making the "my feet are my life" jokes that my family seemed to love to tease me with, and I really didn't want to hear any of those tonight.

We were greeted at the front desk and told to pick out polish colors.

"Red," Glynnis insisted when she saw me pick up a bottle of pale pink. "Toenails are meant to be red. And they'll match your shoes."

I put the pink down and chose a red color that would look good with the new shoes and followed her to the back of the room where a row of spa chairs awaited us.

Glynnis sat and plopped her long skinny feet into the water, leaned back, and closed her eyes with a sigh. So this was supposed to be relaxing? Big deal. I soaked my feet on a daily basis.

I pulled up the legs of my sweatpants. I regretted not having shaved since Sunday. I shuffled my feet out of my shoes and plunged them into the bubbly blue water before the lady could get a good look at them. I didn't like people looking at my feet, either. I flopped back into my chair and my skull collided with a hard lump.

The nail lady picked up a remote control, pushed a button, and handed it to me. I jumped as my chair started moving and the hard lump poked me in the neck. It rolled down my back, forcing each part of my body to gyrate off the chair in an obscene seated belly dance as it rolled down my body on its mission of mayhem. I had assumed massage chairs were supposed to feel good, but this was more like getting stabbed in the spine.

"Shiatsu," the lady at my feet explained, smiling happily.

Right away I deduced that shiatsu is Japanese for pain. I jabbed at the remote and the poking was replaced by vibrating. I subtly tried a few more buttons, eventually turning the chair off. I hoped the lady didn't notice. I didn't want to hurt her feelings.

The lady tapped me on the leg. A few seconds later she tapped my leg again, a little more insistently, and raised her eyebrows at me.

"Put your foot on the towel," Glynnis explained. I reluctantly pulled a foot out of the water and placed it on the towel. The lady looked at my callouses, missing nails, and bent toes and began speaking to the lady working on Glynnis's feet in a stream of rapid Vietnamese. She shook her head, looking disgusted. She reached for a pair of plastic gloves and snapped them on.

"They're supposed to look like that," I told her. "I need those callouses." I didn't mention anything about my big toenail that was completely black and how my third toe curved under my second toe in a mangled kind of way. She probably assumed I had some form of leprosy.

She reached among her array of shining metal tools and pulled out, I kid you not, a cheese grater. Not a tool that looked like a cheese grater. An actual cheese grater. I had the same exact one at home. It even had "Calphalon" on the handle in the same place.

I squealed and wrenched both my feet up into my chair and hid them under my legs, spraying blue water over the floor. Glynnis looked over in irritation.

"Put your feet down, Eiley. Stop acting like a hillbilly getting her first pedicure."

"But this is my first pedicure, and you know my feet are my life and all. I've worked hard to build up the right amount of callous and tough skin. I need every bit of it."

"Yeah, like a surgeon's hands," she smirked. "Put your nasty feet into that water and suck it up."

I lowered my feet back into the water. "Okay, but no cheese grater." The woman looked sorry that she wasn't going to get the chance to grate my epidermis off. She pulled out another tool that looked like a small pair of scissors and started clipping away at the skin around my nails. I didn't say anything. No way. I was sucking it up, even though the chopping was starting to hurt a little.

I looked over at Glynnis again. Her eyes were still closed. I risked a glance down at my toes and couldn't help but notice that there were some tiny little specks of…blood.

A wave of nausea coursed through me, and my ears started ringing. I bent to put my head between my knees and my hair fell into the foot water. The nail lady yelled something at me that I couldn't understand through all the hyperventilating. (Mine, not hers.)

Glynnis snapped to attention, grabbed some of my dry hair, and pulled my head back up again.

"I'm bleeding. Is there supposed to be blood? Cause I gotta think any beauty procedure that involves bloodletting is a little bit suspect." I swayed in my chair and shut my eyes tight. I fanned myself with my hand.

"I'll fix it," my nail lady yelled and scurried away. Glynnis's nail lady took one of the small fans they use to dry nails, clipped it to the arm of my chair, and aimed it at me.

My lady returned a few minutes later with a small tube. "Superglue," she said triumphantly, and began to dabble at my cut.

"Um, I have to question the wisdom of using superglue to fix a cut. Isn't it going to get into my bloodstream? Am I going to get superglue poisoning? Oh my God, I'm going to die in my sleep tonight." I tried to pull my foot away, but the small woman was surprisingly strong.

"Calm down. I'm sure it's fine. They wouldn't do it if it were dangerous."

"We suddenly think the woman who was about to use a cheese grater on my flesh has good judgment?" I looked at her incredulously.

"Oh for crying out loud," Glynnis said in exasperation. She looked at my nail lady. "Nothing but massage and polish," she told her. "Nothing else. No more filing, no more cutting. Only massage and polish." I couldn't help but notice the lady looked unhappy with both of us.

The nail lady filled her palms with some lavender-scented lotion and went to work massaging my tired calves. The hot towel that followed was nice. I could definitely do some relaxing during that part. The painting was okay too and I had to admit that they looked really good. Maybe I would even get another one when this wore off, as long as they would agree to massage and paint only.

I got home late, toting my shopping bags and waxed to within an inch of my life. I had a new little black dress, red stripper shoes, and toenails to match. Even though my birthday wasn't for another eight months Glynnis made a gift of it all to me. Otherwise I would have had to sell a kidney on the way to Tysons'.

I stumbled toward my bed, stripping off my grubby clothes as I went. My hair was only slightly damp from the foot water and I figured it would be okay to sleep on.

I picked up my cell as I passed it on the table. I had a notification for voicemail. I'd turned my cell off while I was being mutilated in the name of beauty. I checked the message. It was Valerie. "Hey, did you know your cell is going right to voicemail? You can't text me that you banged Lance Manyon then cancel our Tuesday night at Not Frank's and not provide more information. I need details. Length, girth, duration…call me or I'm coming over there."

I'd have to tackle that tomorrow. I was too tired tonight. Barney and I were asleep before our heads hit the pillow.

Chapter 11

Cheers to the Girl in the Thong Underwear

I turned in my chair so that I could see myself reflected in the row of mirrors that hung on every surface of the upscale salon. I'd been surrounded by piping hot hair instruments for the last two hours, and even though I'd arrived sweaty and covered in last night's foot water, my hair was now straight, smooth, and sophisticated.

The perfect hair and makeup were worth the embarrassment of having to explain to Susan and the Bitcherina that I had to leave early today…after arriving late this morning. After the whirlwind of shopping, waxing, and pedicures last night, I'd slept through my alarm this morning. And my freshly pedicured toe had throbbed all day. It was probably my conscience telling me to worry more about dancing and less about Trey. And I would. As soon as I got a little closure tonight.

I paid for my mini-makeover and zipped home from the salon to add the dress and shoes to my new look. I turned around in front of my closet mirror and liked what I saw. The dress was black and silky with a modest sleeveless halter-top, but so ridiculously short I probably shouldn't bend over. It made even my tiny legs look long and alluring.

I hadn't been out on the town in months. Maybe I would pick up Brett and go have fun and forget all about Trey. Maybe it would make up for the whole not-knowing-my-good-friend-was-gay thing.

I checked Frederic's food and water supply, kissed Barney good-bye, and headed out. It only took me twenty minutes to pick up Brett from Adams Morgan, the neighborhood where he rented a room in a three-bedroom apartment.

"You are the best fake boyfriend ever. Thanks for doing this." Brett looked handsome in a light green button-down shirt that was perfect with his brown eyes and short chestnut hair.

"Don't worry about it. This is going to be fun. We haven't gone out together in ages." He gave me a huge smile that was meant to be reassuring, but I already had butterflies.

We made our way up Connecticut Avenue to Dupont Circle and then to Nineteenth Street. Even with the evening traffic we were there in plenty of time for our six o'clock reservation.

I parked the car but didn't get out. "Are we sure this is a good idea? I mean, what's the point? If he's already moved on, he isn't going to care that I have, too. And what if he doesn't believe that this is a coincidence?" The longer I thought about it, the more I realized how many potential disasters were possible with this plan.

He reached over and tweaked my hair. "I know, kiddo. This revenge plan isn't really your style. Let's go have dinner. I'm hungry. It's a big restaurant, and we probably won't run into each other. If we do see him, we'll figure out what to do when the time comes."

"Glynnis says to play it off like I'm so surprised to see him and Nicole. But I don't think I have the same skill set that she does." I fiddled with the keys in my lap.

"Come on, don't waste the new dress and perfect hair. Besides, I can't wait to eat something that wasn't cooked on the Grudge's forty-year-old grill. I can practically hear a baked potato calling my name."

I perked up a bit. "That's true. I did have salad and water for dinner last night. I'm due for something good. Maybe a baked potato will take my mind off how much my toe hurts." Especially if it were covered in bacon and sour cream—the potato, not my toe, although at this point I was ready to try anything for a little relief.

We headed out of the car and into the restaurant. Brett stopped at the hostess stand while I went to appease my nervous bladder. Maybe I could soak my toe in the sink for a minute. I was pretty sure that was something that had never been seen at The Palm before.

As I neared the restroom the door swung open and Nicole emerged. She was wearing a bright red dress and what looked like a two-inch chrome dog collar around her neck. I assumed she had a fresh spray tan, judging by the aroma of two-day-old wontons that lingered near her.

I looked around frantically for some way to avoid her but there was nowhere to hide. We were only a few feet apart and she'd already seen me.

"What are you doing here?" she demanded, pointing her finger at me again. What was it with this girl and her pointy fingers?

"Well, gee, Nicole. It's a steak house. Clearly I'm here to buy a power sander."

"Nice dress. Did you buy that at Justice, Just for Girls?"

"Sorry, I didn't have time to go to Hookers R Us to get a dress like yours."

"That's probably for the best. You wouldn't have been able to fill one out." It was bad enough that she was having dinner with my ex-fake-boyfriend. Did she have to insult my chest as well?

"Oh really? That's not what Trey said last week at my apartment. In my bed."

"So what. So you had sex with Trey one time. Who hasn't? He was with *me* for months."

"One time? No, Nicole. I had sex with Trey for *hours*." Brett had returned. He grabbed my arm but I shook him off. I was going to say what I had to say, and then we could leave.

"Sex that was so good and so loud the neighbors thought I was being attacked." Brett tried again to take hold of my arm as I waved it to make my point. I would wipe that smug look off her face even if it was only for a few minutes.

"Sex in every room of my house in every position I could think of. Positions *Cosmo* hasn't even heard of yet." I looked away from Nicole to see that people were starting to stare at us. That was okay. I was almost done.

"Eiley," Brett tried to cut in.

I shushed him. "I'm talking breaking things and screaming orgasms, Nicole. Screaming. Orgasms."

I heard a clink of pottery and turned to see a cluster of waiters gaping at us, their trays full of food forgotten. A live lobster climbed the shirtfront of one waiter, making a desperate bid for freedom from the tray and the eventual pot of boiling hot water. I understood that feeling all too well. I felt a sudden kinship with that lobster. I plucked him from the waiter and held him protectively in front of me, waiting for Nicole to come back at me with something else.

What had she meant by being together for months? Trey actually dated her? For months? I looked at Brett, who had a pained expression on his face.

"Well, Myrtle, I guess your grandson is a hottie," a voice behind me said. I spun around on my new fancy red heels with my lobster held aloft. A crowd of old ladies had materialized behind us. Some of them were giggling but the rest of them stood staring, open-mouthed. Right in the middle was Trey, holding the hand of a sweet-looking lady in a purple pants suit and a red birthday hat.

"Hi, Eiley," My head snapped to the right. Chad was standing with an older couple who were probably his parents. "I didn't know you were coming to Nana's eightieth birthday celebration."

"She's not," Nicole hissed. "She wasn't invited."

Trey's face was red. "What is wrong with you?" he asked me. Again.

"You dated her? For months?" I clutched the squirming lobster to myself protectively. It was probably suffocating. Like me.

He rubbed his face with his hand. That was all the answer I needed. Tears blurred my vision as I turned and ran toward the exit as fast as I could hobble, frantic to escape all the horror. I blindly reached for the door as someone else opened it. Right into my forehead.

My arm circled in the air as my feet scrambled for purchase. I fell flat on my back. Stars circled my head like a Tom and Jerry cartoon. Or maybe they were those little tweeting bluebirds.

My bag had spilled and Brett frantically grabbed at ink pens and breath mints. He stuffed my old retainer back inside. "Oh honey," he whispered to me, "let's get you and Larry the Lobster out of here."

I couldn't agree more. Humiliation dripped off me like three-day-old flop sweat. I shook my head to clear it and valiantly swayed to my feet. And fell right back down to my knees, woozily. I looked at Brett through my tears. "Help me."

"Man overboard," Brett said, sliding an arm around my waist and hoisting me to my feet. Unfortunately, my shimmery little black dress did more hoisting than the rest of me. Brett hustled us out the door with me dangling from the armpits of my dress like a slutty marionette.

"Is that one of those thongs?" I heard Trey's grandmother ask. "I always wondered why people wear those things. They look so uncomfortable."

Brett and I made it to the safety of the parking lot. "Let's walk," he said. "I don't think driving is a good idea right now. And besides, you need a drink."

"What should I do with Larry?"

"Bring him along. He looks like he could use a drink. He had a near-death experience."

"Yeah, me too."

We walked a few blocks more to the Science Club. The DJ was playing reggae house mix and it was still happy hour. I ordered a Guinness and Brett took a Yuengling. He also ordered a Persian salad but I didn't feel like eating. I put Larry down on the bar to rest while we had our drinks.

"Come on, honey." Brett rubbed my shoulders. "I've heard some of those stories you and your sisters tell. It isn't the worst thing you've done. It's nowhere near as bad as the sea lion enclosure debacle."

I nodded. This was true. "But it's the worst thing I've ever done in front of the best guy I've ever been with. Present company excluded."

I raised my bottle, suddenly overwhelmed with how grateful I was that Brett was there with me. "Here's to you, old friend, bringer of bacon, and all-around good guy." I glugged down several swallows into my empty stomach. "Tonight I lost the guy of my dreams and tomorrow I'm probably going to lose the job of my dreams." I put my foot up on the stool beside me and slipped the shoe off my aching toe.

"Work sucks, life is unfair, cheers to the girl in the thong underwear," Brett replied, and we drank some more.

"Yeah, Trey's grandmother certainly enjoyed them."

"And her whole canasta club, or whoever that gaggle of old ladies was." Brett started laughing and after a while, I did too.

"I guess it was sort of funny. Showing my nether regions off in 'the place to see and be seen in Washington DC.'"

"You were seen all right. And, oh honey, when that door opened up and you flew backward, clutching a hot lobster..." He did an enthusiastic imitation of me right there in front of the bar, arms flailing in the air, feet pedaling. "And we both know you won't be paying for dinner next week at the Grudge."

"Ah, the silver lining to having made a fool of myself." I ordered another Guinness. My Irish forefathers certainly knew how to make magic out of barley and hops.

"And when you shouted at Nicole about having sex in every room of your house. And your screaming orgasms. Everyone in the whole place was paying attention." He was laughing so hard tears were in his eyes.

"Well, that part was true," I said, pointing my beer bottle at him. "It was all true. I'm talking about the most amazing sex ever."

"I can't believe they let you walk out of the place without paying for that guy." He gestured toward Larry.

I put my head down on the bar. "I can never go back to The Palm again and I didn't even get a baked potato." I studied the wood grain and wondered if I needed to write a letter of apology to Trey's grandmother. And to the manager of The Palm. Maybe a half page ad in the *Post*. Above the fold.

I remembered the rest of my brief conversation with Nicole. "Did you hear the part where Nicole said that she slept with him for months? And he didn't deny it?"

"Yeah, I caught that. Did he tell you he didn't sleep with Nicole?"

"Yes," I threw back the rest of my beer. "He told me that he wanted me to be his pretend girlfriend so that he wouldn't have to go out with Nicole."

"And?" Brett asked.

"And what?" I asked, signaling for another beer.

"Saying he doesn't want to go out with her now isn't the same thing as saying he'd never been with her in the past. And slow down on that beer. You're way past your half a beer limit."

I took a big swallow of my new beer and blew out a sigh. "Then it's a lie of omission. He could have supplied a few more details."

"Before or after you rode him like a theme park?"

"I guess you have a point." I sneaked a tomato out of Brett's salad.

He tapped his beer bottle to mine. "Here's to the girl with hot red shoes. She'll drink your beer, and she'll steal your food."

"That's right." I added a cucumber to my plunder.

"It seems pretty obvious they weren't there on a date. She was a part of the party and probably hoped to turn it into something more," Brett pointed out.

I nodded. The same thing had occurred to me…a little too late to prevent me from doing anything stupid, but hey.

"Did you see the way she was dressed tonight? Who thinks showing up as a dominatrix is appropriate for an eighty-year-old grandmother's birthday party?"

"It matches her personality," I snarked.

"You're saying she's been banged more times than a snooze button on a Monday morning?"

I cackled. "If she were a flower, she'd be a penis flytrap."

"She fell out of the easy tree and banged every guy on the way down."

I went from laughing to depressed in a drunken instant. "Including Trey."

Brett reached out and took my hand. "I know. But he's not with her anymore. He even made you his fake girlfriend to stay away from her."

"I guess that's true. It probably doesn't matter anyway. Not that he was paying any attention to me anyway, but after tonight he'll never speak to me again." I stuck my tongue in the top of my bottle to get the last drops of Irish champagne.

"Come on." He pulled me away from the bar. "It's time to go home."

We piled into an Uber and headed for my apartment. I snuggled under his arm, with Larry on my lap. I dozed off, despite the unfortunate odor of ketchup and feet that permeated the car. It was late and the Black Nectar had gotten to me.

We pulled up in front of my apartment and I gave Brett a big hug. "Thanks for tonight. You went well above and beyond the call of duty, my friend."

"Anytime, sweetie. It's actually kind of nice to see you out of the studio and having a life." Was a sucky life better than no life at all? Hard to say.

He got out of the car, handed me my shoe, and helped me lurch out of the door with Larry. I got to my feet painfully.

"I've been a terrible friend. I don't even know why you would ever bring me bacon." Tears sprang to my eyes.

Brett pulled me in close. "That's the Guinness talking. You're a great friend. Always have been."

My nose was really sniffly but I couldn't figure out what to do with the shoe and the lobster, so I wiped it on his shirt. "No. I'm not. I didn't even know for sure if you were gay. What kind of friend is that?"

"Maybe it's the best kind, honey."

I pulled back and studied his face with bleary eyes. He seemed sincere.

"Think about it, Eiley. You liked me for me. You didn't care one way or the other so much you didn't even bother to ask the question."

"But…" I felt like it was still wrong, but couldn't put it into words. "But it's a part of who you are. A huge part. An important part." I figured it would help me get my point across if I thumped him on the chest with my shoe with each sentence.

"It's okay. I forgive you. I love you anyway. Now come on, the Uber's waiting."

Brett put his arm around my waist and we walked toward the door together. Trey was leaning against my building with his arms crossed in front of him. He was still dressed from his grandmother's birthday party, and he looked angry. I decided it didn't matter, because I was angry, too. I didn't even pay attention to how good the suit looked on him. It must have been hand sewn to his exact body dimensions by the finest Italian craftsmen. Or angels.

"Well," Brett said, "looks like this is where I say good-bye." He gave me another quick hug and walked back to the car. I stumbled unevenly over to Trey, holding my shoe and my lobster.

"What are you doing here?" I asked him, concentrating on making my words come out clearly.

"Waiting for you."

"No kidding. Why?"

"We need to talk. Do you even know what boundaries are? What happened tonight crossed a line."

"I know." My anger suddenly deflated.

"You can't decide to show up wherever I am like that."

"I know," I said again, and a small tear sneaked out of my eye and ran down my cheek. "If it helps, I feel really bad about it."

He let out a frustrated groan. "Do *not* cry."

I was so not going to cry. I snorted loudly and another tear slid out.

"Please?" He wiped the tear away with his thumb and then gently traced the huge black-and-blue lump on my forehead. "You almost knocked yourself out on that door."

"Wish I had. Woulda been less embarrassing if I'd been unconscious."

"How did you end up at The Palm tonight?"

I hung my head. "Facebook." I mumbled. It was turning out that this was pretty embarrassing, too. "Saw you had plans to meet Nicole on Facebook. Wanted to see what was going on."

"Eiley, I didn't have plans with Nicole. I had plans with my grandmother, and Nicole happened to be included in those plans. Our families have been close for years. We live on the same street, remember?"

"Yeah, 'parently you've been *really* close to Nicole." I looked at him accusingly. He threw his hands up, but I didn't want to hear it. I'd had enough humiliation for one night, even if it was self-inflicted. I decided it was time Trey understood exactly what I had on my mind.

"Yanno, I let someone touch my feet. I never do that. And that lady poked me. It was bleeding. With blood." I shuddered a little. "She didn't even need to grate cheese. She put superglue on my toe." I noticed Trey looked a little confused, so I made an effort to be clearer.

"I may never dance again 'cause I wanted you to be jealous. I got a thong. And a Brazilian. D'you know what they do to you when you get a Brazilian? It's…it's…" I struggled to find the right word.

Trey shook his head and turned to leave. He took a step away, then turned back to me.

"Dammit."

He shook his head again then pushed me into the side of the building.

The bricks against my back were still warm from the heat of the day. He stroked my hair away from my face, leaned down, and kissed me. His hands moved from my shoulders down my arms, leaving a trail of goose bumps. I wasn't exactly sure what was going on, but I was guessing he wasn't so mad anymore.

"Everyone at The Palm knows you got a Brazilian, sweet cheeks," he said in between kisses. "And that thong…" He kissed the corner of my mouth. "Were you going to let that guy see it?" He kissed my jaw. "Or is that thong for me?" He kissed my neck, which almost distracted me from noticing his hand had slid up my thigh and under my dress. His fingers deftly found a path to the exceptionally smooth South American landscaping down there. "'Cause I want to think this thong was meant for me," he whispered.

"Who's got boundary issues now?" The rough pad of his thumb brushed against me. "Not that I care. You can invade France for all I care."

I had whiplash from the abrupt switch in conversation, and the Guinness wasn't doing me any favors, either. I tried to remember which one of us was mad at the other but I couldn't focus. His fingers were causing the little woman in the canoe to be extremely happy. I could sort the details out later. I moaned into his mouth and worked my hand under his shirt.

"I hate you, you know that?" I told him.

"Uh-huh." His fingers stroked more firmly. I might have wrapped my leg around him at that point. Simply to elevate my sore toe, you understand.

"Why didn't you call me?" My words were breathy and not at all as angry as I wanted them to sound. I might even have been panting. Just a little. Multitasking can be tricky.

"I'm with you now."

"But you wouldn't be if I hadn't shown up at The Palm tonight." He pressed more closely into me, his fingers moving quickly. I was totally right about busy hands and the devil's playground.

"I think I might have been." His mouth was hot on my neck. It felt so good I almost dropped my lobster. "I can't seem to stop thinking about you, you crazy stalker."

This seemed like important information, but before I could follow up I had to bite into his shoulder to avoid screaming out some creative expletives.

"Wow," I breathed, resting my head against the bricks.

He touched his forehead to mine. "You are so hot, you know that?"

"But not hot enough, right?"

He took a sudden step away from me and I slid down the wall. "Let me take you inside." His voice—like oozy warm honey a moment before—felt cooler now. I had probably pushed the issue of him not having called me too far. I sighed and followed him to the door, clumsily sifting through my handbag one-handed. After a few minutes Trey pulled the bag from me, found my access card, and swiped it to open the door.

My ears buzzed as we walked to the elevator. I clomped along unevenly in my one sad stripper shoe. My toe still really hurt, even with the alcohol anesthetic.

Trey unlocked my door and scooped me up into his arms. I couldn't help noticing how good he smelled while I may have been nuzzling his neck. Tomorrow I would find a good self-help book on willpower and self-control, I promised myself. And unlike *Cosmo*, I'd read it.

He put me down on the couch and sat next to me. I leaned my head back and closed my eyes.

"I'm not sure this is the best time to be having this conversation. Are you listening?" I nodded my head. His voice sounded like it was coming from a long way away.

"You're wrong about one thing. I noticed you at Not Frank's a long time ago. I never pursued anything because I thought that you weren't like most of the other girls there."

I opened one eye and tried to focus on his face. "Spray tanned?"

He chuckled. "I thought you were the boyfriend type, not the friends with benefits type. That's why I made up Lia."

My other eye flew open. "Huh?" It was the best I could do.

"She's not really my girlfriend. She's a friend."

"You made up two girlfriends?" I asked incredulously. "Why would you need two fake girlfriends? Wasn't I fake girlfriend enough for you?"

"I needed you to keep Nicole away, and I needed Lia to keep you from getting too serious." I shook my head in disbelief. "I was worried, okay? I thought you might want more from me than I had to offer."

Was he talking about his penis? Because that was pretty much all he'd ever offered me. "You weren't exactly worried about keeping your distance last Sunday night." *Or five minutes ago.*

"I don't want to keep distance between us."

"And how does not talking to me for four days accomplish that?"

He ran his hand through his hair. "When you told me that your only experience was two serious relationships, you scared the hell out of me."

I shook my head again. He seriously had Y-chromosome-induced relationship paranoia.

"I'm hoping we both want the same thing," he said.

"You'd better spell it out for me because I'm getting a little sleepy." I closed my eyes again. "And maybe leave it on a sticky note in case I forget tomorrow morning."

"We can talk about it another time." He laughed softly then stood and rearranged the pillows so that I could lie down comfortably. He pulled a blanket over me, stopping when he saw Larry still cuddled on my lap.

"Give me the lobster."

I cuddled him closer. "No. He's mine. He's going to live with me."

"You're going to kill him. He needs to get back in water soon."

"Okay, put him in the tub for me."

"Salt water. Let me take him." He held out his hand and reluctantly, I handed Larry over.

"Chad's got a saltwater tank. I can put him in there until we figure out what to do with him."

"Next to his water bed?"

"How did you know that?"

"I assumed…" My voice trailed off.

I felt him kiss my cheek before he turned out the light and left.

Chapter 12

Jazz Hands, Mon Dieu

I struggled to extract my left leg from the couch cushions. My head pounded and I had to blink several times to clear the fuzz from my eyes. I could see enough to know that I was going to be late again today. Frederic swooped over me, squawked, and pooped on my head, and although there are cultures that consider this to be a harbinger of good luck, let me tell you—not so much.

I jumped from the couch to shake my head to dislodge Frederic's gift from my hair and fell to my knees in pain. My toe was swollen to twice its normal size and the color looked off to me, unless you consider purple to be a reasonable color for any appendage on your body. Good thing my job wasn't dependent on my toes or anything.

I hopped on one foot, my arms stretched around my body awkwardly to unzip my dress. My shin crashed into my coffee table and I gave up on the zipper and pulled the dress over my head in a tangled mess.

I would need a good excuse for showing up late to the studio again today. I could say that I had car trouble. I hadn't used that one in a couple of weeks. Traffic was always a good one. Although, considering I'd be biking to work today since I'd left my car parked at The Palm last night, those probably weren't my best options. Maybe I'd leave the poop in my hair and go with pigeon attack. That sounded completely reasonable.

I threw on some dirty clothes from the floor and, after walking Barney, and applying a liberal dose of dry shampoo, grabbed my keys and hobbled to my bike as quickly as I could. I pedaled my hung-over, sore-footed self to the studio and made it there only thirty minutes behind schedule.

I pulled the squeaky studio door open and rushed inside. I got into dance gear and combed my hair over the spot where the bird poo had been in under a minute, and then spent the next five taping up my toe as best I could. I laced up my pointe shoes and swallowed some Aleve. Hopefully those warnings about taking more than two pills in a twenty-four-hour time period were more of a general guideline than a strict policy.

I decided to sneak into the practice room and hide behind some people. Maybe no one would notice I hadn't been there on time. I mean, it's probably easy to miss a five-foot woman, right? Okay, fine. Four eleven. And a half.

Today we were scheduled to rehearse the end of the adagio, first section of the grand *pas de deux*. Originally this part of *Swan Lake* was choreographed by Petipa and Ivanov in 1895, but each choreographer likes to put her own spin on it, and over the years it's been changed—sometimes a little and sometimes drastically.

One of our principal backers wanted to incorporate a version that was done by Christopher Wheeldon at the New York City Ballet. I've seen movies, and the Wheeldon interpretation is genius. But Susan wanted to do an authentic version, close to the original choreography of 1895.

So the backer, a real estate developer named Kris Caposella, decided that a good compromise would be for her to combine the two versions. Never mind that it wasn't really possible. In Wheeldon's version several of the scenes are in the imagination of a dancer who loses track of reality and believes he's become Siegfried. The scenes that Petipa and Ivanov originally staged as being actual events Wheeldon had interpreted as dreams or imaginings. No real way to combine a dream with reality, right?

Susan has settled for simply adding some of the steps from Wheeldon's vision into Petipa's choreography, which of course spoils the authenticity. But what are you going to do when a million-dollar donor threatens to walk out the door?

This act is the most difficult for me, and my left leg, which bears most of the weight of the moves. There's a turn called a *fouetté rond de jambe en tournant*. That's French for "a real pain in the arse." Actually, the turn itself isn't so hard. You stand on one bent leg, whip your other leg around, rise to en pointe, bring your working leg in and land on one flat foot. The tricky part? Thirty-two of them in a row. If you vomit, you lose. And people count. As in count out loud and make sure you do them all. No pressure there.

Today I probably couldn't do a single one. Luckily, we'd practiced this thoroughly last week. This morning we were supposed to be doing a quick run-through as we settled some points with the staging and choreography as Susan tried to add a little more of Wheeldon into her traditional approach. I was desperately hoping "quick run-through" meant no *fouettés*.

Unless you're in the dance world, you'd never guess that so much drama could go into planning a couple of simple moves. This is the act where Siegfried thinks he's dancing with Odette but it's really Odile. He's falling in love with her as she's bewitching him. One change that Susan has considered making is to the ending, when Siegfried is down on one knee and Odile, holding on to his knee, does an arabesque.

You might be thinking no one cares about such a minor point, but you'd change your mind if you'd walked in to the argument I did this morning. Luckily for me, everyone was too distracted to notice my tardiness. Basil and Susan were shouting at each other. The cygnets were wandering around the edges of the room, stretching and drinking water.

"Eiley," Susan called when she spied me skulking about in the back. "Come here. Let's take it from the arabesque." I shambled to the front of the room. Basil knelt down on one knee, assuming his position. I put my hands on his knee and raised my leg to form an arabesque. Flat footed.

"En pointe, please, Eiley," Susan muttered distractedly as she scribbled something down in her ever-present spiral notebook. I grimaced and pulled myself up onto my sore toe.

"Okay, now, Basil, look over your right shoulder," Susan directed. "No, no. Look into Eiley's eyes." Basil directed his gaze at my forehead. My knee began to shake as the pressure and pain built in my toe. Susan continued to write notes, occasionally scratching through something and starting over.

I gritted my teeth. Susan chewed on the end of her pen, deep in thought. I leaned back slightly, trying to ease the pressure on my toe, and lost my balance. I quickly dug my fingers into Basil's thigh for support, hoping to right myself. I'd been in the room less than five minutes and things were already going south. Basil let out a yelp and jerked his leg away. I crashed to the ground. Again. All the activity in the room stopped and the dancers turned to face us.

"You did that on purpose," I accused him, struggling to get myself into a sitting position.

"*I* did? What about your behavior? You're acting like a child. You will never be ready in time for this performance." He crossed his arms resolutely. "Call Corinne. She's prepared," he said to Susan.

I gasped. "No. No Corinne. You're going to have to deal with me." I felt a wave of doubt and turned to face Susan. "Right?" I asked uncertainly. She didn't meet my eyes.

"Okay, dancers," Susan called through gritted teeth. "Change in plans. Let me see the cygnets up here. Get ready for Act Two. Basil, do some conditioning and then go home. We won't need you today. Eiley, go to the small practice room and work on the choreography. Be ready to go by tomorrow morning." The words *or else* hung in the air, unsaid.

Several dancers moved to the front, the only sound in the deadly silent room the shuffle of their dance shoes against the worn wooden floorboards. Dismissing the principal dancers during a rehearsal was bad. Extremely bad. And it had been my fault. Basil threw his hands up in the air, turned, and left the room. The disgusted look on his face was more demoralizing than any insult he could have thrown my way.

I left the practice room, my face burning. I'd been sent to time-out. The only thing I could do to make this right was to master the part. I found a smaller practice room that wasn't in use, cued up the music, and got started. I would work through the pain and gamble with a few more Aleve, if needed. After the first twenty minutes my toe was numb anyway.

I started from the beginning and tried to work my way through. It's actually pretty difficult to rehearse ballet alone. Most of the movements I make are done with Basil. There's a lot of lifting and turning. There's one lift where I'm over his head, belly button to the ceiling, head and feet pointing to the floor. Thankfully, he'd never picked that moment to drop me.

I did the best I could, focusing on the parts that had been giving me the most trouble. There were thousands of steps and combinations to remember. Luckily, I had Susan's Benesh notations—diagrams of each section of dance that look like little stick figures—to fall back on.

I'd been practicing most of the day when the door opened and Basil slipped inside. He leaned against the wall, arms crossed, watching me for several moments.

"Having trouble?" He gestured toward the notations in my hand.

I nodded. He didn't seem angry anymore. He took the remote for the CD player from my hand and restarted the music. "Show me." He leaned against the wall again and re-crossed his arms.

As I repeated the sequence of steps, my face flamed and big red blotches popped up on my chest under his scrutiny. He stopped the music abruptly.

"You're off. You've missed a small step. See here," he demonstrated, "step, step, point, arabesque, attitude, tendu. You're leaving out the point and not ending up with the music." I tried the sequence again and realized he was right. He knew both his part and mine better than I did.

"Thank you," I said simply. I didn't know why he was helping me, but it felt like an olive branch and I wanted to take it.

"Have you been in here all day? It's after six."

"Is it?" I shrugged. I was too sore and tired to bike home, so I'd texted Brett earlier in the day to pick me up at 7:00. I'd planned to keep working until he showed up and I hadn't been keeping track of the time.

"Actually, I was hoping to find you here. We must find a way to work together. What happened today was unfortunate."

I nodded. "I'm sorry about that. It won't happen again."

He sighed. "I am willing to set our disagreement aside for the sake of the performance. Can you agree that our personal differences must not be allowed to interrupt our work?"

It was indeed an olive branch, of sorts. "Absolutely. I promise." I stuck my hand out awkwardly and he shook it.

"Would you like to run through the *pas de deux*?"

A *pas de deux* is like the name sounds, if you know French. Only two people. And hard to practice alone. He was already taking off his street shoes.

Okay then, it looked like the decision had been made. Basil and me. No choreographer, no extras. And no witnesses.

Basil found the music and we started working our way through the movements. After several minutes he took off his shirt, wiped his forehead with it then tossed it aside. We continued working until we reached the part where we'd been having the most trouble.

I'm supposed to do a series of arabesques then Basil turns me around. I stand in front of him and my leg curls backward and around him until my right foot is behind his head. After that there's a few steps and a few turns, and the movement repeats.

Hopefully we could figure out why the sequence wasn't working. I stepped away from Basil and started the turn. The music stopped abruptly. "No, Eiley. You're off again. Two steps between me and the turn." Well of course it would be my fault that we were off.

"I thought it was three steps, not two." I glanced at his shirtless torso. Dancers have outstanding bodies and Basil's was even better than most.

"It has to be two, because then I take two steps and we start over again."

"Maybe you take three."

"No. Look, you do this." He demonstrated my part, throwing his leg behind him, taking two steps, and waving his hands frantically back and forth.

"Since when does *Swan Lake* have jazz hands?" I followed the direction of his gaze to my foot. My pointe shoe had a growing bloodstain on the front.

"*Mon Dieu.*"

My brain turned into cotton candy and my stomach flipped over. I slunk to the floor and took deep breaths to fight the dizziness. My stomach flipped again and I heaved.

"*Mon Dieu.*"

My five bottles of water, zone bar, and half bottle of Aleve made an unfortunate reappearance. I grabbed the nearest thing to stem the tide of the unfortunate lunch reversal, which happened to be Basil's discarded shirt.

"Ugh," I groaned as my stomach started to settle. "Sorry. I have a thing about blood."

"Blood makes you vomit?"

"All bodily fluids, really. Blood, urine, vomit. Pus." He was sitting on the floor beside me now, with my foot in his lap. "I'm sorry about your shirt. You look better without it, anyway." He untied my shoe and eased it off my foot.

"What is this? All this medical tape?"

I rolled my head around my neck, stalling. I sighed, and straightened my spine. I owed him an explanation and I might as well get it over with. And hey, maybe the story would get less embarrassing each time I told it.

"I got a life-threatening pedicure from a crazy woman with a cheese grater. And then I tried to tape it up but it didn't help much. It's killing me. This morning when I squeezed your leg I wasn't trying to hurt you. I was trying to relieve some of the pressure."

Basil gently put my foot on the floor and went to the shelf in the corner of the room where we kept various supplies. He sat down beside me again and used some scissors to cut away my tights and the gauze and tape that I'd wrapped around my toe.

"*Mon dieu.* A dancer's feet are sacred. Why would you do such a thing?"

"To impress a boy," I said in a small voice, trying not to grimace as he poked around my toe.

Basil gave me a long look, saying nothing. Finally he gave a brief nod and an even briefer smile. "It so happens, I've been there a time or two myself." He quickly looked away.

My eyes widened in surprise. Did he mean...? I was burning with questions, but decided to keep my mouth shut rather than risk our fragile peace. He picked up a pair of nail clippers and I focused on not jerking my foot away in fear. He bent over my foot, still not making eye contact.

We sat in silence as he clipped away at my nail. It felt like our relationship had really turned a corner. I decided I should explain why I'd been so unfocused lately to further cement our new bond.

"You see, I've liked this person for a really long time. He never paid any attention to me until recently, and now that he's paying attention to me I don't know what to do about it. I let myself get totally distracted from the ballet. It felt like my one chance to have something I really wanted." He continued to poke and prod at my nail, not saying anything.

"And then you and I weren't getting along." I looked at him expectantly. It took two people to mend a bad relationship, after all. "I really wanted you to like me," I blurted. Basil grunted and threw the clippers aside.

"That's why I tried to fix you up with my friend Brett." I studied his face. I wanted to clear the air once and for all, but had I gone too far? "I'm sorry for invading your privacy. I honestly was trying to help. I thought you'd be happier if you weren't lonely." I hoped he would take my apology in the vein that it was intended, and not point out the fact that dating had not been a positive experience for me so far.

He took a deep breath and let it out slowly. "I don't wish to discuss my personal life with you, Eiley."

I nodded. "No. I understand. I know I crossed the line, and I've learned my lesson. Plus, now I know better than to do something stupid to try to get someone to like me."

He nodded in agreement. "It's not important to be liked. It's important to be respected."

"Well, you didn't do that either," I pointed out. Basil dabbed some Neosporin on my toe. "You didn't think I was ready to be the lead."

"No."

I sucked in a breath. I'd kind of hoped he'd deny it. He opened a package of gauze and wrapped my toe. I wiggled it around a little, surprised that it didn't hurt as much now.

"I didn't think you were ready."

"I *am* ready," I told him indignantly. "I've been an understudy for two years. I was working hard to learn the part." Most days, anyway.

"Not ready in here." He tapped my chest. "Or in here." He tapped my forehead. "You must feel it and believe it with no doubt. And you aren't there yet."

He was right. I wasn't. "Thanks," I said, not meeting his eyes. "You've been kinder to me than I deserve."

He lifted my chin with his finger so that I had no choice but to look at him. "You and I have begun wrongly. But we must work together, so we will make the best of it. I believe that you can do this, Eiley. Don't let me down. Or yourself."

I gave him a brief nod and began to pick up the mess around us. I would work harder, until all of my doubts were gone. As I was throwing the old bandages in the trash Brett arrived to take me home.

"Hey," he called, as he came into the practice room. I could see the question on his face as he took in my shoeless, bandaged foot,

Basil without his shirt, and what could only be described as the pungent, fermented cheese smell of vomit permeating the room.

"Brett, thanks for coming to pick me up. This is…"

Basil put his hand out. "The Bitcherina," he said, taking Brett's hand in his with a smile.

My hand flew to my mouth. "You knew?" I asked from behind my shaking fingers.

One eyebrow shot up. "*Oui*," he replied.

"Why didn't you say anything?"

He shrugged. "It wasn't as bad as what I called you."

Brett laughed. "Nice to finally meet you. Eiley's told me so much about you."

"*Enchantè*," Basil replied, leaning in toward Brett as he shook his hand. I groaned. Hopefully this wouldn't get any more awkward. For me. I took my time cleaning up while they made small talk. They certainly seemed to be attracted to each other. Maybe it wasn't too late for them.

"Why don't you come out with us Tuesday night?" I suggested when I rejoined the conversation. Both men turned to look at me. "Brett was going to come to Not Frank's with me for moral support. Would you like to join us?" I hadn't actually had plans with Brett, but I couldn't resist making one last effort to fix them up. Besides, it would be nice to have some additional support when I had to face Trey again.

"Moral support?" Basil looked confused.

I gestured toward my bandaged foot. "Pedicure boy. You want to meet him?"

"Why not?" He smiled at Brett. I was pretty sure I could have offered dinner with Genghis Khan or the entire Kardashian clan and he would have agreed.

We said good-bye, and Brett loaded my bike into his car. I was so tired I didn't bother changing out of my dance clothes. I leaned my head back on the headrest and closed my eyes while Brett slowly navigated the evening traffic.

A small piece of dried-up bird poo fell onto my shoulder and I brushed it onto the floor. The day had started out horrible but it had ended up pretty good.

Chapter 13

Dirty Bacon

After the disaster on Friday I'd made sure that I was the first one in and the last one out Saturday, Monday, and today. I'd even gone in on Sunday. Although I still had no idea what to say to Trey, I felt like I'd really earned some downtime tonight at Not Frank's. My phone chimed with a text from Valerie. *I'm in your parking lot. Let's go get your car.* I kissed Barney good-bye and grabbed my bag.

When I got to the lot Valerie was standing beside her Mini Cooper. The Union Jack paint job looked freshly washed. I don't know how she hasn't developed scoliosis getting all six feet of herself into and out of the thing. She looked me up and down as I approached and wrinkled her nose.

"What are you wearing? You look like Malibu Barbie."

I looked down at myself. "It's a romper. Glynnis gave it to me for Christmas last year. It's too hot for jeans." I refrained from commenting on the three-inch wedges she was wearing that caused her to loom over me.

We climbed into the car and headed out into the evening traffic.

"How many days has your car been sitting in the lot at The Palm?" She pulled down her visor, partially obstructing her view of the road.

"Uh, five. Counting today. I've been too busy to go back and get it." I stared at the traffic intently to make up for the fact that Valerie was busy with her lip gloss in the vanity mirror.

"You mean too embarrassed, right?"

"Basil is meeting us at Not Frank's," I told her, changing the subject.

Valerie dropped the eyeliner pencil she'd been trying to sharpen one-handed. "What? Why would you want to bring the Bitcherina to our favorite bar?"

"We've reached a truce. He's meeting Brett there, plus he knows the whole Trey story."

She high-fived me. "See? I told you our plan would work. You should trust me more, instead of underestimating my good judgment." Her head barely above the steering wheel, she stretched her long arm to pat the floor mat blindly in search of the missing eyeliner pencil. "What's the deal with Lance now, anyway?"

I groaned. "I don't know. Things are kind of weird right now."

"Why? What did you do?"

I filled Valerie in on what had happened at The Palm and afterward, as best as my foggy memory would allow.

"Weird? He's probably afraid of you. That's taking stalking to a whole new level."

"He didn't seem too scared when he had his hands up my dress."

"That was the testosterone. It poisons them. It eats away at the part of the brain used for good judgment." She turned to look at me and the car drifted dangerously close to a metro bus in the lane next to us. Horns honked. I waved apologetically at the terror-stricken faces framed in the bus windows and wondered what exactly had eaten away the good judgment section of her brain.

"What about Nicole?" she asked.

"She was there for his grandmother's birthday party. They're not together."

"Sure they're not? You told me they have a past. Maybe it's not over yet."

I shrugged. "He went to a lot of trouble setting up the whole fake girlfriend thing with me to avoid her. It wouldn't make sense for him to be interested in her now."

"You're kidding me, right? Because I thought you were smarter than that. When do men ever do anything that makes sense when it comes to sex?"

I grabbed the door handle as she made a left across three lanes of oncoming traffic. A box with a half-eaten Big Mac flew off her dashboard and onto my lap. "So you think he wants to be with Nicole?" I asked doubtfully, trying to wipe special sauce off my leg with the cover of a Kohl's catalog from the floor. Hopefully Valerie hadn't been interested in getting thirty percent off any small kitchen appliances.

She shrugged. "Maybe. Who knows? Maybe he wants to be with you."

"Yeah, about that…" I tossed the Mac mess into the backseat. "We talked about it last Thursday night after the whole Palm fiasco."

"And?"

"I think he wants to keep things pretty casual. Lots of hooking up, no commitments."

"Is that what he said?" She glanced over her shoulder and did a quick lane change. A man in a silver Prius gave her a one-fingered salute.

"I can't really remember what he said, to be honest. But I think it was leading in that direction."

"What did you say?"

I squeezed my eyes shut as she turned into the parking lot without slowing down. "I think I fell asleep."

Valerie turned to face me. "Lance Manyon offered you an illicit relationship and you dozed off? I find that hard to believe." She pulled into a spot beside my car. Thankfully, it hadn't been towed.

"It was a long day. I was tired. And I'd had too much beer."

"And you haven't talked about it since last week?"

"I've been avoiding it." We'd exchanged several texts but not about anything serious. Mostly they had involved Larry and the new home Trey had found for him at a local aquarium.

"Okay then, what do *you* want to do about it?"

I gathered up my bag and sunglasses and pushed the door open with relief. "I don't know. I need some time to think about it."

"Too late for that. You've got twenty minutes to figure it out." I stuck my tongue out at her. "See you at Not Frank's," she called out as I slammed the car door shut.

***

I pulled into the lot at Not Frank's and saw Basil waiting for me near the doors. He would have been hard to miss in the skintight V-neck T-shirt and jeans he was wearing. A few of the regulars would probably be locking in his direction tonight.

"*Ça va?*" I called out to him as I approached, happy to have remembered the French greeting he had taught me earlier that morning.

"*Oui, ça va bien,*" He leaned in to kiss me on each check. Flustered, I tried to copy his suave movements but ended up bumping my nose into his and making a smacking noise with my lips. It was good to know that I could be awkward on any continent.

"I was surprised that you invited me here tonight," he said, gesturing for me to walk ahead of him into the building. That made two of us.

We worked our way through the restaurant to my usual table. We spent a few minutes locating two free stools and squeezed them around our small space. Basil ordered a beer, but I decided against it. I didn't want to do anything that might risk me being late to practice again when things were going so well. Instead, I ordered some wings and cheese sticks and settled down to wait for Brett and Valerie. It really shouldn't surprise you that Valerie and her lead foot had left The Palm before I did and still managed to be late. Tardiness is her special gift.

Basil and I stared at each other in uncomfortable silence. Hopefully the food would arrive soon to provide a distraction. "It's been so sunny and warm lately," I began awkwardly, then rolled my eyes at myself. Of course it was sunny and warm. It was June.

"Yes. It makes it quite warm in the studio as well," Basil offered.

I nodded. "Maybe we should ask for a fan?"

"Yes a fan…would…" His voice trailed off and his gaze drifted away from mine to a point over my shoulder. I looked behind me to see Valerie and Brett skirting the crowded tables and stifled a smile.

The waitress materialized with our food as Valerie and Brett arrived at the table. Valerie pushed Brett into a chair beside Basil.

"You two get to know each other," she ordered, grabbing my arm and pulling me out of my seat. "Eiley and I need to talk for a minute."

"What are you doing? I'm hungry." Plus everyone knew cheese sticks weren't as good once the cheese got cold and gummy.

"I saw Nicole and Trey out in the parking lot," she hissed at me. "And something. Is. Up."

"No it isn't. And even if it was, it's none of my business. William Cuthbert Layton the Third can do whatever he wants. I don't really know if I'm even his fake girlfriend anymore."

"Cuthbert?" Valerie snorted. I waved her off.

"So you don't care."

"I'm telling you, it's nothing."

"It sure looked like something."

I crossed my arms and shook my head stubbornly.

"Knowing that right now Nicole has her hands all over Trey—that doesn't bother you a single bit?"

"That's right."

"If I told you we could watch them from the window of the women's restroom, you'd have no interest whatsoever in doing that?"

I was in the restroom in under a second, straining to see out of the window. Valerie might have a point about the testosterone poisoning. It wouldn't hurt to check it out. Unfortunately, the window was set high on the wall for privacy. Stupid peeping Toms.

"I can't see. It's too high. Be my eyes. Look out there and describe what you see."

Valerie looked out. "Well, Helen Keller, Trey is standing with his arms crossed. Nicole is saying something and is poking him in the chest with her finger."

"I'll bet she is. She's a poker. She's got shiatsu finger." I poked Valerie a few times to be sure she understood me. "What's she doing now?"

Valerie looked out again. "I changed my mind, you're not Helen, you're Ethel. Trey's talking now."

"How does he look? Upset? Angry? Happy? Is he touching her? And why am I not Lucy? I really think I'm Lucy."

Valerie turned to look at me. "Because you're the short one. Ethel is the short one."

"But I have red hair. Lucy had red hair. Look again, what's going on now?"

Valerie turned back to the window. "Oh my God."

I vaulted onto her back to get a look for myself. My eyes darted around the lot until I found them. They had their arms around one another and Nicole's hands were tangled in his hair.

"Well that doesn't look good," I muttered.

"Not particularly. So, what now?"

"I don't know. We were supposed to talk tonight. I guess I could ask him."

"You can't do that, stupid."

"Why not?"

"Oh, well let me see. How would that conversation go, exactly? 'So, Trey, I was watching you out the bathroom window and I couldn't help but notice…'"

"Ugh, you're right. I should keep my overt stalking to a minimum until the Palm fiasco dies down."

"You know, you probably shouldn't have slept with him."

"What? You told me to sleep with him." I smacked the top of her head. "You told me to go for it. You can't close the fence after the cows have left the barn."

"Hey. I'm willing to cut you a little slack since you're confused and all, but my goodwill is wearing off." She smacked up at me, missing and hitting herself. She spun around to the mirrors.

Two girls stood in front of the sinks, phones out and aimed at us.

"Oh my God, Erin," the blonde one said. "This is so going on YouTube."

I jumped down in a hurry, remembering the last time I was on YouTube. "That's already been done," I huffed.

"Look, Regan, I added it to my story." The brunette held her phone up to show her friend.

Valerie squared her shoulders and squeezed her six-foot (and three inches, thanks to the wedges) frame up close to them. "I'd better not see that video anywhere."

"Take it down a notch, Yeti." The blonde looked nervous.

We backed out of the bathroom, Valerie still giving them the stink eye. As the door closed I heard Regan say, "Hash tag, Not Frank's," as Erin laughed. Great. Might as well make a fool of myself on all forms of social media, right?

We paused outside of the bathroom to regroup.

"Now what?" Valerie straightened my romper, then patted my shoulders.

"I don't know. Let's go hide out with Brett and Basil. That'll give me time to think about it."

"I thought Trey wanted to talk to you. How are you going to avoid that?"

I threw my hands up. "I'll pretend like I don't see him. It's the only thing I can think of right now." I turned and stalwartly marched toward our table.

"You're in luck. You can practice your ignoring. Here he comes."

I cut my eyes to the side and saw that Nicole and Trey had walked in the door. As soon as he saw me he quickly put some distance between himself and Nicole.

"Eiley."

I turned my head and kept right on walking, giving him what Rowan would call "the cut direct." It was the worst possible insult someone in a romance novel could give you, and the best I could do at the moment.

"Hey," he called, running to catch up to me, oblivious to my Victorian slight. "What are you up to?"

"I'm going to my table."

"Hold on a minute. I was hoping to get a chance to talk to you."

"But you're a guy," Valerie burst out incredulously. "Guys don't talk."

"Um, maybe after the show." I kept right on walking, head down. Trey stepped in front of us so that we were forced to stop.

"I need to get back to my, uh…" I nodded my head in Basil's direction, then looked to Valerie for help.

"Our dates," Valerie interjected. My eyes widened at her outrageous lie.

Trey's head turned in the direction of our table and then back to me. I risked a quick glance at him. He was smiling.

"Who has the fake date now?"

"Not us, that's for sure." Valerie put her hands on her hips and tried to look offended.

"He's wearing leg warmers."

"They go with his shirt. He likes to match."

"He's kissing Eiley's date."

Oops. He had us there.

I whirled around to see Basil and Brett leaning across the small table kissing. And people say I move fast.

"I tried. You're on your own." Valerie patted Trey on the shoulder. "Good luck, Lance." She joined Brett and Basil at the table, carefully reaching around them to procure a chicken wing. I took some small comfort in the fact that she couldn't reach the blue cheese from where she was sitting.

I took a small step away from Trey toward our table, but before I could get too far Trey put his hands on my shoulders and pulled me back to him. I melted a little. As much as I wanted to run away, more of me wanted to lean into his warm body. Even more than that, I wanted to ask him what he'd been doing in the parking lot with Nicole.

"Just listen," Trey started, his mouth close to my ear.

A small bubble of panic lodged itself in my stomach. "I don't want to listen. I don't need to listen." I swallowed nervously. "I'm sorry about what happened at The Palm. I shouldn't have done that. That was wrong."

Slow down, my brain said. *You sound a little frantic right now.* "And it will never happen again, assuming I don't die of embarrassment right now. But I guess you'd revive me, since you're an EMT and all. Unless you were still mad at me, then maybe you wouldn't. Except you probably took one of those oaths and all, so you'd have to. Revive me, I mean."

And also crazy. "I hate that you lied about Lia. Why did you do that? I'm not that pathetic, am I?" My voice wobbled, and "am I" had come out as an imperceptible squeak.

I stared straight ahead, my back against him, unable to see his face to even attempt to read his expression. I glanced at my table and Valerie, Basil, and Brett all looked away quickly, pretending not to watch us.

Trey moved my hair off my neck and my nipples immediately responded. Why wasn't he saying anything? I shifted uncomfortably and felt him growing hard through the soft fabric of my romper. Hadn't he heard anything I'd said? Was this the twilight zone?

"You know, I get it. I do," I babbled on. "You didn't need to invent a girlfriend. You could have told me you weren't really interested in a relationship. I mean, not that you needed to tell me. I kind of already figured that out for myself, considering it took a year for you to even notice I was alive."

He rubbed my neck and I sucked in a breath. I shifted ever so slightly to feel him against my bottom.

"But, see, the thing is, I thought that I was okay with that, but it turns out, I'm not." I think.

He bent and kissed me behind my ear.

"And so, you have to stop kissing me." I felt like I finished fairly strong, considering how hot his mouth was.

I turned around slowly and tried unsuccessfully to avoid looking at his crotch. My cheeks flushed and I forced my gaze to his face. His features softened. He cupped my face in his hands.

"Wait, what did I say? No. No more kissing."

That's right, my brain said. *You tell him.*

Trey still didn't say anything. He didn't move, except to brush his thumb over my lower lip.

Hold on a second, my can-do attitude said. *Let's not be hasty.*

"Eiley, listen," Trey began again.

"No, you listen. The problem is, Trey…" I tried to forget about the urge I had to suck on his thumb, "and that's a big problem."

"What's a big problem?"

That erection in those skinny jeans?

"You. You're the problem. I have a weakness. It's sick, really. Sick enough to make you invent a second fake girlfriend to keep me away."

"I'm not trying to keep you away, Eiley." He lowered his head, stopping before he was close enough to kiss me. "I'd like to be with you right now."

I nodded jerkily. "Be with me? As in…" My stomach clenched. I was trying to play it cool, but as you may have noticed "cool" isn't really in my wheelhouse.

And then he hesitated. I lowered my eyes. What was coming next was going to be hard to hear.

"I like you. We could be really good…friends."

My eyes flew back to his face. "Friends? Like you're *friends* with Nicole?"

"I talked to Nicole in the parking lot."

"You did?" I tried to sound surprised.

"Yeah. I wish I'd been honest with her from the start, but I told her everything tonight."

"Well, better late than never," I babbled.

"And now I want to be honest with you." I girded my metaphorical loins for whatever was coming next. "I think we should spend some more time together." Well, that was vague.

"Spend some time together," I repeated, hoping for clarification.

"Mm-hmm." He bent to nuzzle into my neck again. I was pretty sure this was what people were referring to when they called something a "hard sell."

"So, we'll be friends," I supplied, since he didn't seem in any hurry to define our potential future relationship.

He smiled. "Closer than that."

"Friends with benefits?" I asked.

"Mm-hmm." He slid his hands through my hair and down my back.

"And no commitments?"

"Something like that. We can keep things open and see where it goes."

I took a deep breath in and let it out slowly, not sure what to say. Would the amazing, call-the-police and break-the-furniture sex be enough for me? Or would I spend too many nights with a pint of Half Baked, Googling him and wondering who he was with and if he would ever care about me?

The second one, I decided.

Definitely the second one.

"So what do you think?"

"Maybe." Whoops. That was supposed to have been a firm no.

"That's it? Maybe?" He crowded in closer to me. "What about now? Can I make you change your mind?" I risked a quick glance south again.

He kissed me, and I was aware that Nicole and her friends were watching us. I may have let my hands wander to his skinny-jeans-clad behind ever so briefly for their benefit. And mine.

"Still maybe," I told him when the kiss ended.

"We'll see," he said and then he left to join the band.

I returned to the group at the wobbly-legged table in the corner. All of the chicken wings were gone, but I wasn't hungry anymore. They all looked at me expectantly when I sat down.

"Well?" Valerie finally asked. "Has he filled out a restraining order yet?"

"It didn't look like there was a whole lot of restraint going on over there," Brett stated.

"He wants to be friends with benefits. All the hooking up, none of the responsibility."

Valerie was busy wiping smudges of blue cheese off the empty platter and then licking them off her finger. "What about Nicole?"

I shook my head. "Nicole knows the truth now. He told her the whole story. She's not a problem."

We all turned to look at the woman in question, who was currently pulling her tube top down to reveal more of her Day-Glo yabbos.

Brett took my hand. "So what is the problem?"

"Me. I don't think I can be in that kind of relationship."

"That's it then? *C'est finis?*" Basil asked me.

I watched Trey sing and play for a few moments, his T-shirt tight across his pecs. He noticed my attention and flashed a smile at me.

"Well…"

"You could always take it day by day. See what happens and how you feel about it," Valerie suggested.

"But that way she could get hurt." Brett took the empty platter away from her and handed it to a passing waitress.

"But she also gets to have sex," Valerie pointed out. "Think about it this way: if you walk away from this, you might always wonder what would have happened if you'd given it a chance. It might keep you from forming any real relationships the rest of your life, because it's unresolved. One path is the safe path, and the other path could go either way, but if you don't try it'll haunt you. I like to think of it as the penis not taken."

Valerie, the Robert Frost of our times.

I nodded slowly. It made an odd kind of sense, plus I got to have more sex. "You're probably right."

Huzzah. The little woman in the canoe and my can-do attitude high-fived each other.

We watched Stripper Monkey work their way through some more songs and I continued to consider my options. I was starting to feel a little more confident. Not at all like the same woman who'd scaled her best friend and ridden her like a circus pony in the bathroom mere moments ago to spy on her…ex-fake-boyfriend. Yes, sir, this felt like personal growth.

When the set ended, Trey jumped down from the stage and walked to our table. There was no room for another chair at the precariously overloaded table so he stood behind me. I leaned back against him and smiled and he wrapped his arms around me. I was making the right decision. Probably.

Chad, still on the stage, tapped the microphone a few times and all heads swung back in his direction.

"All right, listen up, people, 'cause you're going to want to hear this." Trey's arms tightened around me. "The drummer from Ugly Hole had to go back to rehab. Now you might not know this, but Ugly Hole is the act that opens for the opening act before the opening act for Blink-182 on the Summer Solstice Tour. And thanks to my close personal friendship—he pumped his hips back and forth. Classy—with a certain tour manager's assistant, Stripper Monkey will take their place for the rest of the tour. That's right, we're going on the road." The regulars in front of the stage cheered wildly.

"Wow." Valerie looked at try. "I can't believe that. You're like, the fifth least important opening act for Blink."

"We'll probably go on around four in the afternoon. The seats will all be empty," Trey told her from behind me.

"But still, the Summer Solstice Tour," I said. "That's huge. We saw Blink last month when they were at Jiffy Lube in Bristow. They're Kyla's absolute favorite band. And now you're going to be on that tour. I can't believe it." I turned my head, trying to get a look at Trey's face, but he was still mostly behind me. "This is huge for you guys," I continued on, trying to move so that I could see him.

"You'll be on the road the rest of the summer, going from town to town, playing a shows like a real band."

"And groupies," Valerie noted. "Imagine all the girls who'll be throwing themselves at you."

Groupies? I blinked a few times. "Oh," I murmured into the uncomfortable silence that had fallen over the table. He couldn't be thinking about...

I spun around in my chair, upsetting our table. Valerie and Brett caught it before it went over, but empty plates and full cups slid onto the floor. I searched Trey's face, hoping that I was wrong about his intentions, but all I saw was guilt in those damn gray-blue eyes.

"Eiley, I was going to tell you all about it when I had a chance."

"I think I get it." My voice was flat. "Enjoy your tour." I slipped off my stool, tossed my hair over my shoulder, and tried to put some distance between us.

"Let me take you home and we can talk." What was it with him and all the talking tonight?

"No, thanks. I don't need you to take me home. I don't need your friendship, and I'm really not interested in your benefits plan, especially not if you're planning on sharing it with a different girl every night." I gave him a hard look, one last foolish part of my heart hoping he'd contradict me.

Crickets.

There was nothing left to say. I stood awkwardly in front of him, not sure of how to make an exit without embarrassing myself. I searched the crowd for Valerie and my eyes met Nicole's. I expected some smug gloating, but all I could read on her face was sympathy. We exchanged a brief glance of solidarity and then my six-foot (and three inches) guardian angel grabbed me by the elbow and pulled me away from Trey and toward the exit of Not Frank's. Trey trailed behind us.

"Never mind him," Valerie said in her loudest voice, "my cousin Thomas asked about you again. I gave him your number and he's going to call you. And," she added, turning to speak to Trey directly, "Thomas is six foot six and totally gorgeous, just so you know."

This was all true. Thomas is six foot six and totally gorgeous. He's also a parochial vicar. That's a priest in the Roman Catholic Church, in case you didn't know. Valerie and I refer to him as "Father WhatAWaste" behind his back. I'm slightly ashamed to admit that I've checked out his ass a couple of times when he wasn't wearing his chasuble, but not so ashamed that I've stopped doing it altogether.

"God bless you, Valerie." I grabbed her arm, and we both burst out laughing as we stumbled out the door onto the gravel parking lot.

We stopped underneath a cracked yellow porch light. Valerie shooed a few moths and beetles away then suffocated me in a bear hug. I sniffled back the tears that threatened to emerge.

After a year of making a fool of myself I'd finally reached my limit. He'd been honest that all he wanted was a casual relationship, but I hadn't realized that had meant with me and every other woman on the Eastern Seaboard. I thought about all those girls raising their hands on Nicole's deck. I knew some guys liked to sleep with as many people as they possibly could. Apparently Trey was one of them.

I'd thought that he was different. He took care of his grandmother and found a home for Larry. But underneath it all he was really a bass-playing man-whore in skinny jeans. The hot ones always were. He'd probably boiled Larry and eaten him. With melted butter.

The door creaked open and I prayed it wasn't Trey. No one wants to be seen wiping snot onto her sleeve. Or Valerie's sleeve. Luckily, it was Basil and Brett.

"Hey." Brett squeezed my shoulder. "Tough one, honey. And me without my bacon."

"Bacon would be really good right about now."

"With cheese," Valerie added.

"And sour cream," Basil suggested.

"And bacon bits on top," Brett added.

We all turned to look at him. Bacon bits on top of bacon? He was right. It had been a double bacon kind of night.

"Sounds like an idea for a new appetizer at the Grudge," I told him.

"And your sisters would be first in line to try it. We'll call it the 'Friends with Benefits.'"

"Slow your roll there, Brett," Valerie said, wrinkling her nose. "Call it the Dirty Bacon Double Cross."

"I'd eat it," I admitted, leaning into Brett for a hug. The rough fabric of his shirt brushed across my cheek as he wrapped his arms around me and squeezed me tight. "Even if it does sound like you're eating bacon that's been on the floor."

The only thing I wanted now was to go home and climb into my bed with Barney. I broke away from Brett and turned to Basil. "See you tomorrow?"

"*Bien sûr.*" He and Brett exchanged phone numbers and made plans to meet again before he left.

"So, do you like him?" I asked Brett, nodding at Basil's retreating form.

"Did he like him?" Val snorted. "I'm surprised they're going home separately."

"No way. I like him, but I've learned from watching this one here that it's better not to jump into bed with someone you hardly know, no matter how hot he is."

Nice. I'd always wanted to be a cautionary tale.

Chapter 14

An Array of Maple Syrup Taps

Sunday stretched ahead with nothing to do. I stirred my spoon through my favorite Greek yogurt—the blueberry and açai flavor that's good enough to make me forget I'm eating Greek yogurt—and considered my options. I could clean bird poop off my furniture or give Barney a bath. Neither of these sounded appealing. Ditto for the laundry pile on my bedroom floor. I had another day or two before it really began to smell. No sense rushing things.

Valerie was working and I had no rehearsals. And who cared what Trey was doing with his time. Not me. I hadn't heard anything from him since Tuesday night at Not Frank's, and it was probably better that way. He was already on the road. You might think that I'd be the type of person to look him up on Waze and try to track him, but you'd be wrong. He hadn't even been on Waze all week.

Okay, so yes, I did check—a couple of times. I figured it was healthier than trying to quit cold turkey. A cyberstalking taper-off plan, if you will. It's not like they make a patch for this sort of thing. A shrink would probably think this was a sound strategy. (Call me, Dr. Phil.)

I threw my yogurt container into the recycling bin and headed to my room to change. I might as well get started on helping Psyche with her boxes.

I piled into the car, cracked the window so Barney could stick his nose out, and steered toward 66 West. I passed the exit for

Haymarket, where Kyla lives, and the view opened up to fields with blue-tipped mountains in the distance. Interstate 66 connects Interstate 81 to Washington DC. The eastern end of it is one of the most congested roads in America. The western end, where I was currently driving, is less traveled and winds through farmland. No fast food or shopping centers as far as the eye could see.

Eventually, we reached the end of 66 and the beginning of the Shenandoah Valley. I took the exit for I-81 and drove the rest of the familiar path to my parents' farmhouse. In a couple of months this drive would be spectacular with the changing foliage. During the fall people from the DMV, (District of Columbia, Maryland, and Virginia area), flock to Skyline Drive to enjoy the season. Today, though, everything was green and full of life, my favorite time of year. I love everything about the summertime.

When I reached the beginning of my parents' driveway, I stopped and let Barney out to run alongside the car. It's a ritual that we have. He doesn't get much chance to let loose in the city and he loves coming here.

He ran the distance full out, ears flying behind him, feet skimming the ground, and a big smile on his face. He'd also enjoy the two hours I'd spend combing through his fur for ticks tonight. Me, not so much.

I crested the last hill and saw the Winnebago parked on the lawn in front of the house in all its glory. It was light brown with darker brown stripes in the shape of mountains with a big brown sun shining down on them, and roughly the size of a small city. I got out of the car and Barney and I approached the behemoth. The door swung open and Aunt Psyche stood on the top step.

"Come here, come here," she trilled to me, her be-mumued arms outstretched, blinged-up fingers waving. Her red hair was in a messy bun with a chopstick protruding from it. I ran up the steps and she wrapped me in yards of polyester and Hawaiian white ginger perfume. I would never admit it to Glynnis, but I was really happy to see my crazy aunt.

We broke apart and moved into the RV. I had to stifle a groan. Boxes were piled on every available surface—more boxes than it seemed possible for an RV to hold. She'd left one small area open for living space at the kitchen table and had a small TV set up there.

"Welcome to Shangri-La." she proclaimed. "Once you help me with my boxes I think I'll be happy here. I'll live in the house, but this will be my satellite office. Your mom, you know… "

"Speaking of boxes," I said, avoiding the topic of my mother altogether, "what exactly am I doing with all of them?" I really hoped the words *burn them* would be involved in her answer.

"Well, I need all of my clothing out and hung up. Some things will have to go into a closet in the house. This place has tragically limited closet space. Then my collections will have to be unpacked and displayed."

"Which collections did you bring?" Like my nephew Finn, Psyche liked to collect.

"Well, let's see. My QVC Marie Osmond dolls, of course. My menus from IHOPs around the country, my array of maple syrup taps, and a truly inspiring diorama featuring oddly shaped Skittles. Those will also go in the house. I can't risk them to any acts of nature like a hurricane or a tsunami. And the humidity here. Havoc on the coatings of the Skittles."

"God forbid." Never mind that we were six hours away from the nearest beach.

"Then, there are fifteen or so boxes of my personal effects. Important papers, tax documents, medical records, things of that nature. We'll need to sort through those and get them all organized."

"We will?" I asked weakly.

"Yes, darling. And then there's my mementos: photo albums, assorted correspondence, and the autographs of the entire cast of the *Muppets Take Manhattan*."

"But aren't they puppets?"

"Of course they are, dear."

Well then. "I guess I'll go say hi to Mom and then come back to help you get started on all the sorting." And make a quick call to let my sister know she's not getting a birthday gift this year. Cleaning up bird poo suddenly sounded really appealing.

Why had I volunteered for this job? I didn't even like cleaning up after myself. This was Trey's fault. Trey and his stupid perfect abs and Epiphany guitar. If I hadn't been so depressed about his tour and probable philandering, I would never have volunteered for this mission.

I trudged down the RV steps and whistled for Barney. We met my mom on the steps of the rambling front porch. I opened the door and took in a deep breath of the scent of home.

"I love coming back to visit you." I struggled to hug her as Barney jumped between us in excitement. "So does Barney." I laughed.

"You both should come more often then. Dad and I are always here." Her face clouded. "And now Aunt Psyche."

"How's that going?"

"About as well as you'd imagine." She bent down to rub Barney's ears. "She's brought all of her things. You've got a lot of sorting to do."

I groaned. "I saw the stacks. I guess I should get started. Right after I check out my room."

"Come in for tea when you're ready to take a break. Barney and I will keep each other company while you work."

I gave her a quick kiss on the cheek and ran upstairs to take a walk down memory lane. I do this every time I visit. There's something so nice about knowing that your childhood home is exactly how you left it.

Glynnis didn't have a room of her own because she'd spent so much of her time away at boarding school, but I did a quick walk-through of Rowan's and Kyla's rooms. Although everything was neat and tidy, not much had changed in the years since they'd moved out.

I headed down the hallway to my room and paused outside of my brother Adam's closed door, not sure if I was prepared to see the picture of him in his Marine dress uniform that my mom kept on his dresser. I glanced down and rubbed my toe over the stain where Adam had spilled apple juice on the hall rug. I ran my fingers down the smooth oak door and continued on to my room. Maybe next trip.

I jumped on my bed and squeezed my old stuffed dog, Snorkel. I took in the pale yellow paint and the homemade curtains and matching spread covered in daisies. This was where I had grown up.

I had sat on this bed doing math homework and talking on the phone with friends. Had there been any boys whom I'd obsessed over? All I could really remember were dance classes. I stood and smoothed out the bedspread, then carefully placed Snorkel back on my pillow. It was time to tackle the RV full of boxes.

I trudged out to Psyche's Shangri-La and set to work. I unpacked each of the collections from packing cartons filled with copious amounts of fluffy packing peanuts. You haven't really lived until you've unpacked thirty-five Skittles each individually secured in bubble wrap.

After the priceless collections were secured, I made careful stacks of the photo albums and loose pictures, all the while keeping an eye out for anything that had Seamus's name or the words "treasure inside" on it. I carted armfuls of clothing into the house, passing Psyche's sleeping form on the couch with each trip I made, and hung them in the empty closet in Rowan's room. Hours went by, and my shoulders ached as I made slow progress, box by box.

I'd saved the most tedious for last—five boxes of miscellaneous papers and files. As I wrapped a rubber band around a teetering stack of EOBs from her HMO, dated between 1990 and 1996, my mother came in the door with two cups of tea.

One of my earliest memories is of sitting with her at our old wrought-iron kitchen table drinking tea. She was in her fuzzy blue chenille bathrobe and I was in Tinkerbell pajamas. She used to keep sugar cubes in a crystal bowl and would let me put as many as I wanted into my cup.

She took in my haphazard stacks of paper. "Oh Eiley. Throw it all out. There can't be anything useful in there. She's hoarded every scrap of paper that ever came into her life. She's a fire hazard."

She was probably right but I couldn't bring myself to do it. "It's not like I have anything better to do today anyway," I told her. "And who knows what treasure may turn up in here."

"Treasure? Not you too?" I looked at her sheepishly. "Has Psyche convinced you to look for the lost family treasure?"

"Well, I would like to hear the story again, in case something turns up in one of these boxes," I replied, standing up and moving toward the little table to sit with her, shaking out my numb feet as I went. "What should I be looking for? Stocks? War bonds? Gold bars? Bubblegum comics? Anything to keep me going."

"Nothing but old family legend, honey. And you know what that amounts to in a family full of Irishmen. The tales get taller as the years go by."

"Or as the bottles get emptied." I nodded. I certainly knew this was true from my own experience at family reunions. Each uncle, brother, and cousin trying to outdo the other in tall tales, racy jokes, and examples of poor judgment.

"So tell me anyway," I asked, as I set aside a few of Psyche's old photo albums to take with me. She had pages of old pictures from her dance days and I wanted to spend some time going through them. I also planned to copy and frame a few of them. Psyche would like having them to decorate her Shangri-La.

"Family legend has it," my mom began, "that your great-great-uncle Seamus hid something valuable. Long ago, back in the Boston days. No one has been able to find it."

After arriving from Ireland, my family had settled in Boston, living there for several generations before moving to the Shenandoah Valley in the seventies. My great-great-great-grandfather and my great-great-uncle Seamus were policemen, as well as my great-grandfather, grandfather, and father after them. My brother, however, is a Marine.

"Did he ever say what it was?"

"No one knows. It was something important to him, and he put it away for safe keeping."

"Where? In Psyche's stuff?"

"No, but she probably has the letter."

"What letter?" I asked, hopeful. That sounded like a clue.

"Well, Seamus wrote his sister Fi a letter, telling her all about it. Then Mary Therese found the letter in a book after Fi died. I think Mary Therese probably gave the letter to Psyche, who clearly saves everything."

"But if there's a letter, why don't we know what the mysterious item is, or where to find it?"

"The letter didn't say. It was all very confusing."

Stacking the last album, I wandered over to the pile of boxes, trying to choose one that might have a treasure map in it. I picked a worn box labeled "Family Things," dusted it off, and dived in.

"I'll leave you to it," mom said. "I'll be out front throwing a ball for Barney when you're ready to come up for air."

I did a quick calorie calculation in my head. "Or you could make pork chops and mashed potatoes."

"I've already peeled the potatoes." She laughed as she pulled the door closed.

It took four more boxes until I found what I was looking for. In a box labeled "Kitchen Necessities" I found a stack of letters tied together with a piece of twine. I shuffled through them until I found a few from Seamus to his sister Fiona. I smoothed them out and started to read.

Letter writing is really a lost art—pen and ink, the letters small and perfect, leaving an image of the person long gone. I got a chill thinking about Seamus writing these words, touching the paper, pouring out his story, never imagining me, a hundred years later, reading them.

Seamus had been in love with a girl who had died. He'd decided he would be a bachelor forever and wanted Fi to know about his treasure before he left for WWI. I read aloud from the last letter that Psyche had of his.

And, sweet Fi, since you and your babes are the dearest to me in this world, I want you to have anything of mine that you might want. If anything happens to me, my most valuable treasure is tucked away safely where we used to spend our summer days. You'll know the place, I'm sure. I've wrapped it tight to keep it safe. All my love, Seamus.

I ran to find my mom and Psyche to show them the letter. "I found it," I exclaimed, my face flushed with excitement. I shook the letter at them. "There is a treasure. See? It's all right here." This seemed like solid proof to me.

"Will you look for it?" Psyche asked. "Someone needs to finally find that treasure. You can do it, Eiley." She was as excited as I was.

My mom turned from the stove and gave me a Glynnis-worthy eye-roll. "Where? Where are you going to look? Never mind that it was over a hundred years ago and even if you found the right place it would be long gone by now."

I thought for a moment. "The house on Eliot Street." Seamus and Fi had grown up there, and when their parents died, Fi's daughter, Mary Therese, had lived there. It had been in our family for many years before it was sold.

"Someone else has lived in that house for years now. What are you going to do? Drive to Boston, knock on their door, and ask to snoop around? Anything you find is going to belong to them now if they haven't already found it." She turned back to the stove and gave the potatoes a stir.

"Okay," I replied slowly. "That's true. But I'm not giving up yet."

"What are you going to do?" Psyche twisted her fingers in her lap. My heart melted a little for how hopeful she looked.

"I don't know yet, but I'll figure it out." I was determined to find this treasure for the both of us. "Besides, I need a little distraction in my life right now."

My mom pulled the pot of potatoes off the burner and dumped the boiling water into a colander. "What do you mean," she asked, taking off her glasses to wipe away the steam from them. "Distraction from what?"

"You know, all the dancing and practicing." I nodded at her.

My mom crossed her arms. "Hmm," she hummed, squinting at me. "You're awfully red all of a sudden. Is there something going on with the performance?"

"I bet it's a man," Psyche chimed in.

My mouth opened and closed a few times. I was torn between the urge to keep up the façade of being a capable adult and the need to unburden myself. It might be good to get some advice more competent than Valerie's. "It's both," I answered finally.

"Go sit at the table. I'll make more tea." My mom dumped the hot potatoes into the stand mixer, added butter, salt, and cream and started it up. She then put the teapot on the burner before she joined us at the table. "Okay, start talking while the water is boiling."

My mom and aunt both turned to me expectantly. "Well, I think I mentioned that I was having some trouble with my dance partner, Basil," I began.

"The Bitcherina," my mom agreed.

"Yes, well. Things got worse, then they got better. We're almost friends now." My mom gestured for me to continue when I hesitated. "I'm worried that maybe I'm not ready for this. The lead, I mean." I looked at my lap, surprised I'd said the words out loud.

"Of course you're ready. How could you not be ready after so many years of lessons and practices? Not to mention the dancing degree your dad and I are still paying for?"

"I don't mean that exactly. But…" I turned to Psyche. "How do you know when you're ready?"

"Dancing isn't about knowing, it's about feeling. Inside of you." She took my hands. "When that feeling hits you, you'll know."

"Okay, but—"

"You'll go from dancing to live to living to dance." She nodded emphatically. I sneaked a glance at my mother. She looked like she'd like to ship Psyche off to a hippie commune somewhere. "You see what I mean? Dancing won't be what you do anymore. It will be who you are."

Pain, fatigue, doubt, and jealousy were all things I'd felt. Living to dance, not so much. "Right, thanks. I appreciate the…advice."

"You're welcome, dear." She squeezed my hands and leaned in closer. "You mentioned something about a man?"

I let out a huge sigh. "I was kind of dating this one guy, but it didn't end well."

"You were dating?" my mom asked in surprise.

"For a little while, sort of."

"What happened? Did you end up not liking him?"

"No. I liked him. A lot."

"Of course you did." Aunt Psyche nodded. "Was he young and hot? With big muscles?" She was still holding my hands, and the squeezing had become uncomfortably tight. "Well-endowed?"

My mom gasped.

"I-I don't really know," I lied, pulling my hands from her grip. She had a surprising amount of strength for an old lady. I turned to my mom. "We weren't on the same page so it seemed better to end it. That's the right thing to do when two people want different things, isn't it?"

"It seems like you still have some feelings for him."

I dipped my head. My mom could always read me. The teakettle began to whistle. My mom rose from her chair and gave me a quick hug. "Give it some time. You never know. The two of you might end up on the same page eventually."

I was pretty sure if my mom knew what page Trey was on she'd tell me to never talk to him again and whisk me off to a convent somewhere. I was also pretty sure that there was no chance that Trey and I would ever be on the same page.

Our pages weren't even in the same book.

And the books weren't even in the same library.

Chapter 15

Well-Placed Sequins

"Did you see Brett last night?" I asked Basil, as I leaned into his arm so that he could help me balance as we practiced a fish dive. We were rehearsing the last scene of Act II until it was time for our final costume fittings that morning.

"None of your business, *ma chère*," he replied as he lifted me off the ground. It was a simple lift, but one of my favorites.

"I'll ask him tonight at the Grudge," I told him smugly. It would be my first night back after a long hiatus. I was looking forward to it, although, with the opening performance only days away, I'd have to be a spectator in the bacon-eating Olympics.

I'd been spending so much time at the studio my friends and family had probably forgotten what I looked like. There'd been no time for anything other than work and sleep, with an occasional shower thrown in. For which the world was grateful, I'm sure.

"What about you? Have you heard from your guitar player?" he asked as he lifted me again, smoothly and easily. Susan smiled at us from across the room. I turned so that she didn't see the frown that came to my face. The choreography was going well, and Basil and I were on friendly terms, but something was still missing. Maybe I needed to get Aunt Psyche's "live to dance" feeling.

"Nope, not a thing."

It had been three weeks since that awful night at Not Frank's. I hadn't heard anything from Trey. I hadn't tried to contact him and

I'd managed to limit my cyberstalking to only a couple of post-practice, late-night reconnaissance missions when my resistance slipped due to exhaustion. There wasn't a lot of information out there anyway. Apparently it wasn't that big of a deal to be the first opening act out of five, even on the Summer Solstice Tour.

"You know, Eiley, I have a friend you might be interested in." He smiled self-consciously. "Maybe meeting someone else would help?" My mouth hung open. Basil was trying to fix me up. I must be more pathetic than I'd realized.

"I need some water." I extracted myself from our lift and retrieved my bottle from the corner of the room. "It's miserable in here today." The DC Metro area was overpowered by the July heat and humidity, and studio air conditioning only went so far.

"Who's ready for final costume fittings?" Serena, the head seamstress, her arms laden with plastic garment bags, stood in the doorway to the practice room. Basil and I looked at each other.

"You go first." He laughed.

"Thank you." I toweled myself off and bolted to the locker room, giddy with excitement.

"What do you want to try first?" She hung the bags up on hooks.

"Let's start with Odile, and save the best for last," I told her, then immediately felt bad. It probably sounded like I meant that one of the costumes wasn't as good as the other.

"I mean," I floundered, "I've really been looking forward to Odette. Like, looking forward to it since I was seven." The Odile costume would involve a lot of black feathers and Odette's would be a white tutu. It helped the audience distinguish which swan was which since they were typically played by the same dancer. Susan wanted something classic, so they were almost exactly like the ones Pavlova wore in 1943.

Aside from Aunt Psyche, my idol has always been Pavlova. Back in the day people told her that she was too small to dance, but she became the epitome of grace and elegance and made it possible for smaller dancers, like me, to have a chance. Wearing a costume like hers and trying to emulate her poise was a big deal to me.

"I know what you mean." Serena smiled and her blue eyes lit up. "And it really is the best. Wait till you see it. Cinderella's fairy godmother couldn't have bibbidi-bobbidi-booed up a costume this good."

My face flushed. Princess had been my other aspiration as a young lady. My inner child broke free and did a few cartwheels. "Who needs a fairy godmother," I told her. "I have you."

"Turn away from all these mirrors," Serena instructed me. "You need to get the full effect all at once."

I turned away from the trio of floor-to-ceiling mirrors and faced the row of beaten and scraped lockers. I stripped down to my underpants and tights. She held the costume out and I stepped into it and pulled it up, trying not to look at it in the process.

She tugged here and there, making some adjustments and checking the fit before pinning the headpiece onto my hair. I'd already met with a stylist, and I knew my hair would be totally different than the simple French braid I had worn today, but this would give us an idea of how it would look.

I took a deep breath and spun around to the mirrors. The black costume was a sharp contrast to my pale skin. It was meant to be seductive and it was. The cut of the bodice, and some well-placed sequins, gave the illusion that my breasts were twice their actual size—almost a B cup.

Feathers covered the bottom and rested on top of the tulle of the small tutu. It was slightly higher in the back and gave my waist a deep V in the front. Even my normally flat butt looked perkier. I briefly considered showing up at Not Frank's in my Odile costume.

"Wow," I gushed, surprised that I liked it so much. I mean, tutus were not meant to be black, after all.

"Not too shabby, huh?" Serena laughed, her curly brown hair floating over her shoulders. "And wait 'til you see the tights that I found to go with this. They're black, but opaque so that they'll highlight all your muscles. And I have glittery black body paint for your arms and face."

"How are we going to have time to do all that between costume changes?"

"Don't you worry about that. I've got a whole team of people. We're going to do several practice runs and we'll have it down to a science. It'll be like those racecars that drive into the pit crews. We'll have your tires rotated and your pistons lubed in thirty seconds."

"Do they lube pistons?"

"They do now," Serena answered. She took a few notes on her tablet and marked a couple of areas that she wasn't happy with and then helped me slip off the black costume.

I bit my lip as I heard the zipper shush open on the next garment bag. I closed my eyes and stuck my arms out, letting Serena do all the work to wrestle the costume onto me. I could feel right away that this costume was much more substantial than the other one, the skirt longer and heavier, almost bulky.

I turned to the mirror and slowly opened my eyes. I blinked several times. I was not going to cry. Was this what a bride felt like? Say yes to the tutu?

The costume was a brilliant white. The bodice was covered in feathers with tiny wisps over the shoulders that continued along the back in a low U shape, leaving my back bare.

The almost-knee-length skirt was in three tiers, the bottom two made of tulle and sequins and the top one made of more of the blindingly white feathers. There were two clusters of feathers at each hip to symbolize wings. I sank to the floor and bent over my extended leg. It was perfect. The feathers at my hips sprang up like wings and my skirt made a perfect circle around me, exactly like the picture I have of Pavlova on my wall.

Serena helped me to my feet.

"It's amazing. It couldn't be any better." Tears sprang to my eyes again and I blinked them away.

"Don't cry on my costume. Do you have any idea how long it takes to hand-sew on that many feathers?" She pulled at the skirt a bit and fluffed the tulle. "It was worth it," she told me, pulling me into a careful hug.

Reluctantly, I took the costume off and found my sweaty, balled-up leotard under the bench. It was too disgusting to put back on, never mind that I'd been wearing it all morning. I went to my locker and was pulling on a replacement from my stash when my phone chimed.

I fished it out of my bag, expecting a message from Val or one of my sisters, but Trey's name flashed across my screen. I threw my phone in my locker and slammed the door, then leaned against it for good measure. Why was he texting me? I banged my head against the metal door.

Serena looked up at me questioningly. "Did someone send you a picture of his junk?"

I banged my head against the locker again. "It's…" I didn't know how to finish the sentence. My ex-fake-boyfriend? "You see…" A guy I banged so loudly my neighbor thought I was being attacked? "I mean…" Someone I thought was a part of my past but I still couldn't stop thinking about?

"I can't even," I finished lamely.

"I have to be honest, I don't know what it means when people say that." She sat down on the bench near my locker. "So you like this guy?"

"No. And how did you know?"

She laughed. "Honey, people don't act like that when the dentist calls."

She had a point.

"Plus, those giant red splotches on your face and chest kind of give you away."

"I gotta take a knee." I slid down the locker and sat on the floor. "So what do I do?"

"Do? It's a text message, not a nuclear arms treaty. Read it and send one back." She wiggled around on the bench trying to get comfortable, then smiled at me. She was probably thinking that all dancers are a little crazy. And she was probably right. It came from years of wearing our hair in tight buns. Not enough circulation to the medulla oblongata.

"I can't. And by that I mean, I shouldn't."

"Right. Because you obviously don't like him."

"It's complicated." I actually liked him too much.

"You slept with him."

"What are you, Nostradamus?"

She took off one of her shoes and massaged her toes. "What's going on with this text sending complication?"

I groaned. "Nothing."

"But you wish it was something."

"Seriously, you could read palms at carnivals," I told her.

"Why don't you give me the backstory here?" She took off her other shoe and massaged those toes as well.

"I liked this guy for a really long time, but I never did anything about it. Then he asked me to pretend to be his girlfriend to keep this other girl away. And while I was pretending to be his girlfriend, I jumped into bed with him. Well, the bed, the floor, the shower, the, uh, toilet. But that's probably TMI right there." I paused to see if she was following the story.

"Okay," she said cautiously. "I have a lot of questions, but keep going."

"After the sex, I don't hear from him again."

She nodded sympathetically. "I think I get the picture."

"Then I think he has a date with the girl he was trying to avoid so I show up at the place and end up crashing his grandmother's birthday party." Her eyes got wide. "The next thing I know he tells me he wants to be friends, but still fool around."

"Have you gotten to the complication yet?"

I blinked a few times. "What do you call a guy who tells you he only wants to have sex with you?"

"An honest one."

"But…"

"How many times did you go out with this boy?"

"Well, that depends on how you count it. Somewhere between one and three, though."

Serena threw her head back and laughed. "After three dates you're upset that he wants to keep things casual?"

"Well, I mean…" I didn't have an answer for that.

"You've liked this guy for how long now?"

"A month or two. Plus or minus a year."

"Why don't you give him a chance to catch up to you a little?"

"He's not ever going to catch up to me," I admitted sadly. Trey and I would never be on the same page.

"Well, maybe the next guy, then."

I shook my head. I couldn't imagine having to go through all this mess again. And I really couldn't imagine anyone being more perfect than Trey. Minus the whole man-whore thing, of course.

"That's how people date, Eiley. You meet someone, you get to know them, and you see where things go. Sometimes, you fool around with them. Because you want to and not because you're going to marry them."

"I know, I read *Cosmo*." What? I was planning on reading one of them.

"You've got to come out of the studio occasionally and be a part of the real world."

I frowned. "I tried that, and almost got thrown right out of *Swan Lake*. It turns out I'm really not great at doing both ballet and life."

"You need a little more practice. You've already made progress with Basil. Besides, I'm not convinced this guy isn't still an option," she said.

"Oh, well, I left out the part about how he went on tour with his band and is probably with a different girl every night."

"Ew." She wrinkled her nose.

"I know, right? That's exactly what I said."

"You're killing me, you know that, right?" I looked at her blankly. "Are you planning to ignore that text? It won't go away, you know. Get that phone out and let's see what this complicated boy has to say." She looked at me expectantly.

Reluctantly, I got to my feet and opened my locker. I found the phone mixed in with my musty dance clothes and pulled it out. I tapped on the message and read it through a few times.

Hey, just wanted to say that I'm sorry for that night at Not Frank's. Take care.

Take care. There it was again, words that seemed so nice but really meant good-bye. I read the text to Serena.

"I guess it doesn't matter how I feel. He's done with me."

"I don't think either one of you are done."

"What do you mean?"

"You've got to decide if you're ready to let this guy walk out of your life forever. 'Cause it sounds to me like you haven't really made your mind up about that yet." She adjusted my leotard straps. "And *he* definitely isn't done."

I threw my phone back in my locker. "You can tell that from one text?"

"Well, I am Nostradamus." She chuckled. "Think about it."

"I'll think about it after the show opens. Right now I need to focus all my attention on not screwing anything up." I grabbed her hands. "Thanks for listening, for the advice, and for the fabulous costumes. You're the best fairy godmother."

I slammed my locker shut and returned to the practice room.

You're probably thinking I was distracted after hearing from Trey, but I wasn't. Fairy princess tutus trump abs and skinny jeans every time—not to mention an opening night around the corner.

No way was I going to spend the rest of my day pining after a prince charming with a loose moral code.

I guess this is growing up.

Chapter 16

What's My Age Again?

I looked around the table expectantly. I'd finally had a chance to tell my sisters all about the letter I'd found, and was waiting for their reactions.

"What?" Glynnis asked. She picked the longest piece of bacon off the platter. I kept my hands in my lap. I'd already had my three-piece maximum for the evening, but I couldn't help noticing how the cheese was melted perfectly and clung to the edges of the crisp piece.

"What do you mean 'what'? It's proof. We have to find it, whatever it is. Not to mention, Aunt Psyche has been emailing me relentlessly asking why I haven't found anything yet. She doesn't seem to realize I've been at the Kennedy Center ten hours a day doing staging."

"You're lucky. All I get from her are forwarded ads for penis enlargement creams." Kyla shook her head and loaded more bacon onto her appetizer plate. "The last one came with the comment, *Why are there no vagina shrinking creams? Must investigate this male conspiracy.*"

"She sends me ads for cougar dating sites." Glynnis frowned.

"Can we get back to the treasure?"

I once read that beavers build dams because the sound of running water makes them crazy. At this moment I could commiserate with my semiaquatic rodent friends. The sound of crunching bacon was about to put me over the edge.

"Stop saying it's a treasure. It's probably some knickknack that was hidden away years ago. It's not like it's a pirate chest filled with Spanish galleons," Glynnis admonished.

"Oh. Doubloons. Maybe it's doubloons." Rowan clapped her hands.

"I know it isn't a real treasure, but it was something that was special to him and I want to find it. It's a family mystery. I want to solve it."

"That's going to be tricky," Rowan said. "Where do we even start?"

"It's going to be junk." Glynnis crunched happily into another piece of bacon.

"The house on Eliot Street," Kyla suggested. "They lived there for ages, I bet he'd feel safe leaving something there. His letter said where they'd spent their summers. It has to be there." I nodded eagerly. That was exactly what I'd thought.

"They sold that house years ago." Glynnis pulled her phone out of her Chanel bag and began to skim her text messages. "It's probably been torn down after all these years, anyway."

"Okay then," Kyla paused, warming to the idea, "Where else?"

I'd been thinking about this for the last few days. "What if someone in the family found it when they moved out of the house, but didn't realize what it was? Maybe it's been boxed up somewhere in some attic all these years."

"Trudy." Glynnis threw her phone back into her bag. Trudy is my cousin and Mary Therese's daughter. "If anyone would know, she would. She may even have some of the old boxes and things from when they sold the house."

"Let's call her now." It would give me something to do with my mouth other than shove bacon into it. I fished my phone out of the small backpack I used as a purse and dialed my cousin's number. After a few minutes of small talk—precious few since neither of us had much of a life outside of work—I got right to the point.

"I'm trying to find your Grandmother Mary Therese's old boxes and papers. Where did all that stuff from the house on Eliot Street end up when it was sold?"

Trudy groaned. "Not another family member with treasure hunt fever."

"Psyche wants me to look for it," I replied defensively. "Besides, you have to admit, it's kind of cool. I feel like Nancy Drew. You know, the clue in the old letter."

"Some of it's in a storage shed behind my brother's house."

"Great, I'll get in touch with him, then."

"Eiley, you aren't going to find anything. You know that, right? When my mom re-boxed all that stuff she went through everything."

"You never know."

"Well, good luck, titian-haired girl detective," Trudy teased before she hung up. Where were Bess and George when you needed them? Not to mention Ned Nickerson. I tried to picture Ned in skinny jeans with a bass guitar. And leg warmers.

"I'm going to text Brion. Trudy says some of the boxes are in his shed. I actually have a little time off on Friday afternoon, maybe I'll drive over there and check it out."

"Great. Now, let's get on with I Hate My Life," Glynnis suggested. She looked around the table, but no one said anything.

"Okay, fine, I'll start." Kyla wiped her hands on her napkin. "So I have this enormous can of air freshener in my bathroom, you know? And it's blue. So, I was up there doing my hair so I could go to the store and buy some notebook paper. I was going to spray a little bit of hairspray on my hair to kill the static, which, coincidentally, comes in a blue bottle…"

"I can see where this is going," Glynnis interrupted.

"I accidentally grabbed the air freshener by mistake, and since I squeeze my eyes shut and hold my breath while I spray hairspray…"

"Hey, who needs the extra fluorocarbons?" I asked, still eyeing the bacon.

"It was some time before I noticed the error. My hair looked awful but my head smelled like the forest in a spring rainstorm."

"That's it?" Glynnis asked. "Air freshener on your head for I Hate My Life?"

"Let's hear yours then." We all looked at her expectantly.

"I don't have much either," she admitted. "Remember me telling you about how Fischer/Rowland is hoping to get a huge new contract for a redevelopment project?" We all nodded, but I was pretty sure none of us had been paying much attention.

"We found out today that the company has decided to transfer someone in from the New Mexico office. Apparently he does the same job there, and they want him to work for me." She shuddered.

"*For* you?"

"With me. Whatever."

"What's wrong with that?" Rowan asked.

"What's wrong with it? I work alone. Besides, New Mexico is filled with sprout-eating hippie freaks. He probably wears Birkenstocks, makes homemade organic kale chips, and does Bikram yoga."

"I do Bikram yoga," I told her.

Glynnis gritted her teeth. It was killing her to let my comment pass.

"Well, I had a good week, except for the air freshener episode. And kale is a delicious, healthy vegetable." We all stared at Kyla in horror.

"What? I'm just saying."

"I don't see you eating it." I pointed out.

"Yes, but I give it to my kids, so that counts." We all nodded. That seemed reasonable.

"I had a good week, too," Rowan concurred with Kyla. "I figured out two of my urban murals and they're going to be *amazing*. One of them is a face on a half wall and the grass on the top is the hair. No ears or chin, only eyes, nose, and mouth. Like he's watching you. Because someone is always watching you, you know. Usually the NSA."

"How can it be a face with no chin? Do you stop at the lips?" I asked her.

"And," Rowan charged on, "I'm meeting with the person who's going to work with me on the stamp next Friday. Things are proceeding apace."

"Another artist?" Glynnis asked.

"No, some sort of hobbyist. He's going to help me figure out a theme and then we'll do four different designs. Some sort of awareness campaign."

"Awareness of what?" I wanted to know.

"Well, I'm not actually aware of it yet. I think it's phlebotomy."

"Why would anyone want to be aware of phlebotomy?" Glynnis scrunched up her face.

"Phlebotomists would, although I guess technically they're already aware of it, considering they're phlebotomists and all. I know. *Vampires*. Maybe he's one of those Goth types who thinks he's a vampire." She made it sound as if working with a vampire wannabe would be a good thing. On the plus side, she definitely had the wardrobe for it.

"Why would the United States Postal Service create a series of stamps for vampires?" I asked. Glynnis quickly grabbed the last piece of bacon off the platter as Brett arrived with three steaming plates of spaghetti and meatballs and one green salad.

The smell of buttery garlic bread wafted to me, and my stomach sighed in disappointment. Seriously, do you know how much willpower it takes to eat salad when everyone around you has garlic bread? I don't think the word "hero" would be entirely inappropriate here, people.

"I've missed your face around here," Brett told me as he off-loaded the plates from the tray to the table.

"Take a good look because I won't be back for a while. We open on Saturday."

"Are you ready?" He set down his tray and massaged my shoulders. It felt amazing. I leaned back into him and sighed. Was I ready? Probably.

"More importantly, is Glynnis ready for our after-party?" I asked.

"Of course I am. My assistant Kathy set the whole thing up and ordered the tickets. We're all ready. You need to do your part."

"You okay, honey? Your shoulders got as tight as a duck's arse." Brett shook his fingers.

"That is a good question, though, isn't it? Why is there no shrinking cream?" Rowan asked thoughtfully. We all looked at her blankly. "Psycho could be on to something."

"You've been pondering that all this time?" Glynnis rolled her eyes.

I figured it was a good time for a diversion. "Today was costume day."

"Is that why you're only eating a green salad with balsamic vinegar on it?" Brett asked.

"That's part of it." And by "part of it" I meant that was totally the reason. It would be a little hard to pirouette in a form-fitting be-feathered leotard with a food baby. I'd look like a cobra after it's eaten a small villager.

Brett left to check on his other tables and I took advantage of the momentary lull in conversation to launch into a full description of my costumes. I would have a captive audience until the food ran out.

"So not one thing for I Hate My Life?" Glynnis asked, desperate to interrupt the costume chatter.

"Kind of. I got a text from Trey today."

"And?" Rowan asked.

"What did it say?" Kyla followed up.

I shoveled a sad, soggy romaine leaf into my mouth. Salads were not the Grudge's strong point. "It wasn't much. Basically it was see ya, wouldn't want to be ya, have a nice life, sorry I'm not sorry."

"Let me see this text." Glynnis wiggled her fingers.

"I'm paraphrasing."

"What did he say exactly?" she probed.

"He said he was sorry for how things ended ,and that I should 'take care.'"

"That doesn't exactly mean good-bye forever," Rowan pointed out.

"That's true. Complete silence is good-bye forever," Kyla agreed.

"What do you want it to mean?" Glynnis expertly twirled her pasta around her fork in the bowl of her spoon. I always felt ridiculous when I tried to do that.

Good question. I shrugged and stuffed another mucky forkful into my mouth.

"Tell me again how you left things the last time you saw him," Kyla mumbled around a mouthful of meatball.

I swallowed my sea-weedy mush reluctantly. "Okay. I told you about crashing the birthday party, right?" They all nodded. "So a few days later we saw each other at Not Frank's."

"And he was still speaking to you?" Glynnis wiped her hands off on her napkin. At least I wouldn't go home smelling like garlic tonight, not that Barney cared.

"Crashing the date at The Palm was your idea, remember?" I snapped.

Glynnis shrugged.

"He was still speaking to me. We talked about where things were going."

"Things were going somewhere?" Kyla looked up, surprised.

"He suggested we keep things casual. No commitments."

"And that's bad because...?" Glynnis asked.

"There's more. It turns out that his band was asked to fill in as the first opening act on the Summer Solstice Tour."

Kyla's fork clattered to her plate. "You have got to be kidding me. The same Summer Solstice Tour we went to in June?"

"Yep. That's the one. Apparently he needed to be free to go hang out with random women every night."

"Ew." Rowan scrunched up her face.

"Right?" I shook my head in agreement.

"Wait, he told you that?" Glynnis asked.

"Yes." I shook my head harder for emphasis.

"What were his exact words?" She sounded dubious.

"His exact words were no words," I told her, exasperated.

"You're saying he didn't deny it, right?" Thank God for Kyla. It was about time someone around here got it. "So what did you say?"

"I said no. Then I walked out," I told her.

"Is that your final decision?" Glynnis asked.

"Maybe. I don't know. It doesn't matter because he's moved on."

"What if he hasn't?" Kyla asked.

I shrugged again. I'd been asking myself that since my earlier conversation with Serena. "I have to think about it." That was the safe answer, right?

"That's crap," Glynnis stated. "You already know what you want to do."

"Well of course I know what I *want* to do. I don't know what I *should* do. What the best decision is."

"You know what you should do?" Kyla asked me.

"Not take advice from the three of you anymore?" They all stopped eating and looked at me in surprise.

"Oh please." I pointed to Kyla. "You married the first guy you slept with when you were nineteen years old." I pointed to Glynnis. "You won't keep any guy around longer than two weeks. And you," I said, pointing to Rowan, "learned everything you know about relationships from romance novels."

Kyla's head bent as if she were studying her dinner plate. I'd probably hurt her feelings. Glynnis, however, snorted and threw her napkin at me. "I still know more about relationships than you can ever hope to, you socially stunted mutant." I glanced at Rowan, who smiled.

"You're not mad?" I asked her.

"Nah, you're right about me. On the plus side, if I ever meet a renegade privateer with amnesia who's sailing the high seas and is secretly the illegitimate son of a duke about to inherit the title because his family was killed off in a freak stagecoach accident, I will be on that boy like white on rice."

"Maybe try match dot com for that," I suggested.

Kyla squeezed her shoulder. "Sure. Every pot has a lid to fit it."

"Am I the pot or the lid?" Rowan asked.

"What I was going to say," Kyla quickly changed the subject, "is that you should try some essential oils." She pulled her shoulder bag onto her lap and started rummaging around. "I went to an essential oils party last week. Did you know that essential oils can help you with pretty much any problem you may have?" She pulled out a handful of glass vials. "What do you want? I've got calming, stress reducer, clear thinking, or revitalizing." She looked up at us.

"I don't think essential oil is going to help me figure out my life, but thanks anyway," I told her.

She dropped the vials back into her bag. "Okay then, why don't you go to one of his shows?"

"So I can watch him hook up with random girls rather than imagining it?" The essential oil was sounding better and better.

She shrugged. "For closure. You need closure."

What was she talking about? Things were pretty well closed at this point.

"I'd even go with you."

Glynnis snorted again. "There it is."

"What?" Kyla asked, eyes wide.

"The real reason you want Eiley to go to a show, so you can squeeze in one more concert this summer," Rowan accused. We all looked at Kyla suspiciously.

"What is with you?" Glynnis asked. "You're an adult. You're married. You have a litter of children. Shouldn't you be over this sort of tween obsession with boy bands?"

"Eiley's not."

"Hey, don't drag me into this."

"Besides, I'm not obsessed," Kyla protested.

Rowan and I exchanged a glance. "Remember that time you made us drive four hours to go to a concert in Atlantic City?" Rowan asked.

"And when we had to drive five hours to go to the Virginia Beach concert, and we got stuck in traffic in the tunnel and you had to pee in a 7-Eleven Slurpee cup you found in the back of your minivan?" I reminded her.

"And it had a hole in it," Rowan noted.

"I can't unsee that," Glynnis grumbled. "And the time you seriously considered selling your kids' toys to buy plane tickets to go to Vegas and see the show there?" she asked.

"They were old toys." She threw her hands up. "So I like live music. Is that so bad? It makes me happy, like when I was in college and we used to listen to Blink all the time."

"That was ten years ago," I reminded her.

"That's it," Glynnis exclaimed in a voice that was uncharacteristically loud for her. "I've tried to figure this out for years. You have arrested development. You had to drop out of school and get married. You're stuck in your junior year of college."

No one said anything for a moment as we considered Glynnis's statement. It made sense. Kyla listened to the same music, had the same hairstyle. and dressed in the same clothes as she had in college.

Kyla picked up her fork and began mutilating a defenseless meatball, not looking at any of us. Two bright spots of color stained her cheeks.

"Don't worry about it, honey." Rowan slung an arm around Kyla's shoulders. "What do we know about psychology anyway? A dancer, a painter and a…" she paused, looking at Glynnis.

"You were going to say witch, weren't you?" I joked, trying to lighten the mood.

"Maybe *you* don't," Kyla told her, "but *I* do. I was a psychology major before I left school."

Aha. That was it. Beer pong, boys, and psychology.

"So fix it," Glynnis told her. "Go back to school. Finish your degree or start a new one. Move. On."

Kyla glanced up from her spaghetti twirling, her face pale. It was time to change the subject.

"You guys haven't heard about the black tutu yet."

Someone tried unsuccessfully to stifle a groan, but I bravely forged ahead. It was about time they started taking an interest in my career, and besides it gave me something to do while I watched them chew.

Chapter 17

Eau de Cow

My cousin Brion is a sheriff in Culpeper County, and thanks to watching a lot of late-night reruns, I can't get the image of him driving around in an old black-and-white squad car and rolling a drunk Otis into a cell out of my mind.

Barney and I drove down Route 29 to Brion's farm with the windows open and the radio on. As he'd promised, the shed was unlocked when we arrived. I let myself into the dusty outbuilding and used my iPhone flashlight to take a look around. Barney took off at top speed to sniff himself into a coma.

There were a variety of cast-off items: winter coats, watering cans, and what looked like old college belongings, including a moldy futon and a beer bong with fraternity letters glued to it. I finally found a neat but dusty pile of boxes in the back corner underneath a blue painter's plastic drop cloth.

My Aunt Kathleen had thoughtfully labeled each box's contents in permanent marker. Huzzah. I found a couple that were likely suspects—*Old Letters* and *Photos and Knickknacks*—and pulled them from the stack.

I started with the letters first. Psyche had one letter but there were bound to be more. I flipped through the envelopes and organized them chronologically, based on their postmarks, and started to read.

Although the paper was yellowed and crumbly, I could see why no one had thrown these away. Within a few moments I was taken away by Seamus's sweet teasing tone as the story of his life as a young man in Boston unfolded. He became a police officer in 1912 and wrote often about how much he loved the city. He walked the same beat every day, past the marketplaces and schools until he eventually reached Fenway Park. His letters were filled with descriptions of the people he met along the way.

I wished that I could go back in time and meet Cornelia, with her hair in a bun, selling flowers in her blue gingham apron. I could imagine Mary-Kate with her six children playing in the front yard. I pictured myself sitting with Seamus in the empty stadium as the Red Sox practiced on their field. But most of all, I wished I could have met the young man who had written about them all with such fondness. His letters felt more alive than I did right now.

I found the letter that told about the day he met a girl named Elizabeth at a newsstand on Brooklyn Avenue. He'd been sharing some neighborhood gossip with the newsboy when he saw her, *a trim figure dressed in pink, her brown hair swinging down her back.* And it sounded like he'd fallen in love with her at first sight. *She turned, like she could tell I was studying her, Fi. I may be a fool for saying it, but I knew right then she was my own.* Apparently the gene for falling in love with someone you've never met ran in my family.

I read through all of the letters. Seamus told Fiona how Elizabeth had played hard to get. He followed her home that day and tried his best to charm her. At first she didn't want to have anything to do with a man who wasn't properly introduced by her parents. The fact that he was Irish Catholic and a cop compounded his problems. But Seamus refused to give up.

He walked by her house each day and sometimes brought her one of Cornelia's flowers or a bit of ribbon from the five-and-dime, trying to get her attention. Maybe I should have plied Trey with ribbons and flowers. Or bacon. It would be pretty hard to ignore a girl bringing you plates of bacon.

Eventually, she couldn't resist his charm any longer. They started courting, and before much longer she agreed to be his wife. I was guessing that Seamus had never asked Elizabeth to be his friend with benefits.

When the sickness first started, no one worried too much. I was in tears by the time I read the letter describing her death, even though I knew it was coming. Barney had come to sit beside me, and laid his head on my leg, offering his sweet doggy comfort, tinged slightly with eau de cow.

I watched her take her last breath, Fi. It slipped out in a whisper and then it stopped. I looked around the room a bit sure I'd see her spirit there waiting for me. The feeling was so strong I thought I should get up and open the door to let it pass out. But there was nothing. She was gone. Away from me, forever.

Seamus wrote less often in the letters that followed and usually focused on Fiona's children or his parents rather than his own life. He had changed in all those pages from a lighthearted young man to this new person, sobered by reality. I wondered if my Uncle Seamus had known how short his time would be with Elizabeth, would he have still pursued her. I decided that he probably would have. He seemed like a *carpe diem* kind of guy who would have wanted to seize every moment of happiness that came his way.

I felt myself perk up when I finally came to a letter that mentioned the treasure. It was right before Seamus had left for World War I.

I leave next Monday. Don't forget to help the kids find my treasure. Don't tell them what it is, but give them this hint—I used to carry it every day. I even have it in Mam's favorite picture.

Well, alert Daphne and Freddy. That sounded like a clue to me. Carefully, I stacked the letters and turned my attention to the box marked *Photos and Knickknacks*.

I removed the items and lined them up on the ground. Hopefully something might be more valuable than it seemed. There were some assorted trophies from teams long forgotten, two broken clocks, and a dented silver teapot. Nothing jumped out at me as being priceless.

I reached in again for the stack of photos. Unfortunately, I had no way of knowing which picture had been his mother's favorite. I figured it was safe to assume that it would be of Seamus, and he'd be in his early or middle twenties.

I sorted through a large stack of pictures, but none of them caught my eye. Most were of dour-faced older people in heavy black dresses and suits. Only a few were of Seamus.

At the bottom of the box I found a framed photo in a protective wrapping. I held my breath and mentally crossed my fingers as I peeled back the brown paper. Seamus in his police uniform stared up at me. It was black and white, but I knew the curls peeking out from under his cap would have been red, like mine.

I traced his smile with my fingertip, feeling the family connection through time and space. "Where's your treasure, Uncle?" I asked the smiling face. I didn't care much anymore about finding something worth a lot of money. I only wanted to know what it had been.

I studied the picture. It was so old and grainy it was difficult to make out the details. His arms were down at his sides and partially obscured by his pants legs, but I could see that he held something in his right hand. It was white and mostly hidden. I had no idea what it could have been, but it had to be what I was looking for. I mentally went back through all the boxes I'd searched earlier. I hadn't seen anything that could possibly be what he was holding.

I bundled up the letters and the picture and walked to my car, a malodorous Barney trailing in my wake. I bypassed the house, hoping no one was home to see me skulking across the yard with my purloined letters and photo. I wanted to do something special with them. They deserved something better than slow disintegration in a dusty box.

Barney and I got home and had dinner. I gave him a nice long bath, scrubbed out the tub, and then stood under the hot water until the ache between my shoulder blades loosened.

This afternoon had been a great distraction, but all I could think about now was the performance tomorrow. I knew the part. I could almost always do all the fouettés with no problem. But I didn't feel as confident as I usually did. *It's just another performance*, I told myself. *You can do this.*

I changed into my pajamas and snuggled into bed.

Hopefully my can-do attitude knew what it was talking about.

Chapter 18

Grapealicious

I splashed my feet in their soak, leaned my head back on the couch, and tried to think of something relaxing.

A fluffy kitten playing with yarn.

A beautiful sunset over the beach.

I took a deep breath in and let it out slowly.

What if the show got a bad review? I took in another deep breath.

A stream trickling through the mountains.

What if I couldn't do all the fouettés? What if Basil dropped me? I let the breath out slowly.

A tranquil rainstorm in the desert.

What if I kicked out my own front teeth? Precedence had proven this was clearly in the realm of possibility. I could hurt myself and lose my job and never dance again. I wasn't qualified to do anything else. I'd lose my apartment and have to move back home with Mom, Dad, and Aunt Psyche. I'd have to sleep on that table in the Winnebago that converts into a bed.

I took a deep breath and let it out slowly as I gently massaged my temples.

Purple mountains majesty.

I tried to remember the opening sequence and drew a complete blank.

Amber waves of grain, I thought frantically.

I was closer to panic now than I had been before all my meditations, and light-headed from all the deep breathing.

I couldn't sit any longer, fretting. I dried off my feet and rubbed on some lotion. I decided it would be a good time to get my shoes ready.

When I was little, I dreamed about my first pair of pointe shoes. I plotted, bargained, begged, and, on one regrettable occasion, misappropriated an older girl's shoes.

Finally the day came and I was fitted for my own pointe shoes. Forget your training bras and high heels. Nothing compares to the thrill of your first pointe shoes. I still have them. They hang in my bedroom next to my pictures of Aunt Psyche and Pavlova.

I pulled my white and black shoes for tonight out of my bag. I could still remember taking my first shoes, beautiful, pink, and perfect, out of their little box for the first time. How I worried that my mom would sew the elastic on wrong, or that the satin would get dirty. I'd already sewn the ribbons and elastic onto tonight's shoes, so I didn't have to worry about that. Good thing, because I'd probably jump out of my skin if I had to sit and sew now.

You might think that dancers use one pair of shoes for a while then throw them out and get a new pair, but that's not really how it works. I always have five or six pairs of shoes going at any given time. Some are brand new, some are in the sweet spot, and some are about to go.

For a performance I use a new pair each time so that I know they'll stay strong for the whole show. But it isn't as simple as taking them out of the box and putting them on. There's actually a lot of prep work involved, and most dancers like to do that for themselves because, like a hockey player taping up his sticks, everyone has their own quirks.

I put the shoes on my kitchen table. "You and I need to have the night of our lives," I told them. "I will do my best to make you look good and you need to do the same for me. I will remember you forever, and if tonight goes well, you might get a spot on my wall next to the others. It's just me and you." The costumes are amazing, but really ballet is all about the dancer's body and the pointe shoes.

My younger self would have cried if she saw what I was about to do. I took the first shoe in both hands and cracked the arch in the middle, wiggling it back and forth to make sure it had plenty of flexibility.

Then I took a file and roughed up the hard outer sole and shaved a tiny bit off the edges. I considered roughing up the toe a bit but decided against it.

I tried it on for fit, made a few adjustments, and then started all over again with the rest of the shoes.

I found a tote bag that Kyla had bought at one of her neighborhood parties and packed the shoes. I took Seamus's picture off the wall and slipped it in as well, along with a change of clothes for later.

Hopefully my after-party would be more celebratory than pitying consolation.

I was enjoying the big fuss my family was making. My mom had been bragging on social media for weeks. She'd even posted some of the publicity photos that were up all over town. Aunt Psyche bought a new dress, which was a little scary. Brett would be there. Glynnis was even bringing a date, a guy she'd met walking her dog. I figured I should meet him now since guys don't last long with Glynnis. All the people I loved would be there to share in my night.

I added some flats to my bag. I'd be in no shape for heels after the performance. I grabbed a bottle of water, kissed Barney Awesome Rocket to the Moon Fife good-bye, and loaded up my car. Mrs. Radice had agreed to walk him for me since I'd be gone for so long today.

I can never find my way to the Kennedy Center, no matter how often I go, so I asked my phone to chart a course, and off I went with my shaking hands, false bravado, and all.

I found my way through the maze of narrow hallways to my dressing room and changed into a practice leotard. I had a room to myself, which was nice, but part of me missed the company of the other dancers. I met up with the rest of the cast and we stretched and did a last run-through of some of the trickier choreography, marking time to save our muscles. I made sure to wear both pairs of my shoes to break them in a little.

"Relax, *petite chou*," Basil told me. "Tonight is your night to shine."

"Our night," I told him, clasping his warm, steady hand in my cold, clammy one. What was it like to be that confident in your abilities? I looked around the stage at our small company and the extras who'd been working with us for months to make the show happen. "All of us, our night to shine," I said, feeling a moment of giddy solidarity, even with the really nasty girls who were probably hoping I'd fail miserably. Luckily Corinne was not currently on stage to test my gesture of goodwill.

Susan came out and gave us a short speech that I was too nervous to listen to. The technicians tested the lights and the stage shifted with colors like a psychedelic, ballet-themed rave. The orchestra pit filled up and snippets of music from different instruments burst from the area under the stage. I felt a rush of excitement. This was it.

Oh dear God.

This was it.

We all trooped backstage for hair and makeup. When only fifteen minutes remained to curtain, Serena adjusted the while tutu, fluffed the feathers, and added a few stitches to tighten the strap on the left side.

"You're beautiful." Carefully, she stowed her needle and thread into the sewing kit that would not leave her side for the next several weeks.

I hugged her carefully to avoid any inadvertent molting. "It's the costume."

I picked up my white shoes, kissed each one carefully on the toe (don't judge me), and put them on. I did one last twirl in front of the mirror, applied a coat of Baboon Butt gloss for luck, and joined Basil in the hallway for some last-minute stretching. And praying. I may not have been to mass in a few months, but I could still whip out the Memorare when the situation called for it.

I stood behind the heavy velvet curtains, waiting. Hopefully the makeup people had put enough product on to cover my red blotches. The orchestra began the first beautiful strains of Tchaikovsky's masterpiece and the audience quieted. I was ready. I heard my cue and took the stage to the applause of the crowd. My eyes met Basil's and he gave me a brief nod.

I could sense that the house was packed and my adrenaline bumped up another notch. Nothing compared to a live performance. I took my first steps as a lead dancer, my confidence buoyed by the energy of the audience. I was totally in the moment and the performance flew by, my poise growing with each leap and turn.

I blazed through the fouettés with no problem. I cheekily added one additional turn as the crowd counted them out and cheered their appreciation. Basil adjusted his steps as if he knew in advance I was planning to add the extra turn. "Susan will kill you," he whispered as I passed close to him.

We worked our way through the acts with two frantic costume changes mixed in. Serena hadn't been exaggerating her pit crew's abilities. Although we'd practiced the costume changes, I was unprepared for the speed and accuracy of them. I'd long ago stopped being self-conscious that six virtual strangers were stripping me down to a thong and redressing me while I gulped water. In fact, I almost wished I had this sort of assistance when I prepared to go to Not Frank's.

Susan arranged the choreography so that Odette never looks at the audience until she's dying. It's supposed to be a really dramatic moment where Odette is searching for help and connects with the audience.

Calling on my inner Pavlova, I did a series of quick, fluttery, dying swan steps as my gaze flitted over the crowd, trying to convey my sorrow and the sacrifice I'd made for love.

Above the glare of the stage lights, I could dimly make out a sea of blurry faces and rows of elegant balconies all the way up to the ornate ceiling high above. Right behind the orchestra pit I saw a small girl in a frilly pink dress on her mother's lap. When her eyes met mine, she stretched her tiny hand out to me. I moved slightly so that I could reach in her direction. Her eyes widened and her mouth formed a small, perfect O, and in that moment I got it. Psyche's born-to-be-a-dancer feeling. I understood.

Maybe the little girl would go home and dream of her own tutu and perfect pink pointe shoes. Because of me.

I brought my right foot around for a front tendu and realized the angle was wrong. My toes were out of line with my foot. Quickly, I snapped out of my thoughts and corrected my line. Thankfully I hadn't roughed up the satin on my shoe or I might not have been able to correct.

The show ended and the house lights came up a bit. I waited backstage beside Basil. My chest was heaving with the exertion of the last act, but I couldn't stop smiling. I collapsed against Basil for a quiet celebratory hug. I had never been this happy in my entire life.

Group by group the performers took the stage to take a bow.

I waited as Basil walked out to thunderous applause. He acknowledged the crowd. I ran out quickly and Basil took my hand

and we did a graceful bow together. He took a step back, and I bowed alone. When I straightened, people were on their feet applauding. Some were throwing flowers onto the stage. I bent and picked up a large bundle of beautiful long-stemmed red roses. I smiled and waved to the person who had thrown them, then pulled one rose out and tossed it to the little girl in the front row. Unfortunately, roses aren't super aerodynamic and the rose ended up pelting the bassoon player. Graciously, he redirected the flower to its intended target.

I blew the little girl a kiss, then quickly stepped back to make room for Susan. Basil, Susan, and I took one final bow together, me clutching my bouquet, and the curtain dropped. I sagged with relief. We filed backstage to the largest of the dressing rooms.

We all hugged and congratulated one other. Picture after picture was taken. Someone poured champagne and we toasted our successful opening before we dispersed. I ran back to my small, solitary dressing room with Serena right behind me.

"Let me get this costume off you." She loosened the fabric over my shoulders and began to lower the top. "You did an excellent job tonight. I knew you had it in you."

"Thank you. It really couldn't have gone any better, could it?"

"Stand still, I can't get at these tiny little hooks with you moving around like that."

I made an effort to be still. "Sorry, sorry. I feel like I'm going a hundred miles an hour. It's like I drank three energy drinks." The costume fell to the floor and the cold air hit me as I stood in nothing but tights.

Serena threw a robe over my shoulders. "That's the leftover adrenaline. It'll wear off eventually, and then you'll crash."

I followed her out to the hallway where she hung the damp costume on a rack. Thirty swan costumes were lined up on the floor of the hallway in small, feathery, white pools.

"Get into the shower and try to relax a little." She squeezed my hand. "I'll see you tomorrow, Prima."

I squeezed her hand back, giddy with the compliment.

Two minutes later, I jumped into the shower and quickly lathered, rinsed, and relived the performance in my mind. I breathed in the fragrance of my favorite apple shampoo and tried to settle my nerves.

Still wound up, I got out of the shower and began to towel off. There was a knock at my door and I threw it open, happy to have someone to talk to. Trey stood in the black hallway, a sheepish smile on his face.

I glanced left and right, my eyes scanning the dark hallway. Where had he come from? Heaven? An Abercrombie catalog shoot? A sex addicts anonymous meeting?

I stood in the doorway, stunned and dripping. I raised my eyebrows and made a helpless gesture with the hand that wasn't clutching the towel. Sadly, nothing resembling the English language was forthcoming. I was in too much shock to focus on nouns and verbs and such. Conjunctions and participles were definitely beyond me, and the overabundance of adrenaline wasn't helping me any.

"Chimichangas?" Trey asked with a laugh, remembering my first word to him.

I smiled, my stupor broken. "What are you doing here?"

He shrugged. "I wanted to see you. Is it okay?"

My face lit up into a smile and I nodded. "It's good to see you." And by that I meant *really* good. It had been four weeks and two days since I'd last seen him and I was desperately aware of each gorgeous inch of his body standing only a few feet away from me. I took his hand and pulled him into the room.

"You know, I kind of missed you," he said, giving my hand a small squeeze.

"You did?" My mouth was suddenly dry. I pulled away from him to grab my water bottle off my dressing table. Did missing me mean that he hadn't been seeing a lot of other women? It was probably better not to think about that right now.

"Kind of a lot, actually." He seemed to take up most of the air in my small dressing room.

I leaned back against my dressing table and crossed my arms in front of me. Hopefully that would prevent me from throwing myself into his arms. "How did you know tonight was opening night? How did you get here? Or get tickets?"

He smiled. "Google, a car, and StubHub," he answered, ticking off his responses on his fingers.

"StubHub? That must have been expensive." I pushed the wet hair off my face. One stubborn soggy curl slipped back down over my forehead. I moved it off my face, twirling it around my finger absently.

"It's okay. We're actually getting paid now." His eyes traveled the length of my towel and back to mine. "It was worth it."

I chose to believe that what he really meant was that I was so amazing I was totally worth all the time and trouble it might have taken to come see me.

"So, better than twerking at clubs?" I asked, remembering his comments in the coffee shop on our first date. It had been a date, I decided then and there.

"You're really amazing, you know that?"

My twirling finger pulled painfully in my hair. "Thanks." I tried to mentally record his words so that I could play them on an endless loop the next time I was feeling pathetic. He gently took hold of my hand and detangled the hair from around my finger.

"It was a beautiful performance. You should be really proud." He held my hand between his own and my heart missed a few beats.

Probably from the excess adrenaline and lack of sufficient breathable air, I reasoned.

"How's your tour going?" My voice was high and squeaky.

"It's not as exciting as you might think."

"Yeah, going to a bunch of new places and being adored by screaming fans sounds like it would be miserable." Carefully, I left out the mention of any potential after-show activities.

"The reality is five guys crammed into a filthy van with not enough showers or sleep. And the audiences have never heard of us, so they aren't all that excited, if they're even in the seats to see the opening act for the opening act."

Would I be a terrible person if I admitted that hearing that made me a tiny bit happy? I shifted my weight off my tired left leg and crossed my ankles.

"So…" Trey said, his voice trailing off.

"So…" I said.

We'd officially reached the awkward silence part of the evening. If I hadn't been such a coward, I would have come to a decision about how to solve my Trey problem days ago. But there I was, naked, wet, and completely out of luck. I didn't know what I wanted in the future. My mind was spinning so much I couldn't even think about what I wanted for dinner later with my family. All I knew, at that moment, was that I wanted him. Everything else, I would have to sort out later. It was good enough for Scarlett O'Hara, and it was good enough for me.

"Should we talk?" Trey finally asked.

"We should, but can we…" I blew out a sigh. "Not? At least not tonight?" I was aching, hungry, and too flustered by his sudden reappearance to have any kind of meaningful conversation.

Trey studied my face, hesitating. "It can wait." He opened his mouth to say something else and I lurched forward on one foot and quickly kissed him.

"I don't want to think about anything. I want to be happy right now. *Carpe diem*."

"How happy do you want to be?" He rubbed his thumb across my knuckles. You might be surprised to hear that knuckles can be an erogenous zone. Then again, you might not be.

"As happy as a monkey with a peanut machine." I ignored his raised eyebrows. "I want to reopen negotiations. I think I may have been a little hasty rejecting your previous offer." I wasn't going to think about whatever girl he'd been with last night, or would be with tomorrow night. I'd be thinking about it later, but right now I was going to seize the day.

"You know, overtime, workman's comp, the whole benefits," I took a deep breath and slowly let it out, "package." My eyes briefly skimmed downward. I was no expert at the flirty talk, but I figured that had to be pretty clear. *Cosmo* would have been proud.

"So you're interested in my package?" The crooked grin was back.

Well, that had escalated quickly. We'd gone from "Hey, how are you" to "Let me see your penis" in a few short minutes. I must be better at small talk than I'd given myself credit for.

I quirked my eyebrow and tilted my head. "Is that going to be a problem for you?"

Trey hesitated then shook his head. "No problems here." He wrapped himself around me, and my damp towel pressed against his suit. He lowered his head and kissed me, putting a little bit of effort and a whole lot of tongue into it.

I walked backward leading us to my small sofa, pushing at his suit jacket on the way. The jacket slid from his shoulders to the floor and was quickly followed by his tie.

I fumbled with his pants. Buttons are tricky in reverse. He looked at me for a moment, shook his head, and then reached down and opened the button, raising an eyebrow in an unspoken challenge.

I reached for him, but changed direction, instead pulling my towel from around me and tossing it aside. Take that challenge. I see your unbuttoned drawers and raise you an awkward, slightly damp, sexually frustrated ballerina.

His eyes traveled over me and I had to fan myself with my hand. I pulled his shirt over his head, which wasn't easy for me, being so much lower to the ground than he was. His unfastened pants only needed a quick shove to be down to his knees.

"Hold on, Eiley." He stepped free of his shoes and pants.

"Hold on? To what?" I looked around.

"Wait." He took hold of my arms before I could go after his boxer briefs.

"Wait? For what?" I was baffled. For what possible thing would I want to wait right now? Not even Ed McMahon and the prize patrol would give me pause.

"I feel like maybe we should talk a little before things get…"

"We did. We talked. Now shut up." I lunged toward him, trying to remove his briefs and get him to the couch in the shortest amount of time possible. I fell backward with him on top of me. The couch shuddered and creaked but held strong. I used my toes to snag the edge of his boxers and pull them down. Prehensile toes. It's a perk of dancing.

Before I could get ahold of any relevant appendages, Trey slid off the sofa and sank onto his knees in front of me, pulling my hips toward him. The night kept getting better. At that moment I would have sold state secrets to the enemy.

My toes curled and I tangled my hands in his hair. "Ten points to Gryffindor," I shrieked, my legs shaking.

"What are you *doing*?" a horrified voice asked from the doorway. I jumped to my feet and bumped into Trey, sending him sprawling. I dove for my towel and wrapped it around myself, literally leaving Trey out in the cold.

"Mom. What are you doing here?" My mom didn't answer. She was staring at us, mouth open, a furious blush creeping into her cheeks. I was sure my cheeks weren't much better. I must get my tendency to blush from her, although I'd never seen her blush like this before. Maybe this was the early stages of cardiac arrest. Good thing I had a naked EMT standing by.

My mom sucked in a deep breath and I braced myself for the lecture that was coming. This was going to be so much worse than the time she'd caught me playing doctor with Bradley Puffinburger when I was seventeen. I was a bit of a late bloomer.

When the room was silent, I cautiously opened one eye and squinted at my mother through my hair.

"Ulk." Her hands fluttered around her throat.

"It's her gum," exclaimed Psyche, who was standing behind her. "The grapealicious bubble gum. She's choking." We all began to talk at the same time. Tears streamed from my mother's eyes. Clearly, it was time to panic.

"Do something," I screamed at Trey. He stepped toward my mom, reaching for her, but she took two steps away. He stepped toward her again and again she stepped away from him. Great. All life-or-death situations called for full frontal nudity and a samba routine worthy of *Dancing with the Stars*. (Bruno Tonioli, call me.)

My mom took one hand from around her throat to point at Trey's naked groin, then squeezed her eyes shut. Apparently she'd chosen death over dishonor.

Trey looked at me, not sure what to do. I didn't know how many more seconds she had before the lack of oxygen killed off a few brain cells. Please don't think less of me because I briefly wondered if she might be stricken with short-term memory loss—just enough to forget everything that had happened after opening my dressing room door. That would be ideal. Maybe I could convince her she'd hallucinated the whole thing thanks to the oxygen deprivation.

I glanced at Psyche and saw that she was going to be no help, unless staring at someone's penis prevented asphyxia. It was going to be really hard to explain to my dad how my mother had choked to death in my dressing room because my ex-fake boyfriend wasn't wearing any clothes. I grabbed her shoulders and pushed her backward into Trey.

"Nice to meet you Mrs. Murphy." He grimaced at me and wrapped his arms around my mom's waist. "I going to have to, uh, well, there's no other way but to…" His face was bright red. It was nice to see splotches on someone else for a change.

My mom pointed at me and glared. Her lips were moving, but no sound was coming out. Lucky me. Although she was choking to death, she still had a few seconds to spare to share her horror about the naked man pressed up against her backside.

Trey quickly brought his clasped hands under her breasts and squeezed. Her eyes rolled back into her head as the gum flew out of her mouth. He gently lowered her limp body to the couch. I ran into the bathroom to get a wet towel. Trey was taking her pulse when I returned.

I wiped her face with the towel. "Is she okay?"

"She's going to be fine. She fainted." Another thing we had in common. The first time I was that close to naked Trey I'd felt light-headed, too.

"You should probably put your pants back on," I suggested, as my mother's lids began to flutter.

"Ahem." Psyche coughed delicately a few times. Trey and I turned to look at her. She waved her hands near her face, batted her eyelashes, and looked at Trey expectantly. He looked at me, mouth agape, eyes wide with fear.

"What's the matter, Aunt Psyche? Are you choking too?" I asked. She smiled a little and nodded. Trey's head bobbed back and forth between us. He gathered his clothing hastily. Aunt Psyche let out another small cough and sidled closer to him, her diaphanous bright pink dress floating around her as she moved.

"You're coughing," he told her, with obvious relief. "You know, people who can cough don't need the Heimlich. Because they're moving air. You need air to cough."

"Run for your life, kid," my mom said from her prone position on the couch. Trey hurried into the bathroom, all three of us watching him go.

I helped my mom sit up slowly. "How are you feeling?" I sat beside her and put my arm around her.

"This has to be the strangest night of my life."

"It's one of the best nights of mine." Psyche looked fondly at the closed bathroom door.

"Me too. In fact, I think I can say without a doubt, this has been the best night of my life," I said.

"Oh Eiley. Of course it has. You were perfect. Dad and I are so proud of you." She wrapped me in a hug.

"Thank you, Mom." I leaned my head onto her shoulder and breathed in her familiar lilac scent, almost weak with relief that she was okay. "I mean it. Thank you. For all the practices you drove me to, the sequins you sewed, for never giving up on me even when I gave up on myself..." My voice caught in my throat. "I wouldn't be here tonight if it weren't for you."

"Thank you, sweetie, that means a lot to me. But don't think I've forgotten the naked man in your bathroom."

"Mom, I'm so sorry. It's not what you think." She raised her eyebrows. "I mean, it kind of is." Her mouth formed a tight line. "We were...celebrating."

"In my day we drank champagne," Psyche stated. "Although your way does look like more fun."

"Could we talk about it later?" Or never, I silently prayed.

"We don't have to talk about it," my mom replied. Wow. God did answer prayers. "You can tell the priest when you go to confession." And he had a sick sense of humor.

"That's not necessary, is it?" I asked.

Aunt Psyche shook her head and I smiled at her gratefully. "She doesn't need to go to confession, she can unburden herself with us." Psyche nodded for emphasis. "Tell us what happened and you'll feel so much better. All the details." She licked her lips. "Specific details."

My mom and I stared at her in mute revulsion. "Look, I'm not trying to pry, but it's important for your mortal soul, dear. You could die tonight and end up in purgatory." I was closer to regurgitory at that moment. "Oh. You should invite him to come to dinner with us."

"I think we've seen enough of Eiley's friend for tonight." My mom stood and straightened her clothing.

"Speak for yourself," Psyche muttered, taking one last lingering look at the bathroom door. I was surprised she hadn't burned a hole through it with her eyes.

"Eiley, we'll see you at the restaurant." My mom pulled a reluctant Psyche toward the door.

"Okay, Mom. I'll be right behind you. I've got to, uh, tie up a few loose ends here."

"If that's what you kids are calling it these days." Psyche snorted. We did another round of hugs before they left.

"It's safe to come out now."

The bathroom door opened and Trey peeked around the corner before opening it all the way and coming into the room.

"You didn't get dressed?"

"Well, I thought your dad might make an appearance and I didn't want to take the chance that I'd miss meeting your whole family while I was naked." He was wearing only the pair of gray boxer briefs. I had been right about his prospects as an underwear model. He was perfect.

"Well, sadly, we're here all alone. But I can make sure your semi-nudity won't go to waste."

My family would be waiting for me at a restaurant across town, but they could celebrate without me, right? I traced a line down his chest, over his waistband, and down the length of him. Hopefully my family would be so busy with an appetizer they wouldn't even notice I was missing. Everybody liked to start off an evening with a nice plate of cheese fries, didn't they?

His hand shot out and grabbed my towel sarong. He pulled it off with one yank and took a step toward me. I took a hasty step backward, scrambling to think up a polite way to suggest he use some Listerine given where his mouth was last. If he was aware of my hesitation, he didn't show it. He stalked in close to me, eyes focused, pupils dilated.

I had almost decided to throw caution, and any basic principles associated with good oral hygiene, to the wind when my left calf muscle seized into a cramp and I crumpled to the ground.

"It's okay," I grunted from the floor. "Occupational hazard. Give me a minute." I knew how to get rid of the cramp, but I hated to do it. I ground my teeth together and tentatively stretched my leg out. God was clearly sending me a message that I had made the wrong choice between immoral activity and family dinner. As soon as I could walk again, I would get dressed and head directly to the restaurant.

Trey crouched beside me and covered me with the towel.

"Don't touch it," I ground out between short breaths. Although it might be surprising to you that I'd told the world's hottest man to keep his hands off me, I knew from painful experience what a disaster the wrong touch could cause.

"Trust me." He sat and pulled my leg gently onto his lap. "I know what to do."

"Because you're an EMT?" I'd never considered calling 9-1-1 for a cramp. I closed my eyes and readjusted the towel. Maybe I should bite it to prevent any embarrassing whimpers from slipping out. This was the mother of all cramps. If cramps were a country, this cramp would be their king. Or something.

"No, because I used to get these all the time in high school."

"You did ballet in high school?" I asked, my leg warmer fantasies taking on new life.

"Rugby."

"Rugby? You couldn't have been on the curling team, or a mathlete. You were a hot rugby player." I gasped as his fingers softly probed my knotted muscle.

His eyes met mine. "Sorry, it's going to hurt a little."

"I would have totally gotten all up in your scrum," I blurted.

One side of his mouth quirked up into a smile. I stuffed the towel in my mouth. Apparently there were worse things than whimpering.

"Relax." Trey's fingers bit into the worst part of the cramp. I took a deep breath in and let it out, but I couldn't release the tension in my body.

"I can't. Today was so over the top."

Gently, he lowered my leg to the floor and then moved to sit behind me, pulling me against his warm, bare chest. "I can help with that, too. My grandma used to do this when I was little and couldn't sleep."

What sort of freaky grandma did he have? I guess you can't trust a woman who shows up to her birthday party in a purple pantsuit.

He spooned in behind me and I wiggled my bottom against him. But only a little, because I was a mature, responsible person who was going to spend the rest of the evening with her family having dinner, in lieu of multiple orgasms.

"Close your eyes." He wrapped his arms around me and began working on the cramp again. I obeyed, leaning my head against his shoulder. I was about to sneak an eyelid open a crack to see what was going on when he started singing.

I'd heard him sing before, of course, but he'd never sounded like this at Not Frank's. His voice was a sweet, clear tenor. I took another deep breath and felt myself finally start to relax as I focused on the song about being held by a diminutive dancer. The cramp began to ease, and an image of the stage and the audience, and the little girl in the pink dress floated through my mind. It really had been a perfect night.

The song ended, and we sat together in silence for a few moments. "Thanks," I whispered. I flexed my foot experimentally, relieved that all that remained was a dull ache. I took a quick glance at the clock and sighed.

"Come on." Trey stood then pulled me up. "Take a few steps and see how your calf feels."

I clutched the towel awkwardly and took a few tentative steps, then smiled. "It's fine, thanks to you."

He smiled and wiggled his fingers. "It's the guitar playing." I stared at his hands, momentarily distracted. He certainly did have talented fingers.

"I guess it's time to get going." I sighed. I pulled my clean clothes from my bag while Trey retrieved his from the bathroom.

"Who's the man with the baseball?" he asked when he returned, pulling on his pants. Surprisingly, he looked as good putting clothes on as he did taking them off.

"There's a man with a baseball in my bathroom?"

"That old picture you have." He walked back into the bathroom.

I zipped up my skirt and followed him. "That's my great-great-uncle Seamus." I studied the object in his hand. It was white, and the tiny bit of it I could see appeared to be round. "You think that's a baseball?"

Trey shrugged. "Could be. Looks like it."

"It's some sort of thing that was important to him. I've actually been trying to find it."

"After all this time? What's it been, like a hundred years?" He slid into his shirt and I took a last, long look at his chest before it was covered up.

"Something like that," I muttered as I finished dressing. I checked myself in the mirror then picked up my bag and loaded it with my dirty clothes and pointe shoes. They had definitely earned a place on my wall. I turned off the lights and we walked into the hallway together.

Trey took the bag from me and slung it over one shoulder then took my hand as we walked down the corridor.

"Don't forget your shoes for tomorrow, Cinderella," Serena called out to me from behind a rack of costumes she was sorting. She handed Trey two boxes of fresh shoes for tomorrow's performance.

"Thanks. I can't believe I almost forgot those."

As Trey turned to put the shoes in my bag, Serena gave him a quick up-and-down leer, then winked at me. "Nostradamus had a feeling you might." She grinned.

I led the way to my car, then drove Trey to his. "Do you want to come to dinner with us?" I asked him when we'd pulled up beside his car.

He shook his head. "Your mom made it clear that she'd rather I didn't. Besides, I've got to get back to the band tonight."

I looked down at my lap. I'd managed to temporarily forget about the stupid tour.

"Eiley," he began, and I looked up at him. "I'll call you when I can. And I'll be back in a month, and then, we really need to have that talk."

I made a dismissive gesture with my hand. "Not necessary. I understand what you were trying to say before, and I get it." Trey started to speak, but I cut him off. "No, I do. Really," I assured him. "Now I've got to get going or I'm going to miss dinner completely."

He pulled me in for a hug. "Thanks for coming tonight," I mumbled into his shoulder.

"I'm glad I did. Totally worth it. You killed it."

I pulled away to smile up at him. "Thanks."

We kissed good-bye, and then he was gone.

***

I raced into the restaurant, dodged past several tables of startled diners, and made my way to the private room in the back. I slowed to a walk, took a deep breath, and parted the heavy curtains that sectioned the back room from the dining area in front. Seated at two long tables were all my family and friends.

"Hey, everyone, I'm so sorry I'm..." As one, they all rose to their feet and started clapping. I choked on my words and tears clouded my eyes. The only other time this had happened was the day I'd accidentally walked through the screen door. I had to take a minute to fan my face. The only thing that could have made this night any better would have been if my brother had been there, too.

My father popped the cork on a bottle of champagne and waiters materialized with glasses. "To Eiley." My father's voice filled the room as he raised his glass.

"To Eiley," everyone called in unison.

I fanned my cheeks a little harder and blinked back tears. "Thank you." I nodded. "Thank you for sharing this night with me." I nodded some more. "I'm so happy that you're all here."

I made my way around the table, hugging each of my family members in turn, ending with Glynnis. "Thanks so much for putting this together. I love it."

"It really was no problem. Kathy did all the work." She grinned. I noticed the man sitting next to her. It was unusual for Glynnis to bring a date to a family event.

He put his hand out. "Chris Swallen," he introduced himself as we shook hands. He was tall, well-dressed, and good-looking. Exactly Glynnis's type.

"Nice to meet you."

"Was traffic bad on the way over?"

"It was fine. I left later than I'd intended to. I'm sorry to keep you all waiting," I said this last part in a louder voice, trying to address the room in general.

"Eiley was talking to her young man," Psyche supplied helpfully. I groaned inwardly.

"Eiley has a young man?" Glynnis eyed me suspiciously.

"No, of course not. I was talking to a friend. I wouldn't call him my 'young man.'" I glanced nervously at Brett and Valerie but avoided making eye contact with any of my sisters. Or my dad.

My mom stood up quickly, her forehead creased in concern. "What do you mean he's not your young man? I'd say he was your young man. When I walked in, he was—"

"Helpful to you, Mom, if you'll remember?" I interjected. Her face flushed bright red. That should be enough to prevent her from sharing with all our friends and family members how she'd discovered Trey. She nodded briefly and sat down quickly. Thank goodness that was over. For now.

Conversation resumed around the table as I found my seat. Orders were placed and glasses filled. There was more champagne, but I drank only one glass. I had to get up tomorrow and do this routine of adrenaline and exhaustion all over again.

I sneaked my phone onto my lap under my napkin, checking to see if Trey texted. Glynnis caught me and gave me a raised eyebrow.

I looked away quickly, hoping she wouldn't pry all my secrets out of me until we were in the relative privacy of the Dirty Grudge Diner.

Ten servers arrived carrying huge trays filled with plates topped by silver domes and served our dinner with a flourish. I'd picked a meal with a good amount of carbs. As I raised a fork laden with noodles to my mouth, I felt my phone vibrate.

I scooted my napkin away and risked a quick glance at my lap.

You were amazing tonight.

I waited until my mom excused herself to go to the restroom to reply. The less she knew about this the better.

You too, I replied, and followed it with a winking smiley face. I was going for fun and flirty. I looked up, hoping no one had noticed, but Glynnis saw.

"Who are you texting?"

"Friends."

She lowered her eyebrows.

"People."

She tilted her head and studied my face.

My skin began to heat up. "Well-wishers offering their congratulations," I stuttered.

"Mm-hmm."

I quickly clicked my phone off and slipped it back into my bag.

"That was Lance Manyon Mom was talking about, wasn't it?" Glynnis whispered.

"He was there tonight. Mom met him in my dressing room. Naked."

"I'm going to assume Trey was naked and not our mother." Glynnis smirked. Kyla, Rowan, and Chris were now following the conversation. Rowan motioned for Brett and Valerie to come to our end of the table.

"Trey was at the ballet tonight, naked," Rowan hissed.

Kyla's eyebrows shot up. "So you guys worked it all out?"

"Uh, not exactly. I mean, sure. Sort of. I mean, we talked some, but I don't remember reaching any conclusions, exactly." They all frowned at me. "But it was good," I hastily added. "I mean, overall, it was going in the right direction. The conclusions were…implied."

"By 'implied' you mean his pants were off, right?" Glynnis smirked.

"Mostly." I tried to keep my voice low so that we wouldn't be overheard by my dad and Aunt Psyche.

"How are you feeling about everything?" Brett pulled a chair over to me and sat down.

I flashed back to how I felt seeing Trey's smiling face standing in my doorway, knowing that he'd made the effort to come to my opening night. "Pretty good, actually."

Valerie sat down on Brett's lap. "So you can handle it?"

I shrugged. "I'm on board the friends with benefits train, full steam ahead." Probably.

"Yeah, the games will be sold out, now that the Caps have brought home the Stanley Cup," Chris said in a loud voice. He subtly tilted his head toward the restrooms.

I turned and saw my mom coming back to the table. I mouthed the words "thank you" to him. The last thing I needed was to discuss my booty call with my mother. Talking about hockey was the perfect cover in this family. We all enjoyed the Capitals' games.

My mom took her seat next to my dad. He looked up from cutting his steak.

"Eiley, do you listen to Elliott in the Morning?" he called down the table. I froze, my forkful of penne pasta held aloft, dripping sauce onto my plate. At this rate, I was never going to get to eat.

"Uh…"

Rowan slapped me under the table. "You look like a deer caught in headlights," she whispered.

"I heard a woman on the radio last month that sounded exactly like you. She even had your crazy fear of blood. It was really funny actually."

"That wasn't me." My voice was loud and defensive.

"Well of course it wasn't you, sweetie. This was a woman and her boyfriend. You would never act like that in a public place."

My mom's narrowed eyes flew to my face, full of suspicion. I slipped my hand under my leg to prevent myself from fanning my overheated cheeks.

"I thought it was funny how much she sounded like you," my dad went on, oblivious to my mother's shrewd gaze.

"They say everyone has a twin," Chris offered. I smiled at him, grateful for the rescue.

I hoped Glynnis would hang on to this one.

Chapter 19

Fire in the Hole

I opened the door of the diner and the aroma of grease put a smile on my face. If you're not the kind of person who gets turned on by fried chicken, you and I can't be friends. This was my first night off since we'd opened and there was no other place I wanted to be after my long bacon hiatus.

This diner, with its black-and-white tiles and shiny silver counter, was like a second home to me. One that had better food than my actual home, and people who were willing to both bring it to me and clean up afterward. It didn't get much better than that. My sisters were all already there waiting for me.

"How's the ballet going?" Kyla asked as I pulled my chair out.

"It's good. So far, no major mistakes. I've almost gotten used to the schedule. At least I'm not as exhausted as I was when we first opened."

"Exhausted? It's been weeks. You should be used to it by now."

I turned to Glynnis. "You have no idea. In the last twenty-one days, we've done the show thirty-two times. If you're tired, sick, hurt, or plain not motivated, you suck it up, put on your tights, and do the job anyway. And you do it with a smile on your face to the best of your ability to appear graceful all while you're trying to remember three hours of choreography because you know that people have paid a lot of money for their tickets and each one of them deserves your best effort. There is no getting used to it."

Glynnis shook her head. "You need some bacon." She turned her attention back to the phone in her hand.

"Badly." I spread my napkin over my lap, ready for a pork belly polka.

Kyla's lips twitched into a smile. "There can't be too many performances left though, are there?"

"Two more weeks." I took a closer look at her. She'd gotten a new haircut and she had on a new shirt. "You look great."

"Thanks. I decided you guys might have a point about all the arrested development stuff. I'm trying out some new things." She pointed to her shirt. "It's from one of those online leggings parties that everyone is doing. I have leggings that match."

"Good for you." Rowan adjusted her low-cut, retro hippie shirt. Too bad she wasn't the one with new fashion inspiration.

"I also went online and researched some classes at George Mason. It's too late to apply for this fall, but I should be able to get the application done in time for the spring semester."

I glanced from Rowan to Glynnis. And then back to Kyla. We all sat in silence for a few beats, stunned. "Great," Glynnis finally said. "I'm really happy for you."

Rowan threw her arms around Kyla. "My warmest felicitations, sister," she bubbled.

"Thanks. I'm a little scared, but I think it'll be a good thing. I might need some help with the kids, if you guys are willing?"

"Of course we are," I told her. "We'll all support you. It's probably a good idea for us to have a shrink in the family."

"Let's not get too excited yet." Kyla pushed at Rowan's arms, trying to escape. "I haven't gotten accepted."

"You haven't even applied," Glynnis pointed out.

I shot her a look. "But when she does apply, she'll get in. They'll be lucky to have her."

"And you'll fit right in," Glynnis said.

"You think?" Kyla beamed.

"Oh yeah. They've got a lot of older students and commuters." Kyla's face fell. Time to change the subject.

"Hey, listen, I forgot to tell you, I think Seamus might be holding a baseball in that picture I found."

"That you stole," Glynnis corrected.

"Why would he have a baseball? And why would it be so special?" Rowan asked.

"Balls are always special to guys." Glynnis smirked.

"He did like baseball," I said, remembering his letter about watching the Sox practice.

"You know, it might be a good idea to research this whole thing." Glynnis finally put her phone back into her bag and gave us her full attention.

"You mean at the library?" I frowned.

"You don't actually have to go to the library anymore. You can look up most things online now."

"What would I be looking for?"

She shrugged. "Anything, really. You could search the newspapers that year, look at old property records, that sort of thing."

"I don't know if I know how to do all that," I told them. But what I really meant was *I don't want to do all that.*

"I'll help you. In fact, never mind. I'll do it myself." I blinked a few times. That was the last thing I'd expected to hear from Glynnis.

I didn't have too long to ponder my sister's sudden interest because Brett had materialized with our appetizer. "Welcome back, stranger."

"No kidding. This has been the hardest month of my life."

"Too much dancing?"

"Not enough bacon." I stood and gave him a quick hug. "Thank you so much for coming to my opening night. It meant a lot to me."

"I was only there for Basil."

"He sure can fill out a pair of tights." All our heads swung in Rowan's direction. "Oh, like you didn't notice," she snorted.

"You were fabulous, Eiley. I knew you were good, but I had no idea you could do that," Brett fairly gushed.

"To be honest, I didn't really know it either. Not until I actually did it." I felt my cheeks flush with pleasure, but I didn't care.

"Fill me in on all the details." He pulled a chair out and sat down with us.

"You mean like backstage gossip?"

"I mean like your boy toy. What's going on with that?"

"Well, we've been texting since that night. A lot, really. Some FaceTime, but our schedules don't always work out." Trey also sent me a daily SnapChat message and sang part of a song to me. I listened to them at night when I went to bed, but I wasn't going to share that with my sisters.

"How many naked pictures have you sent?" Glynnis asked suspiciously.

"None. I would never do that." Because Chad might accidentally see them. "Although I wouldn't mind receiving naked pictures." I'd finished a little louder than I'd intended. Several heads at the table next to us swung around.

"And you're happy with all of this?" Brett asked.

I nodded. I wasn't sure what was going to happen in the future, but for now I was happier with Trey in my life than I was with him out of it.

"You really haven't talked about anything serious since the opening night, have you?" Kyla asked.

"Not really. It's hard to talk on the phone. He's usually on stage or in a van full of people, not exactly the place for a private conversation." This was all true, but the real reason I hadn't been eager to have any serious discussions was because I still didn't know what I wanted.

"No phone sex?" Rowan wanted to know.

"Ah, no."

"When he's back, what's going to happen?" Kyla pressed.

"Please tell us anything that doesn't involve genitalia." Glynnis piled some bacon onto my plate. The table next to us turned in our direction again.

"Okay, enough of that," Kyla said before I could answer or pick up my fork to throw at Glynnis. "New topic. I talked to Mom today."

"How's she doing?" I asked around the first mouthful of bacon that I'd had in too many weeks. I took a moment to savor the crunchy, cheesy perfection. I smiled at Brett and he smiled back.

"Better than expected. She's taken up yoga and pottery and is spending three afternoons a week pushing people around in wheelchairs at the hospital."

"So pretty much anything she can do to stay out of the house," I guessed.

"And away from Psycho," Rowan added.

"And she made me promise that we'd all come home for Thanksgiving dinner."

"It's barely September," I protested.

"We've never missed a Thanksgiving at home, I don't know what she's worrying about," Glynnis said. This was true. We always went home for the holidays—Thanksgiving, Christmas, Easter, Arbor Day—any excuse for a visit and a huge home-cooked meal with all our favorites.

"Now I'm thinking about mashed potatoes," Rowan said. "With gravy."

"Green bean casserole," added Glynnis.

"And homemade bread, fresh from the oven." Kyla licked her lips.

"Stuffing," I put in, looking at Brett. We ordered all the Thanksgiving-related items the Grudge had to offer. It never hurt to do a trial run.

"We should play I Hate My Life while we wait for our food," Kyla suggested when Brett had left. "I'll even start." The rest of us nodded. "So, Shady Pines Elementary decided to kick the school year off with a science fair."

"Science fair, that's right up Finn's alley, isn't it?" Glynnis asked.

"Well, I thought so, but he claimed he didn't want to do it. I was surprised, but I didn't want to push it, since the school year just started. Then Friday night he tells me he's changed his mind. So I'm dreading it, right? You know how it is. Your kid waits 'til the last minute to do a huge project and it turns out to be a big headache for you." Kyla looked around the table at our blank faces. We had no idea, but we nodded anyway.

"But I was wrong. He tells me he's going to do it all by himself. He won't even let me see it until the night of the science fair." She unconsciously fluffed her new short hair-do.

"What did you do?" I asked.

"What do you think I did? I put my feet up and finished off a bottle of wine and streamed season two of *Downton Abbey*."

"Season two? You're years behind," Glynnis exclaimed.

"What was the project?" I asked. "And how is this 'I Hate My Life'? Seems pretty good to me."

"I sure did get to see the project. The whole neighborhood saw it." Kyla paused and gulped down some soda.

"And?" Glynnis demanded.

"Finn's project was a study of the effect of alcohol on problem solving." We all looked at her, not getting it.

"His data went something like this: 'My mom's ability to solve for X after one glass of wine, two glasses,' and so on."

"How many glasses did he get up to?" Rowan wanted to know.

"Eight."

Glynnis snorted.

"Okay, ten. I told you, I had a lot of *Downton Abbey* to watch. It was Friday night. You have to finish the bottle once you start it. Everybody knows that. Now everyone probably thinks I'm an alcoholic."

"There were probably tons of entries. I bet most people didn't even see it," I told her.

"Everyone saw it, the neighbors, his teacher, his principal," she wailed. "He won second place." She hung her head, her short curls brushing the scarred tabletop. "It's going to be part of a write-up in our local paper."

"It could be worse," Rowan offered. "You could have been watching porn."

"Speaking of porn," I interjected and told the tale of the naked Heimlich maneuver and the comatose mother that I had managed to avoid sharing up until then.

"You know," Glynnis said, "all of your I Hate My Life entries have been about Trey and/or his penis lately. Don't you have anything else?"

"I think we should disqualify her. Although that is a lovely story." Rowan patted my hand.

"That's right," Kyla agreed. "No more penis entries for you."

I noticed a few heads turning in our direction again. "Shush. Don't get us thrown out of here before I get my Thanksgiving prequel. I need this food. Do you know how good I've been?"

"Relax," Glynnis scolded, "I don't think these guys are upset about all the penis talk." She winked at one of the openly staring men who grinned and winked back before turning back to his dinner.

"He's cute. You should get his number." Rowan suggested. Glynnis looked the man up and down.

"Solid haircut, good body, nice shoes, quality suit. But not interested. I come here to pick up bacon and other related pork products, not men."

Brett arrived, staggering under the weight of his tray filled with plates of mouthwatering food. When it was all distributed to its rightful glutton, he pulled up a chair again and sat with us.

Rowan was up next with her entry for I Hate My Life. "*Well*," she began with a huge sigh that threatened to cause her flowing peasant blouse to reveal more cleavage than was appropriate for a family establishment. "I was working on a painting, one I was doing for fun, you know. I've been sketching so much for the Urban Spaces thing I was absolutely *drained*, and I needed to do some real art. So I was painting a poppy in a field of poppies…"

"Wouldn't that be a field of poppies, then?" Glynnis asked.

"No, because this one is *special*. It stands out from the others. That's kind of the point, you know. And I was mixing paint to get the right shade, you see, and…"

"And you saw a spider and spilled the paint," Glynnis and I said together. This was not Rowan's first "I saw a spider and spilled paint" story. Her fear of spiders rivaled my fear of bodily fluids.

"…and I saw a massive hairy spider climbing up the leg of my easel. I'm pretty sure it was a black widow. So I threw the palette at it, missed and hit the canvas of all things. Ruined. The whole thing."

"I'm sorry your picture got ruined, I love your poppy pictures." I had two of them hanging in my kitchen.

"Okay." Glynnis reached up to flatten her perfectly smooth hair. "I can't even believe I'm telling you this. I went to a Thai buffet for lunch yesterday with Kathy and we definitely got our money's worth. When I got back to my desk, I couldn't even sit down my stomach was so bloated. So I decided to go to the gym on the third floor. I was jogging on the elliptical, with my iPod on."

"Listening to Blink?" Kyla interrupted.

"Actually yes, but that's not part of my story. Anyway, the Thai food had made me really gassy. I held it in as long as I could, but eventually a few slipped out. I figured it would be okay since they were so quiet no one could notice."

We all grimaced, waiting to hear what happened next.

"Well, when I got off the elliptical I walked past Earl, who was on a stationary bike behind me. I started to say hello and he wouldn't even look me in the eye. And then I realized what must have happened."

Brett started laughing. "How loud was your iPod?"

"Exactly. Too loud to realize that my little toots weren't silent."

"There you were," Rowan laughed, "farting away on the elliptical right in front of your boss."

"Pretty much."

We all laughed at the thought of my perfect sister committing a social faux pas of this magnitude.

"We had a meeting later that afternoon, and I swear he must have told everyone because they were looking at me and smirking when I got there." Rowan let out a loud snort of laughter.

"It gets worse. When I got up to get some coffee, someone yelled 'Fire in the hole' when my back was turned."

"Maybe they'll give you some sort of fart-related nickname," Brett suggested.

"I don't know if they will, but I know I will," I said. "Barking Spider."

"Belching clown," Rowan added.

"Fanny Frog," Kyla chimed in.

"I'm going to yell out 'Fire in the hole' whenever she enters the room," Brett stated.

"Fire in the hole would be a better name for Eiley." Glynnis smirked in my circection.

We couldn't come to an agreement on a winner, so we made Brett choose. "Farting in public, almost killing your mother with your naked hookup, public airing of your drinking habits, or canvas ruined by spider. You ladies have set the bar pretty high this week. I'm going to go with Glynnis, mainly because this is so out of character for her."

My phone rang, interrupting Glynnis's victory speech. I grabbed my backpack off the back of my chair and began to fish around for it, wondering who was calling me. It was late for a telemarketer, unless they were calling from Bangladesh. Assuming the time difference from Bangladesh was roughly six hours behind appropriate business hours. It could be a call from Australia, then it would be tomorrow there, right?

I found the phone and saw that it was Trey calling on FaceTime.

Brett stood up to go get our check, and then sat right back down again when he saw Trey's name on my phone screen.

I clicked and his face came into view. The picture was dark and grainy and there seemed to be a lot of people around. The phone's speakers crackled with background noise.

"Hey, I'm glad I caught you." Trey smiled into the camera. "Are you at the Grudge with your sisters?"

I panned my phone around so that he could see everyone.

"Give the phone to Kyla for a minute," he told me when I'd returned the screen back to myself. I handed the phone over to my sister and shrugged.

"Eiley told me how much you like Blink, so I thought you might like a look backstage," I heard him say.

"I want to see," Rowan interrupted.

Kyla shifted in her seat so that she could hold the phone high enough for us to see the screen too. The picture changed from Trey's face to a pile of cases, wires, and equipment. Standing next to that were several guys in black shirts with the word "Crew" on the back.

The picture jostled and Trey moved closer to the group of guys. As he angled his camera we could see the side of the stage where the band was performing.

I glanced at Kyla. Her eyes were wide and she was holding my phone with a white-knuckle grip. Apparently she wasn't quite over her obsession. Not that I was judging. No one knew better than I did how hard it was to quit an obsession cold turkey.

"What song are they playing?" Glynnis asked. The phone's speakers were overwhelmed and more crackling noises came out than actual music. We all listened for a minute but couldn't make out any specific lyrics.

Trey's face reappeared on the screen. "Why don't you guys come for one of the shows?"

Kyla bit her lip and cleared her throat. She looked around at each of us. This was really going to be a test of her new effort to move on with her life. "That sounds great, Trey, maybe we'll do that."

"I've got to go. Tell Eiley I'll call her later, okay?" Trey asked, and then he was gone.

"Trey came to see you. Maybe you should go to see him," Kyla said as she handed my phone back to me

"See her? Is that what we're calling it these days?" Rowan laughed at her own joke as she poured more gravy onto her mashed potatoes.

"Maybe you should return the favor," Brett suggested, taking a bite out of my half-eaten turkey club.

"The, um, sexual favor?"

"Well, honey, kneeling at the altar never hurts. But what I meant was you should go see his show," Brett mumbled around bites of sandwich.

"And slurp the gherkin," Glynnis said. The man at the next table turned around again to smile at her.

Kyla bent over her phone, Googling concert dates. "It's a good idea, Eiley. You guys can finally talk. In person, with your clothes on."

"In a well-lit public place," Rowan pointed out.

"With at least five feet of space between you," Brett added.

"I thought you were going to cut back on the concerts?" Rowan raised her eyebrow at Kyla, who blushed and looked away quickly.

"I'm making small changes. It's not healthy to do too much too fast, you know," she explained. I nodded. I was a firm believer in the taper-off plan.

"I'm in. Who else?" Rowan asked.

"Pass," Glynnis said. She rummaged around in her Louis Vuitton bag and pulled out one of her business cards then passed it to the man at the next table.

"I'm in," Brett said.

"Okay, it's a plan. I'll be there, and I'm volunteering Valerie. But it will have to be next Friday, it's my only day off."

Kyla did some more scrolling. "Next Friday looks like they're at Jones Beach in New York. That's manageable, right?" She looked up from her phone with hope in her eyes.

I counted the hours in my head. With traffic, a twelve-hour round-trip, plus a night in New York, and a few hours for the concert, the schedule would be really tight. Trey's crooked grin ran through my mind.

I nodded.

I could make it work.

Chapter 20

Verisimilitude and the Last Huzzah

I hooked my fingers into the waistband of Valerie's shorts as she navigated the crowded mass of people who'd arrived early for the show. We'd only been able to get tickets for the pit area, and although the rest of the arena was mostly empty, the pit was full of people who had arrived early to make sure they had a spot as close as possible to the stage for the show later that evening. She came to a stop a few rows back from the stage.

"This is the best I can do for now. You're small, maybe you can work your way through the crowd once the music starts."

Brett and Kyla appeared a few minutes later, carrying three large beer cups and a bottle of water for me. With a performance in less than twenty-four hours and the ninety-five-degree temperature today, beer was out of the question.

"Did you tell Trey you were coming?" Valerie wiped the sweat from her forehead and took a big swallow from her cup.

"I'm going to do that right now." I pulled out my phone and texted: *I'll be the girl at the rock show, stage left.*

A few moments later, Trey and his band mates walked onto the stage to light applause and one earsplitting whistle, courtesy of Valerie. Trey's eyes skimmed the crowd, unable to find me in the throng of people. I needed to get closer.

I tapped the person in front of me on the shoulder. A girl wearing all black with her hair dyed to match turned around. I smoothed my unicorn skirt nervously.

"Excuse me, can I get through here?" She curled her lip at me and turned right back around.

Undaunted, I moved a few feet to my left. Music blasted from enormous speakers at the edge of the stage and the people around me began to dance. I jumped into the middle of the thrashing bodies and worked my way forward. I looked over at Valerie and she gave me a thumbs-up from behind her upturned beer cup.

Only three tall men stood between me and the stage now. I debated for a second then tapped the one with the man-bun on the shoulder. When he turned around, I had to lean back and crane my neck to look up at him. His eyebrow was pierced several times and he had a tattoo of a tiger in a tree on the side of his neck and the Blink bunny on his arm.

"Do you know this band?" I asked. "I mean, probably not, right? You're probably here for one of the other bands, but I came to see this band. Well, specifically the bass player, you see, he's my friend, well more like a friend with benefits, to be honest..." Man-bun shook his head and started to turn back around.

"Wait, wait," I grabbed his arm. "Can I stand in front of you while this band plays? I promise, I'll get out of the way as soon as they're done."

He grunted and pushed me in front of him. Success. I had made it to the front of the pit. I looked up to find Trey and realized I had one more problem. I was staring right into the wall of the raised stage. I looked around, trying to figure out how to solve this latest dilemma. Man-bun grunted, handed his beer to the guy standing next to him and grabbed me around the waist. He scooped me up over his head, then reclaimed his beer. I scrambled to sit on his shoulders.

"Thanks, Mr. Man-bun," I called down to him. I removed my unicorn skirt from over his head, wishing for the tenth time that I'd had time to augment my wardrobe or someone my size to borrow from other than Mrs. Radice. And although I was pretty sure she would have been willing, I wasn't sure the over-seventy look was what I was going for tonight.

And there he was, skinny jeans, Epiphone, and all. I sighed. Trey smiled when he saw me and gave me a small wave as he leaned into the microphone to sing. I waved back happily. My rock star ex-fake-boyfriend was ever so dreamy.

The tempo of the music picked up and more people began dancing around us. The crowd was a jumble of jumping bodies and waving arms. Man-bun threw up his arms and did an awkward thrashing dance move. I tightened my ankles under his arms as I wobbled precariously, but with his hands up in the air I couldn't get any traction.

I listed dangerously to portside. I was going to fall and sustain an injury that prevented me from ever dancing again. Maybe I could learn to knit afghans for the table-bed in Aunt Psyche's Winnebago where I'd be forced to live. I could earn spare change selling them on Etsy. I grabbed his coiffure in desperation, but it was too little too late, and I fell sideways into the swirling mass of people, still clutching his scrunchie.

Rough hands grasped my waist and legs and hoisted me into the air unceremoniously. The next thing I knew, I was crowd surfing. Man-bun's goateed cohort pushed my rear end up into the air, propelling me onward into the heaving crowd.

"Okay, thanks, you can put me down now," I yelled into the throbbing music, unable to make eye contact with any of the Good Samaritans boosting me through the crowd on my perilous journey. I twisted my head to the right, looking frantically around, trying to get my bearings. At last, I found Valerie's head sticking up out of the crowd.

"Help me."

She gave me another thumbs-up then pulled out her phone and began recording. I looked at Brett but before I could do more than make eye contact the person below me spun me around and I was headed in the other direction.

A hand squeezed my bottom as I bobbled past Chad, my body undulating like a dragon in a Chinese New Year's parade. He nodded at me and kept singing. I caught a few of the words but didn't recognize the song from their usual set at Not Frank's.

I needed to get my feet on the ground. I tried to force my legs toward the floor, but someone grabbed my feet, pulling off my left shoe in the process.

"Yeah, she's short and sweet but man, that girl's a stalker," Chad sang.

I slapped someone's hand away from my chest area. Stalker? I listened harder as I continued to smack at the encroaching hands. It was like a game of Whack-a-Mole. As soon as one hand went away, another took its place.

Don't panic, my can-do attitude said. *It's a good thing to have a song written about you.*

"She's like leprosy, but you can't live without that ass..." I spun around dizzily. I lifted my head and looked at Trey. He shrugged.

"If you spend the night, you'll wake up tied to her bed."

Okay, maybe not, my can-do attitude conceded.

My head swung in Chad's direction. What a buffoon. I'd never done that. Normal people weren't into bondage. Were they?

I pictured Trey naked and tied to my bed.

On the other hand, I could see where there might be some perks to the whole situation. I made a mental note to check out the climbing ropes in the back of Trey's jeep. And check out a copy of *Fifty Shades of Grey* from the library.

The crowd shifted and I sailed toward Valerie and Brett. They wrestled me back onto my feet.

"Bad day to wear a thong, honey." Brett pulled my unicorn skirt back into place. "Dude, this song is about you."

I ducked to avoid Valerie's lanky arms as she danced. "You think?" I asked sarcastically. "Listen to it, it's bad."

"It's not all bad," Brett said. "There were some complimentary things about your, uh…behind area."

"She's like a tumor that makes your skull ache," Chad warbled on.

Brett grimaced and threw his arm around my shoulders in sympathy.

"Like herpes or Ebola, she won't go away." He trilled out the last syllable of "away."

I sighed. With any luck Chad would fall as he left the stage and give himself a concussion like I had in the fifth grade on our field trip to Luray Caverns. I'd been trying to impress Tanner Mulroney by climbing on the railings, but it didn't seem to make him like me any better, especially when the post-concussion vomiting started.

"But she's the one you can't live without."

Trey caught my eye and winked at me. Things were looking up.

After another two songs the band was finished. The roadies worked to move equipment off the stage to make way for the next band. My phone chimed with a text from Trey, telling me where to meet him.

"Come on," I told the others, "I want to go find Trey."

"I need more beer anyway." Valerie tilted her cup up to show that it was empty.

"I'm going to stay here and watch the band." Kyla eyed the rows of people between herself and the stage. I knew she was really hoping to find a way to move closer to the front before her favorite band came on.

Brett and Valerie replenished their beer and we skirted our way past all the vendors clustered around the stage entrances. We reached a security fence blocking off the area behind the venue from the public. I looked at Brett and shrugged. He pointed into the darkened area behind the building and I could make out Trey walking toward us. He talked to the security guard, who lowered the chain barricade to let us pass.

"Hey. Surprised to see us?"

"I'm glad you made it. I was hoping you'd be able to find time to come."

"It's my night off and I don't have to be back until tomorrow night. I wanted to see your show, so here we are." We stood smiling at each other. I heard Valerie mutter something under her breath and turned to see her rolling her eyes at us.

"Walk with me. I need to get a clean shirt out of the van." Trey slung his arm around my shoulders. I wrinkled my nose. A clean shirt would be a good idea.

We walked toward a gravel lot filled with tour buses, vans, and semis filled with equipment. Valerie and Brett slowly trailed behind, creating enough distance for privacy. It was a good thing Kyla hadn't come with us. We would have had a difficult time restraining her from invading each bus until she found Travis Barker.

"So, that was some song. You know, the one about the stalker?" I raised my eyebrows.

Trey opened the passenger side of a dented white Chevy Express van, and the smell of week-old halibut drifted out. He hadn't been exaggerating that showering wasn't a priority on this tour. He threw the sweaty shirt onto the floor and turned to face me.

He flashed his half smile. "It was only partly true, you know."

"Which part? The Ebola part, or the tumor part?" I crossed my arms in front of me.

He guided me around the open door of the van and detangled my arms. He pulled me to him, wrapped his arms around me, and rested his hands on my bottom. "This part."

Good enough for me, my can-do attitude decided. I stretched up on my toes to kiss him, pressing him against the side of the passenger seat. I thought about what Glynnis had said about returning the favor. Could I pull something like that off in public? Probably not even in private, if I were being realistic.

I broke from the kiss and checked our surroundings. Several people were milling around, and Valerie and Brett were out there somewhere, but no one was in our immediate area. Besides, I reasoned, the open van door blocked most of our bodies.

I took a deep breath and reached for the button on Trey's skinny jeans.

"Eiley, what are you doing?" asked the man who had his hands up my skirt mere seconds ago.

"Returning the favor," I told him.

"What favor? I'm not so sure this is a good idea." He glanced around nervously.

I pushed his jeans down and steadfastly ignored the part of myself that wasn't so sure about it either.

"Wait a second," Trey said. I thought I detected a note of terror in his voice.

I cupped my hand around him, determined to go through with it. "Shh." I gave him one last kiss for courage.

He looked like he was about to protest so I quickly flung myself in the general direction of his groin.

"Eiley, wait."

My back whacked into the van door, which unfortunately propelled me forward, right into him. I had just enough time to shut my eyes before impact.

My skull thudded into him and then we both crashed awkwardly to the ground.

Someone guffawed loudly behind me. I looked up to see Valerie and Brett standing there along with Chad and Noah.

"I'm guessing that's not the kind of head he was hoping for," Noah commented, and they all howled with laughter again.

"You are the world's worst groupie," Valerie snorted.

"This is so going in the song." Chad typed furiously on his phone.

Trey stood, reassembling his clothing in the process. He gave me a hand up, then slid gingerly into the van to sit down.

In the seventh grade I had an English teacher named Mrs. Dovers. Mrs. Dovers tortured us weekly with a vocabulary book called *1,500 Words You Need to Know*. I hated that class and that book. But thanks to Mrs. Dovers's due diligence, I could easily say at this moment that I was absolutely mortified. And chagrin, I had that too. Possibly some verisimilitude, but I wasn't sure if I was remembering that one correctly.

"Go away," Trey groaned.

I glanced nervously at him but he was looking at Chad and Noah. I blew out a sigh of relief. After a few more jokes made at my expense, Noah and Chad left, taking Valerie and Brett with them.

"Get in." Trey gestured to the driver's side of the van. "I need to sit for a few more minutes, and this will give us a chance to talk." Slowly, I walked around the van, dragging my feet. I couldn't imagine what he was going to say.

I climbed in, averting my eyes from the rear of the van. If there were condom wrappers mixed in with all the fast food boxes and dirty clothes, I didn't want to know. I rolled down the window to keep my eyes from watering.

"I'm sorry." I blurted before he could say anything. He rested his head against the headrest and closed his eyes. Hopefully my red splotches would die down before he opened them again. My face was hot enough to fry eggs.

He shook his head. "Don't worry about it."

I smiled in relief. "It was an honest mistake. It could have happened to anyone, really."

His eyes flew open and he chuckled. "No. Only you, Eiley." He reached toward me and I put my hand in his. "You're definitely one of a kind."

What had he meant by that? One of a kind like the Hope Diamond? Or one of a kind like Kim Jong-un? It was as vague as his favorite "take care" line. I really should have found the time to invest in a *Cosmo* subscription. I needed some guidance—like a life coach or a Sherpa.

"You know, when I came to see you after the ballet, I was hoping we'd get more of a chance to talk."

"I remember."

"What made you change your mind?"

So it was like that then. We were going to dive right into a serious conversation. Not even a little bit of talking about the weather first.

I shrugged. Although "because I wanted to have sex with you" was a fairly accurate response, it seemed like he wanted something more in depth.

"It was a lot of things, really. I realized that I had some unrealistic expectations. And I figured that I could change my mind again later if I didn't like the situation." I looked down at my lap, trying to garner some courage from the shimmering unicorn on my pocket. "But mostly I knew that I wasn't ready to never see you again."

"And how do you feel about it now?"

When I raised my eyes again, he was looking out the window, his face turned slightly away from me. I studied the edge of his jawline and considered my answer.

"I'm really happy to be here with you tonight, even if you are afraid I'm going to tie you to my bed someday."

He nodded, then turned to face me. "Do you remember I told you I moved to the States when I was thirteen?"

I nodded. I'd been harboring the hope that he could still remember the British accent and I could convince him to talk dirty to me with it.

"The first people we met were Chad and Nicole. My sister, Jenny, and I spent most days with them in their pool that summer and we've been friends ever since then."

"And you ended up dating Nicole?" *What was British slang for penis? Willy? Todger? Purple parsnip?* My can-do attitude was having some trouble focusing.

Trey nodded. "Eventually. When I was a senior, and she was a sophomore."

"Did you take her to your prom?"

He nodded again. "I did. And we dated the whole summer after that before I went away to college."

"Did you do the whole long-distance thing?" *John Thomas? Wanker? Was there an Urban Dictionary in Britain? Ye Olde Urban Dictionaire?* I needed to put my can-do attitude in time-out and start focusing. Trey obviously had something on his mind.

"We tried to stay together, but it didn't work out. I think it kind of broke her heart. Chad was so mad he didn't speak to me for almost six months. Jenny and I both lost our best friends. Even our parents stopped spending time together."

I was pretty sure Nicole had no heart, and losing Chad was a bonus but it seemed better to keep that to myself.

"Sounds like things were pretty awkward between your families for a while."

He nodded. "It's a big part of the reason I'm not really comfortable with commitments."

I squeezed his hand. "Because you're afraid to risk hurting someone?"

"I guess so."

"And that's why you thought it would be easier to pretend to have a girlfriend than telling Nicole the truth?"

"Yeah." He smiled weakly. "It sounds stupid now, though, right?"

I twirled a curl around a finger of my free hand. "The fake girlfriend thing worked out pretty well for me, so I'm not complaining."

"Yeah, I've been thinking a lot about that since I left, actually." He looked away from me then, his eyes focused on the front window.

"I guess you have time to kill driving between concerts." I looked around the dirty van.

"The thing is," he paused, still not looking at me, "I want to hook up only with you, Eiley."

I sat in silence, momentarily stunned. This was not new information and I didn't know why he was bringing it up again. Maybe he was worried that things would end up like they had with Nicole and Chad.

"I know," I told him. "I mean, I totally got that message. You've been clear. I told you, I'm okay with it. For now." He turned to face me but I couldn't read his expression any better than I could in profile.

"No. Listen to me. I want to hook up only with *you*, Eiley." He gently held my chin so that I couldn't look away from him. "And a whole lot more than that, actually. Do you understand?"

"I, uh…" I nodded. And nodded and nodded. "No." I kept right on nodding.

"You…don't want that?"

I nodded some more. My face was the surface of the sun.

"I don't understand." He frowned.

"You don't understand? Trust me, your level of not understanding is nowhere near the level of my not understanding. It's like you're Copernicus and I'm Kimmy Gibbler sitting here. I mean, you can't change your mind like that, although, to be fair, I did do that to you, but I mean, this is totally different, even if it is the same. There were like twenty women at that pool party with their hands up, Trey. That's a pretty frightening cross section, you know? And you don't even know that I kiss my shoes. The whole thing is unfeasible." I nodded.

"Unfeasible?"

"That's right." Score another one for Mrs. Dovers. "Because a leopard can't change his spots, that's why. You're from Venus and I'm from Mars, and you're out there sleeping with all the Martians, see? There's no reason you're going to change that. Twenty hands, Trey. You shouldn't forget about that, because I sure can't."

I took a deep breath and tried to stop nodding. I looked at Trey expectantly, waiting to hear what he would say, but he turned away from me, grabbed the door handle, and slid out of the van. "Come on," he called through his open door.

I opened my door and followed him, relieved to be out of the van. He took my hand and led me across the lot.

"Where are we going?"

"Somewhere special."

I followed him past the parked vehicles, deeper into the gloom behind the venue. It was finally starting to cool off after the hot day. A welcome breeze lifted the hair off of my shoulders. I could faintly hear Fall Out Boy playing "Uma Thurman." Hopefully Brett and Valerie were back inside, enjoying the show with Kyla.

We walked around the side of a small building that housed restrooms for the crews and I saw where he was headed. The dumpsters. My feet stuck to the pavement as we came to a stop beside the hulking green receptacles. I really wished I had my left shoe. I looked around nervously for flies.

"I figure I've had good luck with you a few times before beside one of these things." He smiled crookedly and I nodded mutely.

He blew out a sigh. "I was wrong, okay? I was wrong about everything except how much I wanted to be with you."

I shook my head. This was too good to be true. Something was surely going to go wrong. I took a deep breath and held it, waiting for the "but."

"Eiley, I know it's probably hard for you to trust me. But I know how I feel. I've known it for a while now, actually."

Wait. What? My breath came out in a loud puff, blowing my bangs off my forehead. Was he saying what I thought he was saying? A vision of myself in a wedding dress standing next to a dumpster flashed through my mind. It couldn't be true. I shook my head some more and took a step back. Was it progress to go from neurotic head nodding to neurotic head shaking? Probably not.

He closed the distance I'd put between us. "I've never met anyone like you, Eiley."

"Like me?" Like a tumor that makes your skull ache? Like a stalker with borderline obsessive tendencies? I swallowed drily. "I don't know what that means. Like what?"

"Like all the small things about you that I love."

I glanced down at my breasts and Trey laughed.

"No. Like the way you bend your straw when you get nervous, and how you blush when you tell lies."

I took another step back apprehensively. He was right about the straw thing, but anyone could have figured out the blushing.

"Like how you rescue animals. And how you're sweet and smart and funny." He took another step closer to me. "And hot."

I fanned myself with my hand a few times. He was about to see a whole other side to my personality: the nervous breakdown. I needed some air. I needed some distance so I could think. Why was this man always sucking up all the air I needed so that my brain could function? I frantically stepped back again. My head thunked into the side of the dumpster and the dull clang echoed inside the bin.

"I know how hard you work to be good at what you do." His eyes locked onto mine as he took a slow step closer to me. I had no more room to escape. If he broke my heart now, all the corndogs at the Jersey Shore wouldn't be enough to fix it. Even if they all came with spicy brown mustard and a side of curly fries.

"You're ridiculously talented, you know that?"

I smiled. I wanted to say thank you, but I didn't want to interrupt whatever he was going to say next. This was getting pretty good. He hadn't mentioned the word Ebola once.

"I want to be with you, Eiley. Only you. Okay?"

I nodded, at a loss for words. Sorry, Mrs. Dovers. He smiled then bent his head to kiss me.

After several minutes Trey broke the kiss and rested his forehead against mine. His eyes were closed and his hands were tangled in my hair. "I might fall in love with you someday, Eiley Murphy."

Well shut the front door. This was news.

I wrapped my arms around his waist.

"Chimichangas," I said, smiling up at him.

Epilogue

Swan Song

"Did I miss I Hate My Life?" Brett had arrived at our table like a hip, gay Santa Claus, his tray loaded down with all our wishes. He removed the empty bacon plate and replaced it with an order of zucchini sticks, then began to pass out our entrees.

"No." Rowan reached for her plate of meat loaf. "Besides, Eiley's probably not playing any more since she's so happy now."

"Mom can be her surrogate," Kyla suggested. "She's pretty miserable lately."

Brett pulled a chair over and sat down beside me. "More Psycho drama?"

Kyla threw a chicken bone onto her plate with a clink. I had no idea how she'd picked it clean so quickly. "Psycho has a new hobby. She's become a cheese maker."

We all groaned.

"Mom says she's in the kitchen for hours, straining her whey curds. It makes a huge mess and, apparently, smells like feet." Kyla pulled a face.

Brett wrinkled his nose. "Yeah, she's probably hating life pretty good right now."

"She's taken up mall walking," Kyla continued. "To get away from it all."

"But the nearest mall is an hour away." I could still remember having to beg my parents to make the trip on weekends so we could hang out with our friends and shop.

"Well, that makes it even better, doesn't it? Two hours of drive time in the car all by herself probably seems like heaven." Kyla pounced on a fresh piece of fried chicken like a hammerhead shark on an unsuspecting squid.

"Speaking of family matters, have you made any progress on the Seamus mystery?" I asked Glynnis.

"You still need to give me the letters and the picture, so I can see what I'm working with."

I mulled this over for a moment. I didn't want to part with Seamus's things. Glynnis was the type of person who would get bored with the project and throw them away. "I'll bring you copies next time I see you," I told her.

"But I did manage to do a little bit of research on my own," she continued. "We know that Seamus loved the Red Sox. We know that he walked a beat past their stadium most days." She looked around at us and we all nodded.

"I did a little digging, and it turns out that in 1915, during the years that Seamus was on that beat, the Red Sox won the American League." She smiled smugly.

"Do you think it's a game ball or something?" I asked.

"Not just a game ball. A *signed* game ball."

I nodded in agreement. A signed ball probably would have been something special to Seamus. "And, get this," she went on. "Guess who was the pitcher for the Sox that year?"

"I'm pretty sure we're not going to be able to guess so why don't you tell us," Kyla suggested before Rowan could start yelling out random names of athletes.

"Babe Ruth." Glynnis looked triumphant.

"So it's possible that out there somewhere is a baseball signed by Babe Ruth that your great-uncle hid," Brett stated.

"It's possible," Glynnis agreed. "Next week we need to come up with a plan. Eiley, you bring the pictures and letters. Rowan, you call Trudy and get all the information you can on the old house in Boston. Kyla, you bring supplies for us to work with. I'm going to go online and find current pictures of the area and print them out. Sound good?" We all agreed.

"I could invite Psyche," I suggested. "She'd be so happy to see us working on this and she might have some good ideas."

"That's a terrible idea. She'd ruin this place for us," Glynnis protested. Rowan and Kyla nodded in agreement. I wanted to argue but I knew I wouldn't be able to change their minds.

Brett gave me a sympathetic squeeze. I leaned into him appreciatively. "How are things going with you and Basil?"

"I'm thinking about asking him to make things official. Once you guys are finished with all the performances. What do you think?"

We all congratulated Brett. "It looks like things are finally working out for both of us," I told him happily.

"Oh, that reminds me." Glynnis reached into her Stella McCartney bag and pulled out a twenty-dollar bill and handed it to Kyla.

"This was more of a surprise than the return of the McRib, to be honest." Rowan fished around in her pleather bustier and pulled out a rumpled bill and added it to Kyla's pile. "But equally as worthy of celebration." She smiled at me.

My jaw dropped open. "Thanks for betting against me."

"Not me." Kyla smiled. "That's why I'm raking in the money right now."

"Dumb luck." Glynnis blew the steam away from a piece of fried zucchini.

I reached for the plate, retracted my hand then reconsidered. I only had one week of performances left and I was willing to risk damage to my spleen caused by a dangerously snug tutu for the promise of deep-fried perfection. I chose the largest fritter on the plate, gave it a generous dip in ranch dressing, and took a careful bite. I chewed slowly, relishing the flavor that only a robust trans-fat can deliver. Totally worth it. Besides, zucchini is a vegetable. Vegetables are healthy. Everyone knows that.

"Not dumb luck at all. I simply choose to believe in the power of love." A large drop of ranch dressing fell onto Kyla's shirt as she bit into her piece of zucchini. She wiped it away quickly.

"Love?" Glynnis snorted. Even Brett looked surprised.

"That's right. Love. Right, Eiley?" Kyla looked at me expectantly.

"Well, I mean…love is, uh…" I shoved the rest of the piping hot zucchini into my mouth and shrugged at her. Tears sprang to my eyes and I had to open my mouth to let out some steam and fan my tongue. The last thing I wanted to do was gush to my sisters about how much I liked Trey. It would be years before they'd let me live it down. Sisters are like that. Every Thanksgiving, without fail, they bring up the time I threw up on the turkey.

"This is not about love. It's about hooking up." Glynnis looked from Kyla to me. "With someone way out of your league, apparently."

I continued to chew my zucchini.

"That's how it started out, but it's more than that now. Isn't it, Eiley?" Kyla turned back to me.

My hand hovered over the zucchini bowl. I could stuff another one into my mouth, or I could throw one. At her eye. "The truth is," I began hesitantly, "I actually really like him." Hopefully they would be satisfied with that answer and not press it any further.

Glynnis reached under my hovering hand and grabbed the last zucchini stick. There went my ammunition and any opportunity of launching a full frontal assault with a piece of lardaceous squash. "Oh, really? Tell us what you like about him without mentioning the words abs, bass guitar, or penis."

"Well," I began evasively, "there are a lot of things about him that I like. He's smart—"

"Maybe, but he's got some seriously questionable judgment," Glynnis interrupted.

"And," I forged ahead, "he's an EMT, which means he helps people."

"That's a good quality for you to have in a boyfriend," Kyla said. I turned from Glynnis to Kyla and raised my eyebrow. "I mean, you do have a tendency to hurt yourself. Having a medical professional at the ready seems like a good option," she finished.

"And those feet are a full-time job for anyone," Rowan added helpfully.

I decided to be the better person and ignore the remark about my feet. "He lives with his grandmother so she can stay in her house. That shows he's kind. Plus he's funny, and musically gifted."

"Playing the bass guitar does not count as being musically gifted." Glynnis smirked. "And you weren't supposed to mention his guitar."

"I don't care." I smiled. "Those things need to be taken into consideration. He's in a band, his abs are amazing, and he's good in bed." Hopefully no one would notice that I'd accidentally gushed a little.

"Kind of wondering what he's doing with you, though," Glynnis said. Stunned, I put down my half-eaten BLT.

"Don't look at me like that. You know I'm right. You stalked this man on social media for a year," she said.

"And peed on him," Kyla chimed in.

"And flashed his grandmother," Brett added.

"Not to mention almost getting him arrested and beaten up by your building super. It's kind of a surprise the boy kept coming back for more punishment," Glynnis finished.

"That proves he really likes me," I replied triumphantly.

"Or it was that new lip gloss," Rowan said thoughtfully.

"Don't be ridiculous. Trey obviously appreciates all of Eiley's outstanding qualities." Kyla threw the bone from her last piece of chicken onto her plate.

"Exactly. Thank you, Kyla." I smiled happily at my sister.

I know what you're thinking, but don't worry. I plan to get to the drugstore as soon as possible. A trunkful of Baboon Butt couldn't hurt.

ABOUT THE AUTHOR

Elsie is a great writer even though she was a difficult child who refused to eat brussel sprouts, peed in all of her dresser drawers, and tried to flush my shoes. If she sells enough books she can finally move out of our basement and we can have the rumpus room we've always dreamed of. So please feel free to tell all your friends about this book. I'm begging you.

– Elsie's Mom

Here's everything you need to know about me: I've inherited the family chin. For the love of God, please buy my book. Buy one for all your friends. Spread the word. This thing isn't going to fix itself, you know.

So listen, all these *I Hate My Life* stories? Sadly, they're true. If you want to be a part of the next book in the Murphy sisters' saga, send your most embarrassing story to me at: elsieyoungauthor@gmail.com.

HOOK UP WITH ELSIE:

elsieyoungauthor.wixsite.com/website

facebook.com/elsie.young.33?fref=ts

twitter.com/ElsieYo18888440

www.BOROUGHSPUBLISHINGGROUP.com

If you enjoyed this book, please write a review. Our authors appreciate the feedback, and it helps future readers find books they love. We welcome your comments and invite you to send them to info@boroughspublishinggroup.com. Follow us on Facebook, Twitter and Instagram, and be sure to sign up for our newsletter for surprises and new releases from your favorite authors.

Are you an aspiring writer? Check out www.boroughspublishinggroup.com/submit and see if we can help you make your dreams come true.